# Across Great Divides

## A Novel

Monique Roy

"...in spite of everything, I still believe that people are really good at heart. I simply can't build up my hopes on a foundation consisting of confusion, misery, and death. I see the world gradually being turned into a wilderness, I hear the ever approaching thunder, which will destroy us too, I can feel the sufferings of millions and yet, if I look up into the heavens, I think that it will all come right, that this cruelty too will end, and that peace and tranquility will return again."

~Anne Frank (1929–1945), Dutch Jewish diarist; born in Germany. Diary of a Young Girl, entry dated July 15, 1944 (1947).

*For my grandparents:*

*Amid the upheavals of war, you refused to be destroyed.*

*Your resiliency lives on.*

*Your courage prevails.*

*Stories like yours live within us.*

*We will never forget.*

# chapter

# ONE

*Berlin, Germany 1932*

Eva first saw him on a mild summer night at the Berliner Philharmonie concert hall, minutes before a symphony. She watched from the balcony as the hall slowly filled up with people—women in glittering dresses, impeccably dressed gentlemen, and children scrubbed clean and in their finest clothes. Tuxedoed ushers greeted streams of guests as they floated into the great hall, soon to be riveted by sweeping, romantic music.

Eva concentrated on the stage setup—the position of the strings and basses in relation to the flutes and clarinets, as well as the talented musicians who readied themselves onstage, eager to deliver a truly spectacular performance. In fact, Eva always observed the way the instruments were positioned as it revealed a great deal about the performance to come.

Suddenly, her concentration was broken when the hall went silent and the audience's attention was directed to a man who appeared in the second floor's golden balcony. He was a recognizable and popular figure. He was not alone. A beautiful, young blonde woman clung to his side. Before he took his seat, he turned to the audience and outstretched his right arm in a rigid, formal salute. Many in the audience raised their right hands in response. Without a sound or any movement, he acknowledged the guests with his hypnotic, pale blue eyes and spellbinding manner. He possessed a strange and powerful magnetism. Gentle murmurs emerged from the audience and quickly hushed as darkness enveloped them.

Eva leaned over the balcony's rail and stared across the hall at the man. She knew who he was. Everyone did.

"Is that —" her sister, Inge, softly whispered.

"Adolf Hitler," Eva cut her off, maintaining her stare. "The leader of the National Socialist Party. Many say he is a man of great power and may be Germany's last hope."

Inge's eyes, identical to her sister's, grew wide with curiosity.

"He seems rigid and terrifying," Inge said, leaning forward in her chair. "But still, it's hard to believe that little man will be anything. I think he is somewhat comical...don't you?"

"Beyond his physical appearance, Inge, I've heard he is a captivating speaker who has enraptured the hearts of many Germans," Eva said, observing the audience as they waited to be dazzled by the symphony.

Eva noticed the finely dressed audience. Germans had a pride of appearance and a regard for cleanliness, which filled her with admiration. On the surface, there seemed to be prosperity in Germany. But, the extravagant dresses and spotless white collars only obscured the poverty and hardship that lay beyond the building's sturdy walls.

Eva felt fortunate to be at the symphony, considering that Germany suffered greatly as the Great Depression left millions unemployed and the country in shambles. From elected leaders, the people of Germany received nothing but indecision and chaos. The Germans lacked confidence in their befuddled, degenerate government, the Weimar Republic.

Eva recalled a recent conversation with her father who told her that the depression in Germany was merely a gift—a grand opportunity for Hitler to make promises to the people of Germany—vows that would in turn build trust and support. Hitler emphasized rebuilding the broken German state and promised a glorified future as he set out to consolidate power, and force old President Paul von Hindenburg to make him chancellor.

But it would be several months until Hitler ruled Germany. And on that night, like other nights, Hitler wanted to make his presence known. Eva continued to watch him as he finally took his seat and turned his gaze toward the stage. She then forced her eyes back to the orchestra.

A silence permeated the air as the Berlin Philharmonic Orchestra awaited its cue. Conductor Wilhelm Furtwängler stood awkwardly on the podium and bowed to the audience. He then turned to the musicians and lifted his baton. The meandering of his baton in melodic shapes summoned the first note of Beethoven's *Symphony # 9 ("Choral")*. His right hand and baton roughly kept the beat; his left hand weaved round in flowing patterns, while his head and torso constantly jerked.

Rhythmic sounds full of sweeping grandeur wafted through the air. Eva felt pulsating vibrations to the core of her stomach. The ebb and flow of sounds were like a pulse, a heartbeat.

Eva closed her eyes for a brief moment. Even with her eyes closed, she could see the movement of the instruments in front of her. From the thundering dances of the bass and cello, the sound dropped back to a soft dance of full pizzicato strings. This faded ever so slightly and then became an extraordinary progression of beats. The violins slowly initiated a towering climax and then an explosion of full orchestra, giving way to a quieter current of sounds.

She remembered coming to the symphony as a little girl, when she would sit in awe between her parents, Oskar and Helene, her eyes glued to the symphony's sudden quick movements followed by slow and melodic ones. The music always inspired her, infused her with hope, and uplifted her spirits.

As she observed the audience, she sensed the intense emotion of the people around her— how suddenly as the joyful melody enraptured them, they emerged from their dark worlds and their eyes shined like lights.

Distant, locked away memories vividly spilled back into her mind now. Eva stood in glittering shoes on her father's feet as he waltzed her around the parlor of their home. As they weaved around heavy antiques, Eva held onto her father's strong arms as they danced together to the sound of music from an old music box. Inge sat shyly in the background, enjoying the spectacle before her, smiling at the graceful, light movements of her sister's feet as she awaited her turn to dance with her father.

A glint in the distance caught Eva's attention. She peered through the mother of pearl opera glasses across the audience. Her searching blue eyes scanned the audience and stopped at the sight of a beautiful woman wearing the most striking emerald pendant necklace set in harmony with a starry radiance of brilliant cut diamonds. She had never seen anything like it before. Fearing the woman might glance in her direction, Eva directed the looking glasses back to the stage. A few minutes later, she would steal another glimpse at the unique piece of jewelry that filled her with envy. Her eyes shifted to Inge, but her attention could not be broken.

かっく

The mid-afternoon sun cast a soft, golden glow on the autumn foliage along the path to the auction house. The air was crisp and silent, the only sound being the rustle of dried leaves underfoot. Oskar reached the steps to the opulent auction house and paused briefly. Dressed in a fine black suit and gabardine overcoat, he reached for his gold pocket watch.

"*Almost time,*" he said to himself.

For luck, he kissed the inscription on the back of the watch that read: "*Oskar, my love always, Helene.*"

He climbed the stone steps to the entrance. The entryway was marked by arched windows and glass doors that lead to a large foyer, the Great Hall, adorned with high golden ceilings, sparkling chandeliers and marble floors. This was where elegant society with a cultivated taste in art mingled and where time could stand still for a lingering moment.

Oskar entered the rosewood parlor to peruse the dazzling display of estate jewelry, including diamond rings, strands of pearls, gold, platinum and silver rings, necklaces, brooches, and bracelets. Roaming the room, he slowly inspected the jewelry, impressed by the splendor around him. He walked towards a piece a few feet away. The jewel glimmered back at him. When he was only inches from the jewelry, he stopped.

The familiarity of the gem startled him. He went closer and examined the emerald and diamond necklace. A replica or a piece he had cut with his very hands? He recalled the brilliantly green emerald glowing like a ball of green fire. It was one of a kind, a finely cut pendant necklace, fit for a queen. Looking at its beauty, Oskar recognized the stunning emerald set with a gleaming radiance of many brilliant cut diamonds.

Everything from the diamonds to the emerald to every intricate detail would always be etched in his mind. Oskar had inherited the gemstones when his father died in 1925, a time when Berlin culture was considered decadent and sophisticated, amid unprecedented social and artistic freedom. When Oskar took over his father's prosperous diamond business, the city had become an intellectual center where artists, musicians, and writers thrived. It was a special time, even for jewelers like Oskar.

He then remembered the woman who bought the necklace from him five years prior. She was a younger woman with soft eyes, an alluring face, and a lovely, long shapely neck. Her name did not come to mind. He recalled she came alone. She bought the necklace nonchalantly, as if she was buying a loaf of bread, and he never heard from her again. Why was the pendant necklace here? He clenched his jaw in thought and scratched his head.

And then it was time.

As the auctioneer opened the bidding to the eager crowd, a white-gloved porter walked the necklace around the room for all to see. There were five or six players, maybe more. Oskar was not certain.

At Oskar's bid of 25,000 Reichsmarks, applause sounded around the room, and stirred murmurings of astonishment.

The hammer came down. Oskar left the room with a victorious smile.

# chapter

# TWO

*Berlin, Germany 1933*

The ravishing emerald and diamond necklace draped around Helene's neck heightened her beauty and elegance. As she zipped the back of Eva's navy blue rayon dress, the sparkling jewelry caught Eva's eye.

"*Dankeschön*, Mama." Eva smiled and admired her mother in the mirror. Helene was the epitome of fashion and elegance. Her black dress complimented her slim figure and captured her classic sense of style.

Helene smiled back at her daughter.

"Inge, wear your new red scarf, darling," Helene hugged Inge. "There's a chill in the air."

Helene constantly fussed over her twin daughters. She wanted them to look their best at all times and to show them off to the world. They were her pride and joy.

Oskar and Helene were delighted when Eva and Inge were born. They considered the twins a double blessing. Oskar always told Helene that their special blessing was multiplied. The girls were spoiled and were given everything they ever wanted. They were put on a pedestal from the moment they were born.

Eva could see how her parents fell in love. Helene was extremely beautiful, with short, brown curly hair and striking blue eyes. She was sophisticated and aristocratic with strong ideals. It was Helene's strength and refinement that Oskar first saw in her. Oskar himself had a strong personality and an entrepreneurial spirit. He could fill a room with his charm and youthful exuberance. He was easy on the eyes and lavished his family with luxuries – as many as he could afford.

Helene grabbed her fur coat from the Louis XV-style Bergere armchair and checked her fashionably tilted hat in the mirror. She pulled on a pair of short leather gloves.

"You look pretty, Mother," Inge said.

"Thank you, darling," Helene said.

"Are you going somewhere special?" Inge asked.

"I'm going to help your father in the diamond center," Helene said. "That reminds me, girls, meet us there this afternoon at four o'clock. Your father has something important to show you. Don't forget."

"We won't forget," Inge said. "*Auf Wiedersehen!*"

Walking out of their quaint Berlin apartment, she blew her daughters both a kiss. They blew one back.

The scent of Helene's perfume lingered in the air. It was a smell the twins always savored.

೨∼ఈ

After Inge tied the red scarf around her neck and clasped the last button on her wool coat, the twins strolled, arm-in-arm, down Oranienburger Strasse, located in the center of Berlin, in the heart of the Jewish district, and the center of Mitte. The one-kilometer long street housed inviting cafes, frequented by gentlemen and cosmopolitan women who sipped coffee, relished cake and reminisced. Young men and women wandered the streets carefree, finding amusement in Berlin's exuberant liveliness. Rising above the building facades of Oranienburger Strasse stood the golden dome of one of the largest synagogues in all of Germany, an exotic presence above the mundane apartment blocks.

To Eva, Berlin was more than just a place. It was in the essence of her being. She loved Berlin. For a young woman with a deep affinity for fashion and all things beautiful, Berlin was timeless, progressive, and one of the greatest cities in the world. The robust and dynamic city was a true metropolis of its time, a nucleus for the arts and a cultural jewel. Berlin oozed with sophistication and flair, and even displayed some arrogance. The city had become a civilized breeding ground for a stream of visionaries, scientists, writers, and artists.

Eva and Inge grew up in a middle-class Jewish family, and their allegiance to Germany and its strong culture was deep. They considered themselves as German as they were Jewish, but it was mostly German blood that ran through their veins. Their loyalty to Germany was fervent, so much so that they never pictured themselves living elsewhere. Germany was forever.

Being the only set of mirror image twins in the close-knit community in which they lived, Eva and Inge stood out from the crowd. Sometimes all the attention went to Inge's head and she thought of herself as a movie star as she paraded down the street. Many would greet the young women as they passed, admiring their 'Aryan' beauty, sparkling blue eyes and long, straight blonde hair. Few knew they were Jewish.

And very few could tell them apart. Oskar and Helene, and their brother, Max, represented the gifted few—the only ones who could tell who was who. Outside of their immediate family, the one exception was Trudy, their closest friend from school, who could tell them apart from the day they met.

The first time they saw Trudy was in sewing class. Trudy needed a sewing needle and approached Eva and Inge, knowing exactly who was who. They were amazed by her insight. When they asked Trudy how she was able to tell them apart, she said that Eva had a distinct freckle on her cheek. Indeed, she did, and until then, only her parents and brother had perceived it as a unique characteristic that distinguished them. They also admired Trudy's sense of style, as it was similar to theirs. She was a classic dresser and her clothes were feminine and sweet. She had an effervescent personality and witty side that she also expressed in the way she dressed. She wore bold colors like shocking pink, which was revolutionary for the times.

Eva and Inge found amusement in the trickery of confusing others about their identities. They often went to the bakery to buy their favorite pastries and their father's favorite, a Berliner *Pfannkuchen*, a German doughnut with jam and powdered sugar. When Eva and Inge walked into the local bakery, Mr. Bernstein, a short, bald-headed man with a heart of gold, was constantly puzzled by their identical appearance. He would ask, as if he had given up trying, "Is it Inge or Eva?" At first they wouldn't answer him, but make him guess, and unfortunately his answer was always wrong. Messing with people's minds was a benefit of being a twin.

Their childish tricks quickly stopped when they noticed Mr. Bernstein had lost his wits. He was less patient when dealing with his customers. He seemed unnerved and frazzled. And, he had every reason to be.

The street where his shop stood was no longer peaceful. Brown Shirts, members of the storm troopers (*Sturmabteilungen*, SA), poured through the Berlin streets and ruled them with fear and aggression. The swastika appeared on shop windows, a menacing symbol of what was to come. When Eva and Inge entered the shop, Mr. Bernstein would secretly add extra pastries to their order and quickly dismiss the girls.

"Hurry home now, girls," he said, as he handed them a bag filled with warm pastries. "May God bless you."

At first they were baffled by his kind gesture and expression, but they soon came to realize that the statement was really a 'goodbye'. Each time they went to the shop, they wondered if it would be their last.

Great uncertainty began to build. The changing German attitude towards the Jews did not only emerge in the streets of Berlin, but in the classrooms as well.

෨⸱ᥫ

So many times, Eva and Inge were asked at school, "What is it like having a twin?" Neither had put much thought into it; since the day they were born, this was the only life they had known. It was something they took for granted every day. They had a hook, they were twins. In these uncertain times, they were thankful to have each other.

School was the only place where the young women struggled to be individuals. As the atmosphere at school began to change for the worse, the teachers became stricter and less tolerant of disruptions in the classroom. The twins were seen as a disruption, and eventually, they were separated in class.

Eva sat in the front of the classroom and Inge sat in the back corner. They were told they could not speak to one another or look at each other. This was an impossible demand, of course. The teachers were astonished at how they always had similar scores on exams, which did not change when they were separated. Often, they would switch their names and confuse everyone. This resulted in them being referred to as "the twins" rather than using their names. The teachers pulled them apart for these obvious reasons, as well as being haunted by their magical telepathic powers. They would often raise their hands in class at the exact same moment and sneeze simultaneously. The teachers became flustered. The students laughed.

The twins always knew each other's thoughts, could finish each other's sentences, and spoke in a secret language. They also exerted a common force and effect on one another that however far the distance between them, they would always remain close in mind and spirit. The teachers felt that separating them would solve the issue of their interconnected emotions, pains, sicknesses and so on, but to their astonishment, no division would change the matter. They always felt each other's joy and pain. But they did what they were told without a fight, knowing they were still in each other's close company.

Education played a crucial role in trying to cultivate a loyal following of Hitler and the Nazis. Enforcing a Nazi curriculum depended on devoted teachers to deliver it. The curriculum at school changed drastically and the students were being told lies. For instance, they were told that the Jews had contributed nothing to civilization. Every school subject suddenly was connected to "*Rassenkunde*"—race science.

One morning, the teacher told the class that Albert Einstein was not a Jew. Eva and Inge's hands shot up in the air at the same moment.

When the teacher acknowledged Eva, she voiced that Einstein was in fact a Jew. The teacher's face turned stern. Inge froze and quickly lowered her arm to her desk, fearing any confrontation with the teacher. Eva had always been the braver of the two.

"From now on, no one will argue with what I tell you," the teacher said from behind his desk, which formed an invisible barrier of authority. "Does everyone understand?"

"Yes, Herr Faust," the students mumbled.

"Do you understand?" Herr Faust stared at Eva. His bushy eyebrows rose as he awaited her answer.

"Yes, Herr Faust," she said. A lump formed in her throat. "It won't happen again."

"Yes, it definitely will not happen again," he reinforced to his students.

Then, he stood up from his wooden desk and walked down the aisle to the back of the class. For a moment, he stared at the low wooden benches where his students sat until their bones ached. His arms crossed behind his very straight back as he came upon Inge's desk. Inge kept her eyes down on her desk. Her cheeks flushed as he glared at her.

"Did you have something to add?" he asked coldly, standing over her.

"No, Herr Faust," she said softly, keeping her gaze downcast.

"I noticed your arm shoot up in the air at the same time as your sister's," he said.

"I apologize, Herr Faust," she said, finally settling her eyes on his bushy eyebrows.

"A muscle spasm of some sort," Herr Faust replied.

"Yes, Herr Faust," Inge said. "It won't happen again."

"In the future, no one in this room will talk unless called upon," he pointed at his students, walking back to his desk.

As school became a more hostile environment, the twins began to worry about the future.

"Don't worry, girls," their father would tell them. "This too shall pass. Continue to work hard and do your best."

Once they completed their schoolwork, they decided to channel their energies to things they enjoyed most—fashion, boys and American movie stars like Jean Harlow, Katharine Hepburn and Clark Gable.

Their brother, Max, directed his energies elsewhere. He was intellectual and calm, and viewed life through different eyes. At fourteen, he was younger than his sisters by two years. He was handsome with dark, wavy hair, resembling his father. His eyes were a striking color of hazel. Max was into politics and the ways of the world.

Soon, after his fourteenth birthday and as the political climate in Berlin began to change, Max became a member of the *Bund deutsch-jüdischer Jugend* or the Ring, a Federation of Jewish Youth, BDJJ for short. Emigration was an increasingly urgent concern of the BDJJ and its members. Max always stressed to his parents that they must leave Germany. His parents would not hear of it. They did not see the imminent threat like Max did. In fact, he was the only one who saw what was to come. Despite his parents' dismay, Max got so involved in BDJJ that they rarely saw him after school and on the weekends.

They often wondered if Max even went to school anymore. He hated school. He came home one day greatly affected by something that had happened. He told his family that at the beginning of every school day, they had to stand and raise their arms in the Hitler salute and thank the *Führer* for giving them a nice day. Loyalty was demanded; it was instilled in the minds of all young Germans. Max refused to be loyal to the *Führer*, an act of defiance for which he suffered the repercussions at school and beyond its walls. Two boys from his class, members of the Hitler Youth, chased Max after school and beat him up. He arrived home with a black eye, blood pouring out of his nose, and a broken rib. His sisters cleaned up his wounds and he declared that he would never go to school again. Oskar demanded he did and that if the Hitler Youth members ever laid a hand on his son again, they would have to answer to him. Oskar did not stand for disobedience of any kind.

☙❧

After school, Eva and Inge grabbed Trudy, and like their mother instructed, they headed to their father's diamond center, PristineHaus.

Trudy was always included in their family gatherings, whether they were supporting Oskar's diamond business or coming together as a family for Shabbat dinners on a Friday night. Trudy was not Jewish, but Shabbat dinners were a special time where they focused more on each other than religion. However, the family kept the Jewish traditions of Shabbat alive by reciting the Kiddush, breaking bread (*challah*), and singing the blessings.

After years of a budding friendship, Trudy was like a member of the family. Yet, Eva did not know much about hers. Trudy was an open book when it came to matters of the heart, but when it came to matters of family, she was closed off. She rarely spoke of her parents, so Eva never asked, not wanting to overstep any boundaries. All Eva knew was that she was an only child, her mother was involved in several charitable organizations, and her father was an engineer of some kind. Eva had only seen Trudy's mother a few times and found her to be mostly standoffish. She had never met her father. He was never around when Eva was at Trudy's house. Eva began to think that Trudy appreciated being a part of her close-knit family as it made up for her lack of family.

Set in an intimate space in the centrally-located Mitte district, PristineHaus sold fine diamond jewelry of all kinds. Over the years, Oskar became a master diamond cutter and polisher, which allowed for his creativity to flourish. When the young women arrived, Max was standing over his father's shoulder staring at the beautiful jewelry that sparkled from a container on the mahogany desk. Eva and Inge kissed their father and mother "hello".

"Welcome, girls," Oskar said, with a warm smile.

Trudy stood near Max. Whenever he was around, she always wanted to see him or be near him. Eva knew that she secretly had a crush on him. At his young age, his interest in girls had not ripened. They were waiting for that day to happen.

A stunning array of jewelry glimmered before them: distinctive, whimsical designs in pure form that expressed fantasy and elegance. Some were beautifully cut pendants that hung on woven chains, while other pieces were rings in timeless settings.

"It's my new collection," Oskar pronounced proudly. "It's called Pristine Gems."

"Every woman in Berlin will dazzle with Pristine Gems," Helene said. She kissed her husband's cheek.

"And Hitler, too?" Max added, jokingly.

"No more talk of Hitler, Max," Oskar said. "Hitler Shmitler. He is harmless."

"Right, Trudy?" Oskar asked, needing further confirmation.

"Yes, a little man with a big ego," Trudy said, smiling reluctantly. "But harmless indeed."

"I hope you are right," Max said, crossing his arms.

"What are you going to do now, girls?" Helene chimed in, trying to change the sour topic.

The girls looked at each other as if they were reading each other's minds.

"Would you like to go to the bookshop?" Eva said, looking at her sister and Trudy.

They nodded.

"I like the sound of that," Helene said. "If you are not going to let me teach you English, you might as well let that crazy old woman teach you."

"She is not crazy, Mother," Inge said.

"How do you know English so well, Helene?" Trudy asked.

"My father was British and worked for the British embassy," she said. "He taught my mother and me. Sometimes my father preferred that we speak English over German. I want all my children to speak English well. That includes you, Max." She grinned as she playfully pointed at her son.

The bookshop they sometimes visited was unlike any bookshop they had known. It was a cozy and small treasure nestled next to a café on Oranienburger Strasse. It was there where the girls fell in love with books and perfected their English.

The first time they set foot in the shop, they were amazed at the many wonderful books, neatly stacked on the shelves. The little bookshop provided an escape from reality and an entrance into a world full of magic and wonder. It was a place where they could find happy endings.

The shop owner, an older lady named Gertie, was a widow. She was lonely and gravitated towards the young energy of the girls. She also loved the fact that they were so intrigued by the books in her shop. It was not just books that brought them together.

The girls would bring her coffee and pastries from the café next door in exchange for lessons in English.

Amid a large collection of German books, Gertie would uncover a hidden treasure, kept in a secret box at the back of the shop. When she lifted off the lid of the box, the unique American culture came alive. A large stack of great American novels were waiting to be devoured. They would sit for hours reading aloud popular American novels by famous authors, like Ernest Hemingway and F. Scott Fitzgerald.

Inge once asked Gertie where she found the books. She answered from her travels to America, and that she had a cousin who lived there and would often send her some books.

When a year had passed since the girls had first stepped foot in the bookshop, Gertie gave them each a gift. They could choose one book to keep.

"I would like *The Great Gatsby*," Inge said, grabbing the book from the box.

"My favorite," Gertie said.

"Are you certain you want to part with it, Gertie?" Inge asked.

"Yes," she answered. "It's yours to keep, *mein Liebling*."

"That's the book I was going to choose," Eva said.

The old woman laughed. "You do live in the same house," she said. "You can always share."

"What will it be, Eva?" she asked.

"*Little Women*," Eva said.

"Great choice," Inge said.

"Which book would you like, my dear?" she asked, looking at Trudy.

"*The Sun Also Rises*," Trudy said.

"You will learn a lot from this book," she said, handing it to Trudy. "I think it is Hemingway's best work."

"Thank you," Trudy said.

The twins hugged the old woman.

While their meetings with Gertie provided a small diversion to the harsh reality around them, the girls were young and yearned to meet handsome men.

One evening, Trudy, Eva, and Inge were invited to a friend's birthday party, but Inge became ill with a fever and could not attend the party. Eva wanted to stay home as well and not leave her sister, but Inge insisted that one of them make an appearance at the party and persuaded her sister to attend the party.

Always together and rarely apart, Helene would tell her daughters to try to be more independent of each other and make friends on their own. But they didn't want to hear of it. They had promised each other in their younger years that they would always be together, no matter what.

When Trudy and Eva arrived at the birthday party, they knew everyone, except two young men, Frederick and Verner. Trudy had an infectious laugh and that night, when she burst into her peals of laughter, it was impossible not to laugh with her. As she reclined playfully in her chair, she became the life of the party and possessed many likable qualities that Frederick admired, beyond her pretty looks. Verner didn't say much at the party, but every time Eva looked his way, he would smile. She wasn't sure if he was just shy or there was a lack of connection.

When the party died down that night, Frederick and Verner suggested they go to the popular beer garden, which was a short walk from the party. Trudy grabbed Eva's arm and said, "Let's go with them, shall we?" She did not expect *no* as an answer. "Here's our chance," Trudy proclaimed with a smirk. Eva knew what that meant and rolled her eyes in response. Trudy's quest was to fall into the arms of a charming and attractive young man.

When they arrived at the leafy beer garden, Frederick and Verner led them to an empty, wooden table sheltered by a century-old large chestnut tree that was like a sweeping canopy over them. A lively oompah band entertained with rousing songs. Eventually, one-liter beer steins arrived at the table. It was the first time Eva had tasted beer. The bitterness was horrible at first, but the more she sipped the beer, the more she began to enjoy its unique flavor.

Trudy sat close to Frederick, who claimed to be twenty years old and attended Humboldt University, Berlin's oldest university. Eventually, after conversing about normal things like art, culture and relationships, and as alcohol and mutual acquaintance put them at ease, the conversation reverted to politics...and Hitler.

"I am a passionate nationalist," remarked Verner. "Germany has suffered economically, and I think Hitler is the kind of leader who will march us out of the economic crisis."

"I'm strongly thinking about enlisting," said Frederick. "Join me?"

"Do I look like a girl who would join the military?" asked Trudy.

"Why, yes, a very sexy one, indeed," Frederick responded, eyeing her.

Eva just laughed, not commenting. She flicked her hair behind her ears.

"I think everyone should devote part of their lives to society," Verner said. "We need to support Hitler and his cause. Old institutions are dead. It's time to start over."

"Even if Europe has to turn to ashes, Germany must always prevail. We are the master race. And, as for those dirty Jews," Frederick said, leaning forward intently as he spoke in German.

Moments of uneasy silence lingered. Trudy gave Eva an apologetic look.

"What do you think of Hitler, Eva?" Verner asked, turning toward her.

She cleared her throat and hoped that God would forgive her for what she was about to say.

"I think he will be a remarkable leader," Eva said, hating herself, and ready to go home as the night had quickly become less romantic.

"Well, gentlemen, it's getting rather late," Trudy blurted out. "Eva and I need to walk home."

"Could we accompany you home?" Frederick asked, smiling.

"No," Trudy said. "Thank you for offering. Eva and I live quite near each other."

Frederick said, "How about dancing tomorrow night?"

"Sounds nice," Trudy responded.

Eva just nodded, unsure if she wanted to see Frederick or Verner again.

"Potsdamer Platz at eight o'clock?" Frederick said.

For the first few minutes as they walked home, their heels clicking on the pavement, Trudy and Eva did not say a word. Eva finally broke the ice.

"So, Frederick, eh?" Eva said, nudging Trudy in the side.

"Charming and adorable, don't you think?" Trudy asked in German.

"Somewhat," Eva responded. "To be honest, I am not sure about charming, Trudy. That comment..."

Trudy cut her off.

"Sorry about that remark, Eva," she said. "I don't think he meant it, really."

"That made me very uncomfortable," she said. "I hope it never happens again. But, you must promise that you keep to yourself that I am Jewish."

Trudy promised.

As they got to know Verner and Frederick, the anti-Semitic remarks died down. Eva wasn't sure if Trudy had said something to them, but she was relieved the young men had refrained from making unacceptable, racist remarks.

Frederick and Trudy began dating shortly after that first night they all met. They became serious quickly, spending most of their spare time together. Eva found herself in a tough spot. If she wanted to see her best friend, then she had to see Frederick and his best friend, Verner. There was no getting around it.

Surprisingly, Eva found Verner to be an interesting and kind individual. They shared a passion for the arts and Eva's first kiss. Verner tried several times to push their relationship along, but Eva refused to sleep with him. She enjoyed being with Verner, but was hesitant and cautious about anything more with him, for he still did not know she was a Jew. Eva tried to keep things casual between them, and when Verner asked for more, she pushed back, saying, "She wasn't ready." He never became angry or upset by this rejection, which Eva found to be respectful and mature on his part. He liked her enough to continue to spend time with her, and that was enough for Eva at the moment.

Verner, Frederick, Eva and Trudy, along with Inge and some of her friends, often hung out together. Their favorite pastime was swing dancing in the packed dance halls. The halls were an eclectic mix of young and old, rich and poor. But this was the one place where no one judged, where everyone let go of their concerns for a few hours of splendor and entertainment. They danced their feet off to the popular bands and orchestras dressed in tuxedos. Those days, Eva lived for dancing with everyone.

Eva and Inge were always amazed at the magic and ambience of those dance halls. They would often talk about it. Eva was intrigued by the masses of spotlights that changed color as they turned. The colored spotlights would weave among the swinging dancers, wrapping them in a warm glow. It was romantic at the very least. It was intoxicating. Eva loved those nights, dancing with her friends. It made her feel hopeful for the future.

But then, things grew complicated and awkward. As Trudy and Frederick became more serious, Eva saw less of her friend. As this happened,

Verner naturally turned to Eva for companionship, but Eva began to feel uncomfortable seeing Verner on a regular basis. He began to show up on dates in his Nazi Youth uniform. All Eva could focus on was the official Hitler Youth arm band, red with a white strap and swastika. Every time they saw each other, the swastika stood out more than anything else. She quickly ended their relationship in a café, simply by telling him that she needed to focus on her studies.

Then, one day, everything changed. Eva had planned to meet Trudy after school for some supper and had invited her sister to join them. Eva and Inge waited for Trudy for over an hour before they left the café themselves to head home. Trudy never met them that evening. The following day, Eva never heard from Trudy either. She began to worry. Maybe Trudy was ill. Eva did not know what was happening. She decided to go by her house after school.

As Eva walked up the path leading to Trudy's house, the path she had walked countless times before, she noticed Trudy sitting by the window. Eva waved to her friend, but Trudy did not wave back. Instead, she turned away. Maybe she did not see Eva?

Eva knocked on the door and Trudy's mother answered. Trudy had always said that her mother was strict and a true disciplinarian. Eva asked to see Trudy, but her mother said she was busy with schoolwork. Eva told Trudy's mother that she could come by the next day. She responded *no* once more. Eva's heart sank.

"Why won't you let me see Trudy?" she asked, almost begging.

"Eva, Germans and Jews can no longer mix," Trudy's mother said matter-of-factly.

"I'm as German as you are," Eva responded with tears in her eyes. "German blood runs through my veins just like you."

"Yes, but the difference is you are Jewish—Jewish blood runs through *your* veins."

Eva was silenced by these words. She closed her eyes as darkness closed around her mind. She heard Trudy's mother say that Trudy had joined the *Bund Deutscher Mädel,* the female branch of the Hitler Youth, and that she would be trained for her important role in German society: wife, mother, and homemaker. First and foremost, Trudy would self-sacrifice for Germany. Eva could not comprehend any of it as she stared blankly at Trudy's mother. In a haze of sadness and anger, Eva tried to push herself past Trudy's mother, but her mother forced the front door closed, slamming it shut in Eva's face. Eva banged on the door several times yelling Trudy's name, but no one came to the door. Only silence permeated on the other side. She stood on the grass and shouted Trudy's name again. More silence.

Somehow her legs steered her numb body home as tears spilled down her cheeks, soaking her blouse's collar. Her closest friend had instantly become a stranger, someone with whom she could no longer relate. Confused, Eva's heart grew dark.

# chapter

# THREE

On a warm, breezy night in May 1933, walking home from a dinner party, Eva came upon a large crowd of people in the cobblestone public square, Opernplatz, opposite Humboldt University and next to the seventeenth century opera house. Curious about the gathering, she stood at the back of the thickly lined, rowdy crowd and within seconds, fear grew within her. A sick feeling in her stomach emerged twisting it into knots. Nazi storm troopers and German students from universities, once regarded with prestige, stood around a bonfire and tossed thousands of books to the flames. While doing so, they cheered, gave the Nazi salute, and proudly waved the Nazi flag.

To Eva's horror, she realized that these books weren't just any books; they were books that they all knew well, that she had read, and that went against Nazi ideology. The German campaign to purify its language and intellectualism was well underway. When the Brown Shirts (*Sturmabteilung*) threw more fuel to the roaring fire proceeded by thundering "Heils" and rejoicing, she knew this barbaric event would go on for hours and the heaps of books scattered on the ground would all turn quickly to ash. No books would be spared. German spirit would triumph. Her eyes scanned the crowd around her. Who were these people so actively engaged in this heinous activity? Did they not see the wrong? The cheering and laughter around Eva and the enthusiasm from the crowd proved this wasn't just an event, it was a celebration.

People cheered and clapped when a familiar face in the Third Reich, a man named Joseph Goebbels, Reich Minister for Propaganda, appeared in the center of the crowd. He was a small man with a crippled foot, a disproportionately large head and a fragile body. A psychological master, he addressed the crowd with an official stamp from the government.

Immediately silence blanketed the crowd as he mesmerized them with these words:

*"My fellow students, German men, and women, the era of exaggerated Jewish intellectualism is now at an end. The triumph of the German revolution has cleared a path for the German way. And the future German man will not just be a man of books, but also a man of character and it is to this end they want to educate you. To have at an early age the courage to peer directly into the pitiless eyes of life. To repudiate the fear of death in order to gain again the respect for death. That is the mission of the young and therefore you do well at this late hour to entrust to the flames the intellectual garbage of the past. It is a strong, great and symbolic undertaking, an undertaking, which shall prove to all the world that the intellectual basis of the November Republic is here overturned; but that from its ruins will arise victorious the lord of a new spirit."*

The Nazis had declared war on reason itself. As the nationwide campaign unraveled before Eva's eyes, Jewish intellectualism and thought quickly turned to cinder. Literature, science, and philosophy were consigned to the flames. Brilliant books by many well-known Germany writers, such as Sigmund Freud, Albert Einstein, Karl Marx, Stefan Zweig, and even non-German writers like Jack London and Helen Keller were seen as evil and even dangerous, thrown like rubbish into the burning, crackling pile as a way to cleanse anything different or that reflected Jewish thought. Eva placed a handkerchief over her nose and mouth. The stench of burning was repulsive. Her head began to pound and she became so nauseated.

As Eva pushed her way through the dense crowd, she felt a hand grab her arm. "Eva, it's me, Trudy!"

A nervous feeling emerged in the pit of Eva's stomach as she turned to face her. They were both shocked to see each other. It was unbearably awkward, especially with regard to what was happening around them and Trudy's willing participation in such an event. Eva did not recognize the person who stood before her anymore.

Sensing Eva's discomfort, Trudy quickly said, "It's good to see you again." Her green eyes analyzed Eva, breaking her down into little pieces.

"It's obvious what came between us, Trudy," Eva managed to say. "I have to go."

"*Gute Nacht*," Eva said, wishing her old friend goodnight.

"*Auf Wiedersehen*," Trudy said.

As Eva turned to walk away, she heard Trudy say, "Eva, I am sorry." She did not turn around to acknowledge it. Trudy then walked toward her friends, many of them university students who held piles of books in their arms, ready to throw them to the flames.

Walking away from the crowd, Eva prayed that she would never see Trudy again, the face of a Nazi, who was once a friend.

Amid the Nazi songs and shouts of joy, Eva sobbed in the dark corner of a nearby building, afraid of the future. She wondered why this was happening. What was going to become of the city she loved? She heard ugly, hateful words and joyous chants, and as the flames set aglow in the night sky, Eva saw the illuminated faces of close-minded, anti-Semitic young men, women and Nazi youth. This was now personal. As they embraced Hitler, Eva embraced anything and everything Jewish and held it sacred. At that moment, she prayed to God to help make sense of the changing world around her.

# chapter

# FOUR

On the 30th of January 1933, the night of Hitler's appointment to the chancellorship, massed Nazi storm troopers marched through Berlin streets to the imposing Brandenburg Gate, waving torches and singing. They moved on past the Reich Chancellery where Hitler and Hindenburg stood on a balcony that overlooked massive crowds of onlookers. Hindenburg had reluctantly agreed to appoint Hitler as leader after influential politicians, industrialists, and businessmen urged him to do so.

The evening marked the beginning of the end of the Weimar Republic, and Germany was well on a road to an authoritarian dictatorship. Hitler was now master of his own destiny and his country's fate.

It began to snow lightly, and the dawn of a new era had begun, an altogether different era. From this moment, Jews suddenly sensed a different atmosphere, one that didn't have a promising or bright future. Young and old felt very insecure.

As life began to change, Eva and Inge stayed home more often. Their parents worried about them being out, day or night, on the precarious Berlin streets.

One evening, their parents invited their neighbors, the Kleins, over for dinner. After dinner, Eva and Inge excused themselves. Eva sat on the stairs and while she was reading, she listened in on her parents' conversation. She had been mostly sheltered from the cracks that existed in the fragile world around them, but now she needed to know more. She was getting too old for her parents to keep things from her.

"Hitler is becoming a problem for us all," said Joseph Klein, a Jewish banker. "I hardly sleep anymore. I worry all day and all night. Just the other day, I walked by the charred Reichstag building. I tell you, that fire worked to Hitler's advantage. He attacked the Communists, captured them, and made the public believe the country was under attack."

"That is true, Joseph," Oskar said. "After that fire, he placed the nation under his thumb. Hitler's a smart man, always relying on something big, to get the public's attention and win them over. And he wins every time. The people wanted promising solutions to the economic crisis and they got it with Hitler in power. The German people have looked towards radical solutions and extremism for some time now."

"We are sorely hated," said Joseph, taking a sip of his whiskey. "We are blamed for the country's economic problems and failure in World War I. And, it's ludicrous that Hitler blames the Jews for taking over the country, yet we are only one percent of the population."

"Don't worry, Joseph," Oskar responded, putting a reassuring hand on Joseph's arm. "Hitler will get over his feelings. He will have more important matters to attend to other than us. This will all blow over soon. You will see."

Eager to change the topic of conversation, Oskar asked Helene, "What's for dessert, *Mein Liebling*?"

From conversations at dinner tables to the printed words of newspapers, the real story of the moment was that Hitler's problems did not stop at the Jews. He saw a lack of support within the Nazi party and in order to gain control over the government and his political attitude toward the Jews, he decided to act with brutality and test loyalties. The rowdy Nazi storm troopers (*Sturmabteilungen,* SA) were a key force in Hitler's rise to power. By 1934, they numbered over two million men, and some members accused Hitler of betraying the National Socialist agenda. Hitler smelled nuisance and feared upheaval within the unpredictable, undisciplined group, many of whom were rumored to be homosexuals, which Hitler frowned upon. Hitler feared the independence of the SA and their penchant for street violence was a threat towards his newly gained power.

During the weekend of June 30, 1934, what came to be known as the Night of the Long Knives, Hitler slaughtered many of the top leaders of the SA, including the head man, Ernst Roehm, the most powerful man in Germany under Hitler. Roehm readily refused the offer of a pistol to shoot himself, so a vicious high-ranking official of the SS ("Protective Squadron") named Theodore Eicke shot Roehm in the head with the same pistol. Newspaper headlines boasted *"Traitors of SA Shot,"* and now, with his enemies wiped out, Hitler's grip on Germany was secure as Fuhrer, his army swore an oath to fully obey him, and his knives were fully sharpened. If Hitler could easily eliminate those closest to him, then many others did not stand a chance.

Meanwhile, the hostility towards Jews increased dramatically. The Nazis launched a boycott on Jewish-owned shops in Berlin. Helene arrived home one afternoon and told her daughters that two SA guards were standing in front of the bakery and refused to let anyone through the doors. Helene, who did not look Jewish, and a woman of strong will and unwavering fortitude, pushed her way into the shop. Mr. Bernstein willingly served her, threw some extra pastries and bread into a bag, and warned her to not return. Usually Helene would not have listened to someone telling her she could not return to a certain place, but this time she understood. This would be the last time any of them would be able to enter the bakery or any other Jewish-owned shop. Soon, it became a criminal act to support the Jews.

"Where is Papa?" Eva asked her mother one evening.

"Your father said he had to work late tonight."

"But Papa should not be out alone at night," Eva said. "We are forbidden to go out alone, so how can he walk these menacing streets?"

"Don't worry, Eva," Helene responded. "He will be home soon. He had to take care of some business at the diamond center."

These days, Eva always worried about everything and everyone.

❧

As day became night and as concern for his business and family grew, Oskar sorted through the jewelry in his collection. He carefully selected his most unique and valuable pieces. He cut the chains off all the diamond pendant necklaces as he saw the long chains as a hindrance. He carefully wrapped some loose diamonds into *briefjes* and then hid the special kind of paper behind a large bandage on his stomach. He placed more loose stones in his chest pocket for reasons of bribery, if his plan was not successful.

Oskar opened the bag of pastries from the bakery that his wife dropped off two hours before. They were still moist and warm. He carefully stuffed each unique piece of jewelry he had selected into a pastry. Then, he placed the pastries back in the bag and added extra ones on top that did not contain jewelry. Oskar pocketed his gold loupes. He grabbed his coat, and before turning off the lights of his diamond center, he stood for a brief moment, taking it all in. He looked around as if taking a mental picture and made certain that he was not forgetting anything. Then, he switched off the lights, opened the door and walked out, secretly carrying more than 30 carats of diamonds.

"Stop!" announced a German voice. The armed guard who patrolled the street and his center raised his hand in front of Oskar's chest.

Oskar paused and stood before the guard as calm as possible. He noticed the guard's impressive all-black SS uniform with a black swastika armband. His shiny black riding boots made him seem taller than he really was and his menacing look loomed over Oskar.

"*Ja*, Officer?" Oskar responded, staring at the guard.

"*Was ist im Beutel* - What is in the bag?" the guard asked.

"*Frisches Gebäck für meine Familie* - Fresh pastries for my family," Oskar said, breaking into a sweat. Oskar opened the bag for the guard to see. His heart pounded rapidly and his legs felt weak. Panic rose in his chest.

"*Möchten Sie ein Gebäck* - Would you like a pastry?" Oskar asked, trying hard to remain calm and wanting to kick himself for even offering the guard a pastry. He couldn't believe his nonsensical slip of the tongue.

"*Ja*," said the guard, reaching into the bag.

Oskar forced a smile as the guard took a pastry from the bag.

"*Genießen* - Enjoy," Oskar said. "*Gute Nacht.*"

The guard bit off the end of the pastry.

He then faced Oskar, raised his right hand in the air, and said emphatically, "*Heil Hitler!*"

"*Heil Hitler*," Oskar responded in a quiet voice.

Oskar turned and walked quickly toward home. At the corner of the block, he glanced in the direction of the guard. The pastry was still in the guard's hand as he was now talking to someone on the street. Oskar's nerves stood on end. He wasn't certain which pastry the guard had chosen. At last he reached his apartment building. Frantic beyond belief, he opened the door and walked inside.

Eva had never seen her father so unnerved. The minute he walked in the door, he closed the drapes and curtains.

"Everyone, come downstairs!" Oskar yelled, upon hearing their voices upstairs.

"Max, Eva, Inge, Helene!"

Running down the stairs, Eva said, "What's wrong, Papa?"

"Come, everyone, sit down," he said, almost out of breath.

"You are scaring me," Inge said. "You look like you have seen a ghost, Papa."

"I am alright, Inge," he said. "Where's Max?"

"He is not home yet," Inge replied.

"I cannot stand your brother being out at all hours and no one knows where he is," he raised his voice. "I should have put a stop to it long ago. It's no longer safe."

"We'll have a talk with him later, Oskar," Helene said. "Why are you so flustered?"

"Not now, Helene," Oskar opened the bag of pastries. "Here, everyone, take a pastry."

"Why, Papa?" Eva asked. "Shouldn't we save them for after supper?"

"No, Eva, there's no time for questions," he responded, loosening his blue silk tie. "Please do as I say and don't ask questions. We have to find my jewelry inside these pastries. I know it sounds crazy. But I have hidden my jewelry inside the pastries. Then, as I walking out of the diamond center, the guard stopped me. I was so afraid. I told him that I had bought pastries for my family and all I could think to do was offer him one. The guard grabbed a pastry from the bag and then as he took a bite, I was able to quickly walk away. I am petrified as to which pastry he chose."

Inge and Eva looked at each other with deep concern. Helene did not look at anyone, but at the bag of pastries.

In silence, they ripped open the pastries.

Oskar's eyes scanned every Danish and *Pfannkuchen*.

"How many pieces are we looking for, Papa?" Eva asked.

"Five," he said. "Two rings and three pendants. I sold the rest of my inventory last week."

"Here are the rings!" Eva gasped, showing them off after wiping them clean of jam, custard and sugar.

"A pendant!" Helene yelled.

"Another pendant," Eva said, holding up the jewel.

"Anything, Inge?" asked Oskar with worry in his eyes.

"No, Papa," she said, softly.

"Let's look again," Oskar said. "Please, we must have overlooked it somehow."

"Nothing, Papa," Eva said.

"This can't be," Oskar responded, holding his head in his hands.

Helene went over to him and held him.

"How could this happen?" Oskar asked. "I thought I had put enough extra pastries in the bag as a barrier to the pastries that held the jewelry. If the guard took the pastry with the pendant, then why didn't he come after me right then and there? My God, I have put my family in grave danger. I'm so sorry."

Oskar cried. It was the first time Eva and her sister had seen him cry.

That night, none of them could sleep a wink. They searched further, even in the rubbish, but still could not find the diamond pendant. They feared the Gestapo would knock on the door at any moment and take them away, but they never came. Every day, fear and intensity consumed them. Life was changing quickly. Oskar never returned to the diamond center. He was forced to sell it for very little money. As a Jew, he was no longer allowed to own a business.

After that night, Oskar and Helene began to live low profile lives. They rarely left the apartment, only for food. Max, Inge, and Eva went to school and came straight home. Max was still a member of the BDJJ, but Oskar demanded that he spend more time at home with the family and not on the dangerous streets. Oskar also stressed to Max that affiliating himself with BDJJ was not wise. Max did listen, but only for a short time. Several of the BDJJ members became a part of the resistance movement; therefore, young Max began to make some beneficial connections within the movement.

Max tried to persuade his father that they disappear underground and hide from the Nazis. Oskar refused to be known as *"U-Boats"*, to be pigeonholed and live that way. Becoming a "U-Boat", a Jew in hiding, took foresight and planning. Like the submariners the name was coined after, Jewish U-Boats disappeared underground only after careful planning. A secure place needed to be identified, resources needed to be in place, and those who went underground needed to acquire false papers. Money was vital, too – lots of it. And, a certain level of trust had to be put in place. At this point, Oskar did not trust anyone or anything.

"The Gestapo will find us wherever we hide," Oskar said. "It's like they can smell us in the air."

"We must go," Max reinforced. "We cannot stay here. Berlin is no longer a place I can call home."

Oskar shook his head at his son.

"It's too risky to leave," Oskar told Max. "Berlin will always be home."

"Risky?" Max said. "Father, we face greater risk staying in Berlin."

"Hitler will eventually fail," Oskar said. "I believe that things will settle down."

Max sighed, looked down at the floor, and said, "I don't know, Father."

"What do you mean, I don't know," Oskar said. "I know…"

"Stop bickering at each other," Helene said. "Max may be talking some sense, Oskar. Life has become too dangerous. I worry about what will happen to us. All I know is that we have each other and we must stay together, always. It would break my heart to see this family split apart for some terrible reason."

"Ach, Helene," Oskar said. "We will always be together, no matter what happens."

"I hope so, Oskar," she said. "Sometimes families get torn apart in times like these."

"No, not my family," he said, taking his wife's hand.

Helene forced a smile.

Oskar was proud of his German heritage and he would endure discrimination just like other generations of Jews had endured. His threshold was strong and he was willing to withstand what was to come.

He refused to leave the environment that had been his home since he was born. In essence, he feared leaving Germany. It was all Oskar knew, and Germans like him, shared that same fear.

Joseph Klein and his wife, who lived in the same apartment building, offered their extra room as a way for them to hide, but my father refused that as well. The Kleins were Jewish and they faced the same plight.

And then, any form of human rights they had left was vanquished. In 1935, the Nazis passed the "Law for the Protection of German Blood and German Honor," better known as the Nuremberg Laws on Citizenship and Race. The Germans used race to define the Jewish people and these laws determined that Jews were a sub-race of the human species. Consequently, Jews were prohibited from sexual intercourse with non-Jews. Therefore, all intermarriages were also prohibited to protect "German blood and honor." Disgracing the German race or any violations against the law became a punishable offense. Jews could no longer be citizens of Germany. Hitler warned that if the laws did not solve the problem, then he would look to the Nazi party for a final solution for the Jews.

The Nazi symbol was visible everywhere and there was no escaping the contagious propaganda that spread like a virus poisoning people's minds. *Der Sturmer*, a weekly anti-Semitic newspaper, printed non-stop propaganda, such as anti-Semitic cartoons and caricatures, making wild, insidious allegations that Jews were rats and parasites, among other horrible things. The bottom of the first page of the newspaper always bore a horrible motto, *"Die Juden sind unser Unglück!* - The Jews are our misfortune!" The paper was an influential propaganda machine and its readership grew among the working class of Germany. A printed card was even distributed that allowed anyone to mail-in a story for the newspaper regardless of its legitimacy or verifiable evidence. Many readers were the children of Germany and Hitler's youth, whose minds were possessed instantly by the continuous propaganda and anti-Semitic brainwashing.

The chatter within the Jewish community revolved around death camps, and the rumors became widespread, but many Jews did not believe the stories. Nazi deception and the human tendency to deny bad news took over people's minds. Some Jews thought that there was no precedence for such monstrous activities. Many Jews and others believed that the Germans ordered Jews to pack their belongings, leading to the belief that Jews were being resettled elsewhere. However, Eva believed the Nazis were extremely capable of building and running death camps, and of killing Jews.

Life as they knew it diminished quickly and became abnormal, like an out-of-body experience. Every day things seemed to get worse and Eva felt as though she was living in a nightmare. Every morning when she awoke, she hoped that it was all just a bad dream. But it was very real. German society rejected Jews on all accounts.

One day, they were advised that they had to deliver their radios, jewelry and silverware at the nearest police precinct. On that day, they stood in line for three hours and eventually they could enter the precinct house. Rows of tables lined the room, and piles of radios, silverware, and jewelry covered the walls. As they stood waiting for their turn to let go of their valuables, police around them shouted horrible things, like "this place stinks from garlic." The Nazis kept very descriptive and detailed records of the German population. They knew exactly who you were and what you owned. There were no mistakes.

When it was their turn to place their goods on the table, the guard first checked off their names on the master list. They handed over two radios, silver candlesticks, silver serving platters, Helene's wedding ring, and a few smaller pieces of jewelry.

"That's everything?" the guard asked as another guard approached the table. Before Eva could respond, her mother responded, "Yes, that is everything."

As they walked away from the tables, Eva whispered in her mother's ear, "What about the pendant necklace?"

Helene grabbed her daughter in a tight embrace.

"Don't talk of the necklace anymore," Helene said in a quiet voice. "As far as anyone is concerned, it no longer exists. The jewel is hidden away. Do you understand?"

"Yes, Mother," Eva said.

Like criminals, they received identity cards, which included a photograph and fingerprints, as well as a large letter, "J" for "*Jude*", on its cover. In addition, all Jewish males received the additional name Israel and all Jewish females received the name Sara, to be inserted between the first name and the surname. They were forced to sign with this additional name and if not, they would be severely punished. Eva felt like an alien in her own country. As she looked around the room, her heart broke as she watched people of her own kind having to give up part of their lives and surrender their identities to ruthless, evil people who led their beloved Germany. It was the worst feeling: to be stripped of a nationality that was part of a person's inalienable rights.

But it was only the beginning.

The Nazi who came to their home on a brisk November morning was no storm trooper. He wore a black business suit, a grey silk tie, and a crisp white shirt. He looked like a typical Berlin businessman. But he was not in their home on ordinary business.

"The Gestapo has made an inventory of the jewels and it seems some were missing when you handed over your goods at the police precinct," he said, sitting on the couch with his legs crossed. "There is one piece in particular we are interested in."

Oskar squinted at the man.

"We have given up all we own," Oskar replied.

"Oh, Oskar, maybe I need to refresh your memory," the man said, pulling out a pack of cigarettes. He pulled out a red lighter and lit his smoke, staring down at Oskar. "You once owned a splendid emerald and diamond necklace. Do you still own that piece of jewelry?"

Oskar glared at the man, hesitant to answer. If he said no, he knew he would be putting himself and his family in grave danger because clearly the man knew the piece was still in his possession.

"I will ask one more time, Oskar," the man said. "I will give you one more chance."

Oskar looked away in contemplation. He simply feared handing over the necklace that was so invaluable and precious.

"The Nazi wife or mistress who wears that necklace will be one very happy, very satisfied woman," he said. "Do you agree?"

The thought disgusted Oskar.

"Yes," Oskar said softly.

"Do I need to arrest you, right here, right now?"

"No," Oskar said. "Please...I will give you the necklace. Wait here."

The man smiled, taking another puff from his cigarette.

Oskar removed a Persian rug and unlocked a small safe hidden under a floor board in the master bedroom. He grabbed the necklace and held it in his hands. He stared at the diamonds and emerald, glimmering back at him, as if the gems were trying to tell him something. He kissed the pendant necklace and walked back to the parlor where the man was seated.

Oskar handed the necklace over to the man. No more words were exchanged. The man stood up and left the home.

Oskar returned to the master bedroom where the safe lay empty. He gasped and sank to his knees, full of despair and sadness. He no longer felt human. The Nazis were stripping him of everything, from his rights to his valued possessions. He felt powerless and insignificantly small, as the Nazis became the supreme power.

He cried, tears dripping down his cheeks. Exhausted, he dragged himself to his bed and fell into a deep sleep filled with nightmares.

Day after day, the black leather boots of Nazi soldiers pounded against the pavement. The unmistakable Nazi symbol grew even more pervasive, spilling down from the walls of buildings with the Nazi flag flapping in the wind. The extended arm of men, women and children giving the infamous Nazi salute. The nonstop, in-your-face Nazi propaganda that made Jews feel helpless, like the world was against them. As the Nazis rose to power, immense tension rippled through the Jewish communities of Europe.

The future was unknown. The rumors were unsettling and unnerving. The place they called home became unsafe and a breeding ground for hatred. The friends they once knew and adored now looked away when they waved. It was as if they had never met. Other friends merely disappeared, not to be heard from again.

One night, total madness erupted on their street. Their lives as they had always known it ended that night. Germany had disappointed them. From that moment on, everything changed for Jews in Europe. Completely terrified, Eva finally believed that every Jew was in grave danger. She saw the writing on the walls like Max did and she realized that they must leave Germany sooner than later.

It was foggy that night, November 9, 1938. They sat in their dimly lit apartment eating dinner. These days they kept as discrete as possible. Suddenly, chaos and noise erupted in the dark streets. Inge blew out the burning candle and they sat in the dark quietly. They looked out the window and noticed the orange glow of a fire down the street. They could hear breaking glass in the streets. The sidewalks were abnormally empty. Nazi vehicles whizzed by carrying shouting, disorderly young men. They could not decipher what they shouted about or what was happening.

Then, there was a knock at their door and they all jumped from fright.

"Mama? Papa?" They heard from the other side of the door. They recognized the voice and opened the door slightly. Max stood before them, out of breath from sprinting down the street. They let him into the dark apartment and he sat frightened on the couch as his knees trembled. He removed his hat, showing his dark brown hair wet from perspiration and shock.

Oskar gave him some water. After a few minutes, he settled down and told them what he had seen. His hands shook as tears fell from his sad hazel eyes. Eva grabbed his hand and he began to talk, his voice faint.

"I was walking along the sidewalk when all of the sudden I heard a window smash to the ground," Max said. "I quickly looked behind me and noticed it was a Jewish shop, the Bernsteins' bakery. I ran for my life. I noticed a blaze of fire and realized it came from our shul. I stood across the street on the pavement stones and watched as the domed roof collapsed. A Nazi took out the Torah scrolls and books, piled them high in the street, and set them on fire. Nazis plundered the Torah silver. The shul where I had my Bar Mitzvah has been destroyed. Everything important to us is disintegrating before our eyes."

Helene began to cry and moved closer to her two daughters.

"I saw groups of storm troopers and SS men jump off their lorries and smash up shops with great truncheons," Max continued. "They shouted and laughed as they continued to torch and vandalize other shops on the street. Men in cars threw stones through shop windows. Broken glass and wrecked goods from the shops littered the streets. As I hid in the alleyway, I saw our butcher, Mr. Goldman, dragged from his apartment and beaten on the street before my eyes."

Inge looked pale. "What's happening to this city, to our home?"

Oskar held his daughter tightly. "It's only an episode, Inge," he said. "It can't get any worse. It just can't."

"It's not an episode, Father," Max said. "Things are going to get worse. I've warned you."

"We must leave," Helene said. "We cannot live like this anymore."

Oskar eyed his wife. Usually she was right.

Infinite terror gripped them through the night on November 9, 1938. They huddled together, too frightened to move, on the floor in the corner of their parents' bedroom in the darkness and silence of their apartment. They didn't sleep a wink, nor utter a word. They prayed together. Prayers were mixed with tears. They listened to the violence that surrounded them.

Through the night, they heard loud knocks and the sound of Nazis bursting into apartments below them. Nazis screamed in the apartment block and in the streets unspeakable names, such as *Drecks Juden*, *Stink Juden*, and *Schweine*, and threatened the instant annihilation of all Jews. They heard Nazi soldiers trampling apartments with their enormous boots and rifle ends. They sang the horrible words to a song they heard often these days: "*Wenn's Judenblut vom messer spritzt dann geht's nochmal so gut* (when Jewish blood spurts from the knife, then life will be twice as good)."

By the morning hours, exhaustion sunk in on top of nerves and shock. The noise and violence around them had died down, and they were some-how spared. How? God only knows. Maybe they had taken enough Jews. Maybe it was their strong foresight to pull the mezuzah off the door. It didn't matter. They were safe. But they were still hunted.

When a cold dawn finally came and the faint morning sun peeked through the lingering fog, the evidence of the night became visible. Fires continued to smolder. Broken glass crystallized the streets. It looked like they had suffered an air raid. Residents stood in the streets as they watched the synagogues continue to burn to the ground. Everyone seemed to be asking for forgiveness, but no one said a word or did anything to stop the roaring flames or the destruction that had occurred only hours before.

Curious, Eva and Inge cautiously left the building. As they looked more 'Aryan' than Jewish, it was easier to disguise themselves in these situations. They made no eye contact with anyone. They pointed their eyes down at the street and walked without saying a word to each other. They noticed hundreds of Jewish men on their hands and knees. They held little brushes in their hands to clean up the broken glass that littered the streets. Some were forced to sweep up the glass with their long beards. Nazi soldiers stood like giants over the men and whipped them. The scene was shocking and heartbreaking. What was even more disappointing was the crowd of people who were enjoying the show before them, as well as many people who walked by and did nothing to intervene.

Eva wondered how these people were human? Bystanders risked their lives speaking up, but they were perpetrators of violence. They were human beings, witnesses to a crime against humanity; yet silent witnesses, who walked from the scene with only a pang of conscience. The Nazi system was quickly dehumanizing people and eliminating their courage to oppose evil.

Some shops and business were still ablaze from the night before. Jews who tried to enter their businesses to save goods were held back by the SS. They stood by and watched their possessions burn, everything they had worked for turning to ash. Firemen directed their hoses to non-Jewish businesses to save them from the fires. Very quickly and inconspicuously, the twins went back to the apartment and stayed there the rest of the day in quiet darkness.

News transpired through word-of-mouth, through European newspapers, and through an underground newspaper, *Freiheit* (Freedom), written in secret code with cryptic drawings, which slid under their door during the night. The newspaper revealed that the whirlwind of destruction had spread from the streets of Berlin to the smallest towns of Germany and Austria. More than a thousand synagogues were set on fire and destroyed. Tens of thousands of Jewish shops and homes were ransacked and Jewish books were burnt to ash. In the twenty-four hours of violence, ninety-one Jews were killed and more than 30,000 Jewish men and boys were sent to concentration camps. With shattered glass covering the streets of Germany, the Nazi pogrom became known as *Kristallnacht*: the Night of the Broken Glass. The Nazis were retaliating against the Jews for the Paris murder of a young German diplomat by a Polish-German Jew. The event became the turning point toward the murder of six million Jews in the Holocaust.

Soon after that horrific 24 hours, Oskar told them that he had gone to check on Joseph and his wife. When he came upon their apartment, he found their door sealed. Whenever the Nazis captured Jewish inhabitants, they sealed the doors. Their furniture and possessions were confiscated by the German state. It was obvious they were sent to the east, to the concentration camps—their fates sealed forever.

# chapter

# FIVE

The family decided to leave Germany immediately. They could no longer wait out the storm, which would not be over any time soon and would wreak havoc in its path. The promising future in Germany that Oskar once believed in had insidiously faded away. For him, there was never a good enough reason to leave. Now, the reasons became crystal clear. They could barely walk in the streets without feeling like they were in danger every moment. They were no longer allowed to live as normal human beings. They lived in constant fear and panic. They felt like criminals. They were Jewish. They were hunted, every second of every day, like animals. And, they had become strangers to everyone.

Two options existed—flee Europe or become victims. The decision to emigrate weighed heavily on all of their minds and its urgency grew. They knew time was running out and that they needed to set their plans in place as fast as possible. Now, the most important thing was where to go and how to leave Germany. Oskar became depressed and anxious, for he saw the true tragedy in it all—the real need to emigrate became evident, but the German exit door closed tightly and the countries that were once accepting Jews tightened their doors, too. Now, certain conditions and qualifications had to be met in order to leave Germany, and if not, leaving would only be a dream. Nobody wanted the Jews. Quiet despair settled over them. They needed some good luck and a quick solution.

After preliminary investigations, they decided to go to Antwerp, Belgium. Getting there was not an easy feat.

෨෴

Max saw the true value in devoting less time to the BDJJ and more to the underground resistance. Eva admired his courage and defiance. Over time, their parents began to also see the value in his involvement as well. Max hoped that his connection with the underground resistance would help pave the way for his family to securely leave Germany.

The underground network was a small, isolated group led by a man named Erik, an ex-intelligence officer at the Reich Air Ministry. Erik was an anti-Nazi who demanded nothing more in return for his assistance than the defeat of Hitler. The group contained people of various beliefs and affiliations. The core of the group included an author, a nun, a pianist, an electrician, a professor of economics, and a journalist. The rest of the group was a mix of men and women whose main activity was to help Jews leave Germany and distribute information, such as leaflets against Hitler. These were the people who Max became closest to, his comrades. Some smuggled arms, while others ran illegal newspaper presses, and others arranged escapes and false identities.

Max realized that if he helped the group in some way, they would, in turn, help him and his family. So, Max began to assist the group in publishing illegal newspapers, which were typed and reproduced on mimeograph machines. They gathered news from the British Broadcasting Company and Soviet broadcasts on hidden radios. Once published, underground couriers, usually young children and teenagers, since they could move around more freely without arousing suspicion, delivered newspapers to thousands of Jews awaiting news and information.

It was a huge risk and underground couriers traveled under false papers. Many collaborators, police, and spies searched for these underground combatants. They knew how to spot a Jew. Not only that, but the German secret police, the *Gestapo*, and the intelligence agency, *Abtheyhr*, constantly hunted members of the resistance. The resistance groups were smart. They developed secret codes and messages, complex communications networks, and for a short time, they were one step ahead of Nazi Germany. And, for now, so was Max.

As the late afternoon air grew chilly, Max buttoned his coat as he stood in an old cobbled courtyard tucked away at the end of a garbage-filled alleyway. He reached into his pocket for the note and a small hand-drawn map that he acquired earlier that day at approximately 11:30 a.m. at a cozy bookshop near his father's diamond business. The information was hidden on page 78 of a children's book called *Emil and the Three Twins*, written by popular German author Erich Kastner. Just 15 minutes prior to Max's arrival at the shop, at around 11:15 a.m., a nun entered the bookshop, walked to the children's book section, and slipped the note and map into the book. Before the nun left the store, she chatted for a few short minutes with the shop's owner. An avid reader, Sister Lydia, frequented the book-shop often.

Max examined the map carefully, looking around the courtyard. There was no one in sight. Towards the back of the courtyard behind a broken fountain, he noticed the stone steps, marked on the map.

Max sighed as he climbed the worn stone steps. He brushed through his hair with his hands, making sure he looked presentable. He straight-ened the collar of his shirt. He heard a distant drip of water, but everything was silent.

At the top of the steps lay a big iron gate. He stopped, unsure where to go next or what to do. Max grabbed the note from his pocket, scanned the contents, and saw that it instructed him to tap the gate three times. He stared at his shoes, but that seemed like the wrong way.

Then, it occurred to Max that he could use his metal belt buckle. He unraveled the belt from his waist and tapped on the gate three times. He waited only a few seconds when a man suddenly appeared from a dark corner on the other side of the gate. Max jumped with fright, his hand over his chest.

"What's your name?" he asked, staring hard.

"Max."

Max pulled the map and note from his pocket and showed it to the man.

"Okay," the man said, giving Max the once-over and then unlocking the gate.

Max walked through the gate, his eyes on the man. Then, the man held out his hand.

"Sorry to be so cold and intimidating, young man," he said. "We need to be cautious with whoever passes through these gates."

"I'm Anton."

Max shook his hand.

Max followed Anton, a tall, muscular man in his late twenties, through a passageway. They entered the dark, smoky room through a metal doorway. They joined two leaders from the resistance group—Erik and Sister Lydia, a middle-aged nun with a calm exterior and soft-spoken demeanor. Erik was not only a strong leader and an ex-intelligence officer, but he was well-connected. He knew the justice minister of Luxembourg, a noble man with a vast network, who greatly risked his career to help save Jews.

They sat around a small table, drank dark coffee and nibbled on *lebkuchen* (gingerbread). In low voices, they discussed how the escape would unfold. The method was a simple one. Erik was mostly the brains behind the escape plan. He mapped the routes and hid the instructions in fountain pens, which he distributed to the group of people involved in the escape. For the plot to be truly successful depended on every part of the escape to go according to plan and that every person involved knew that they were a vital part to the greater whole. Mistakes could not be made and all those involved needed to be fully onboard and accountable. Erik had hand-selected the individuals who would help them along the way— those who risked their lives for them and many others; righteous human beings who showed decency, courage and hope. Their hearts—pure and simple. They knew the danger to help the Jews was enormous. Death was the punishment.

Train tickets had to be secured from Berlin to Trier, Germany, transport had to be arranged, and the intricate details had to be figured out, everything from emergency food to what was the best and securest route to Antwerp.

Erik scratched his forehead and folded his hands on the table.

"Of course, it's a risk," he said. "I am willing to set the plan in place for your family and make sure you arrive safely in Antwerp."

"Whatever we have to do, we will do," Max said. "My family is strong and we will face whatever we must face."

Max removed an envelope from his jacket pocket and slid it along the table toward Erik.

"The money and diamonds you requested for your services," Max said.

"Thank you," Erik responded as he grabbed the envelope. "And, by the way, thank you for your hard work."

They shook hands and Erik promised he would deliver the necessary visas and travel documents in the next few days.

Max returned home that day to nervous parents who feared losing money and valuable diamonds in exchange for nothing.

"Can we trust this gentleman?" Helene asked.

"Do we have a choice, Mother?" Max said, slightly agitated.

"I worry, Max," Oskar said. "I really worry. Our choices are limited, but I fear we have much at stake."

"Erik is a smart man with strong connections," Max said. "I trust this man with my life. He won't fail us. Everything will work out. I promise. Please trust me."

Days went by, and it seemed that time drifted by slowly as they eagerly awaited any word from Erik.

Then, after five long days, there was a faint knock at their door. A woman from the resistance group came to deliver an envelope that contained immigration visas for Belgium, fountain pens that hid mapped out routes, and important phone numbers. Their wait was finally over.

To their surprise, great fortune and advantage, Max's covert connections within the resistance movement turned out to be their ticket out of Germany.

☜☞

Seven days after Kristallnacht, they fled Germany. They said goodbye to the city that was once home, to the house that once kept them secure and safe, and to a community that once welcomed them with open arms.

The day they left Germany, they threw some clothes into suitcases. They took very little as Oskar instructed, leaving many memories behind. Everything they had earned and accumulated over their lifetime, their furniture, cutlery, beds, books, clothes was left behind. Eva and Inge struggled with deciding what to take as they wanted to take everything, but even they had to leave behind many photos and remnants of their childhood and teenage years.

Diamonds proved to be an invaluable asset and as German currency continued to lose its value, the value of a diamond grew strong. Diamonds were small enough to be concealed and instantly redeemable for money. The gems became the most feasible means to preserve the family's wealth.

One of the most important things Eva would take was a wool blanket her mother made for her many years ago that now concealed carats of diamonds. Eva's heart sank as her teary-eyed sister emerged from her room with one small black suitcase and the red scarf that they all adored on her. Inge also carried her old Steiff teddy bear that she cherished from her childhood and now acted as a secret hideaway for diamonds. Helene sewed the gems into the teddy bear's soft pot belly.

Eva hugged Inge tight. In life, very few things stay constant. Inge remained Eva's constant rock and energy for life.

Helene came downstairs in an outfit Eva and Inge had never seen before or even thought she would own. They looked at each other in surprise and back at their mother. She wore an old, drab skirt, flat black, sturdy shoes that a nun would wear, and a faded green wool sweater. Eva had never seen her mother wear flat shoes before. She wore no jewelry of any kind. Today, fashion and pride went out the door. None of that seemed important now. Their mother would always be the essence of elegance that they had always admired. She carried a small suitcase and a satchel containing the Holy Bible, which hid beautiful diamond jewelry in a carved out section of the book.

Oskar carried the rest of the diamonds, a few stones that were easily accessible wrapped in *briefjes* in his breast pocket, other jewelry and diamond stones in a small leather pouch, and more jewelry sewn into his hat and into the collar of his dark frock coat.

When the grandfather clock chimed at 10 o'clock in the morning, they stood, melancholy, at the door of their home, and took one last glimpse at the place that had brought them much peace over the years. Eva hoped her memories would forever remain intact with the same vividness.

"It's hard to let go, isn't it?" Oskar said to his family as he turned out the lights. Eva took her mother's hand as she had always taken hers in times of hardship. Oskar grabbed Inge's hand and Max followed as they walked out the door. How can they remember this place—this place that was once filled with such vibrancy and life?

So that they wouldn't draw any attention, any suspicion, they split up. Their parents walked down the street, and Max, Inge and Eva took another route. They knew the plan. They had gone through it in their minds at least a hundred times over the last few days.

At the crowded Friedrichstrasse train station, along the Spree River, the floor bore scuff marks of people rushing through checkpoints. Documents were scrutinized and decisions made. Eva noticed a young couple being instructed to wait. The guards stood together discussing them. They looked on nervously, holding hands. Fierce German Shepherds barked at onlookers. Standing close to Inge, Eva watched the dimly lit platforms, patrolled by armed guards, where overwhelmed people waited for their trains to arrive and depart.

They boarded the train. Eva and Inge couldn't speak, for the moment had come to say goodbye to the city they had always known and to face a future of complete uncertainty. Eva stared at the other trains in the station and at the Nazi flags that fluttered in the front of them. The train whistle blew as it rolled slowly out of the station toward Frankfurt and then to Trier—the oldest city in Germany, said to be older than Rome. Sitting in different sections of the train than their parents and brother, Inge and Eva did not make eye contact with anyone, nor speak to anyone. They sat, prayed, and hoped that they would make it to Belgium without being caught. They had a long and challenging journey ahead of them. From the streets to the train stations, Nazi guards with dogs stood on lookout for Jews fleeing Germany. They walked the aisles of the trains, inspecting papers.

The whole time Eva's stomach pained her from extreme anxiety. Her hands shook so much that she had to hide them from view. Time passed slowly. Eva did not know what to do with herself, so she stared out the window. She could not focus on anything. Everything became a nonsensical blur. Exhausted, she blinked several times and when the blur in her eyes cleared, everything became clear and finely outlined. She noticed colors. The speckles of green amid the trees and grass. Fluffy white clouds that lay in a background of blue sky. The many shades of winter—brown, grey and faint yellow. The familiar was becoming a strange, friendless place. She already missed Berlin—the Berlin she once knew, the Berlin that once inspired her.

Eva stared for a moment at her sister. She seemed so peaceful and serene as she lay sleeping upon her shoulder. Eva knew that life could change in mere seconds, that their plan could implode before their eyes at any moment, and that they could be under the thumb of the Nazis in an instant. Eva's one wish was for her family to be safe and secure. For once in her life, Eva wished for nothing more. Eva cupped her hands against the glass window and noticed the towns became countryside. The motion of the train and the long journey began to wear on Eva, too, and she drifted off into a deep, but a short-lived sleep.

Then, she felt someone nudge her arm.

"Ihre Unterlagen?"

Sleepy eyed, Eva looked up at a young, podgy uniformed SS officer standing in the aisle in front of her, demanding her papers.

45

Monique Roy

*"Ja, eine Moment,"* Eva said, fumbling in her bag for her papers, and so that she would not wake her sister, she grabbed Inge's papers, too. Eva didn't know how she managed to control her shaking hands for that moment.

*"Hier sind meine Dokumente,"* she responded as the nervous feeling built up in the pit of her stomach again. The man looked at the papers and then back at her. Then, he did something unexpected. He smiled, said "okay," and moved to the next person.

The sky grew dark when they arrived in Trier, Germany, a small, picturesque, venerable city. Eva couldn't even spot their parents or their brother as they walked off the train onto the platform. They disappeared among the crowd of people. Yet again, they walked separately from the train station to a designated meeting point, the cathedral, about a thirty-minute walk from the station.

Eva and Inge made a wrong turn from the station and had to ask for directions. This added a good twenty minutes to their arrival time at the church. Getting lost turned out to be a small breath of fresh air for them after a stressful couple of months. For a brief moment, they noticed peace and quiet, far away from the hustle and bustle of the busy streets of Berlin and the constant terror that gripped them as Jews in Germany. They found Trier to have the charm of a fairy tale—a medieval town with splendid architecture, fertile fields, extensive forests, and rolling hills surrounded by vineyards; the river Mosel running through it. They finally located the city center, which was mapped out for them, and like their brother instructed, they came upon a small alley. Walking down the alley, they suddenly saw the huge, asymmetrical cathedral in front of them.

Arriving at the door to the church, two middle-aged nuns practically pulled them inside. Helene became so unnerved by their late arrival that she had fainted while waiting for them. They found her lying across the church pew with her head resting on Oskar's lap. With a few hours to spare, the nuns gave them some food and some blankets so they could rest.

Before dawn came, Sister Lydia gave them warm coffee, some rolls and boiled eggs. It was not exactly a great meal, but as hunger took over, they welcomed any food put in front of them. They did not know when their next meal would be, so they ate hurriedly. When they had finished, she hurried them out of the church into a black Volkswagen van, where they lay holding each other, hidden under blankets, while Sister Lydia drove them to Vaux-Sur-Sure, located in the Ardennes in southeastern Belgium, about a two-hour drive from Trier.

"Why do you help us, Sister Lydia?" Helene broke the silence. "We are so grateful, but why? It is dangerous for you to help us. There's enormous risk that you could be shot."

She answered, "This is what our hearts dictate. You are our neighbors. We respect and love you. We open our doors and our arms; we must respond openly and seek the ideal of sainthood, regardless of our different races, religions and ethnic backgrounds. We must have love for one another."

"I'm happy to hear this," Helene responded. "I could never accept the notion that the whole world was against the Jews. Bless you, Sister Lydia. We are forever grateful."

Eventually, they arrived in Vaux-Sur-Sure, a small region with quiet forests and peaceful fields amid a rugged countryside, and headed a short distance to the Sauer River, which traversed Belgium, Luxembourg and Germany. Sister Lydia helped them out of the van. Oskar wanted to give her a diamond in return, but she refused. Instead, she said to them that they should never speak of her again and to forget her good name. They agreed. She drove away while Anton stood waiting for them by an old barn located near the Sauer River.

They spent the day hidden behind stacks of hay, until nightfall. Anton told them stories of the underground movement and how he was helping Jews escape Europe. He claimed to have helped 50 Jews escape into neutral territories from Germany and Poland.

"Why would a young man like you subject himself to grave danger?" Oskar asked. Thankful, but curious, they couldn't help, but wonder why people like Sister Lydia and Anton would put their lives in danger to help total strangers.

Their eyes turned to Anton.

"I have no family," Anton said, sitting on a small stack of hay next to Oskar. "I'm an only child, and I lost my parents in a tragic car accident when I was fifteen years old. When they were taken from me, I had no one to turn to and nowhere to go. I was alone and then a miracle happened. A Jewish man, a friend of my father, opened his door and his heart to me. One day, he came looking for my father and when I told him he had died, he helped me. When the Nazis came to power and life became dangerous for him, the only way to repay him was to help him escape from Germany. He begged me to go with him, but I wanted to help others as well. I dedicated my time to the underground movement and to helping the plight of the Jews."

"What if you are caught?" Max asked.

"Then I will die knowing I did the right thing and that I am righteous," he responded. "After my parents died, I thought I would never feel happiness again. I only felt sadness in my heart. The first time I helped a Jewish family escape, I remember how they were overcome with joy knowing they had made it out of Poland alive and that made me happy. For the first time in a long time, I laughed. Their young boy, who could not have been more than six years old, smiled at me as they said goodbye, and then he saluted me as if I was a soldier of some kind. I will never forget that."

Anton paused and looked at them. "If I refused to help the Jews, what would I tell my children one day?"

They sat for a moment reflecting on what he said, while enjoying the quiet countryside.

Anton disappeared from the barn and returned an hour later with some milk, bread, cheese and fruit, as well as a little Riesling, which was grown in the area. This little treat lifted their spirits. They ate and shared stories of life in Berlin before Hitler's rise to power.

As nightfall came, they continued their journey by boat under the canopy of the starlit sky. Eva could hear the call of an owl, a slow "whoo... whoo," and she knew they weren't entirely alone. She feared the quiet and the cloak of profound darkness that entrapped them as they floated down the free-flowing Sauer River.

Eventually, the air grew colder. As a ghostly mist quietly descended over the river, everyone grew tense. Blinded, Eva focused on the soft swirls of the river near their boat that momentarily soothed her nerves. She stifled a shiver and pulled up the collar of her coat. Eva drew in a long breath and closed her eyes for a brief moment. When she opened them, she noticed the faint glow of a flickering light through the low hanging mist. Her thoughts drifted to the home they left only days ago. She imagined it now sitting empty as darkness and cold inhabited it.

As the wind howled, the boat continued eastward, down a picturesque wooded valley and steep bluffs winding through the Luxembourg Ardennes. Eventually, it traversed its way near Martelange, a quaint town in the Belgian province of Luxembourg.

Anton passed the oars to Oskar, while he grabbed his binoculars and scanned the sides of the river where gentle slopes sustained tall black alder and willow trees. He mentioned that a Jewish man would be waiting for them along the way, so Anton could transport him to Martelange as well.

Out of the darkness about 50 feet in front of them appeared a man waving his arms. Anton grabbed the oars and steered the boat to the side of the river. As they came closer to the man, Eva noticed he was a thinly-built handsome man, with locks of curly brown hair and a light beard. Anton stopped the boat on the side and the man slid down the embankment to where it met the river. Anton helped him into the boat and the sisters moved to make room for him.

"Hello, I'm Isaac," he greeted them, shaking Inge and Eva's hands, as they sat nearest to him.

His soft brown eyes peered at them through small-rimmed spectacles that framed his face.

"Twins," he said in a whisper, with a smile. "You two are so alike... that's amazing. I have never seen anything like that. And, might I add, very beautiful as well."

Eva and Inge smiled at him, while Oskar studied the stranger for a brief moment.

The cold bit at Eva's bones and she wrapped her arm inside Inge's. Inge put her red scarf around Eva's neck. Then, Isaac took off his scarf and put it around Inge's neck, a sweet gesture from a new friend. "Thank you," she said.

"It's fine," he responded. "You must keep warm."

The silence of the night was broken by the sound of Flemish voices drifting from the roadside above. Anton motioned to them to remain quiet with his finger on his mouth. They drifted a short distance down the river where steep bluffs rose above them and they hid from view. The voices grew louder. Eva constantly feared getting caught. These moments created great risk for them, unnerving Eva so much that she wanted to vomit. And, she did, heaving over the side of the boat. Anton gestured to them again to get down in the boat. They lay as flat as they could on the floor of the boat, basically on top of one another, like dead fish. He threw two dark blankets at them so they could cover themselves. The voices continued. Then, the sounds of a car emerged. Eva could hardly breathe under the blankets. She felt Inge grab her hand. Eva squeezed Inge's hand, showing that she was okay. For thirty long minutes, they could hear the voices and the sounds of the running car. Eventually, the car drove away and the voices silenced. They waited on the side of the river a few more minutes until all was clear.

Anton ordered them to stay under the blankets on the floor of the boat. Eva felt the boat move again down the river. She tried to relax again, tuning out the world around her. She kept her eyes closed and imagined that she was sunbathing on a yacht headed toward a deserted island with palm trees and coconuts. She must have drifted off to sleep because she opened her eyes to her mother's concerned face. Everyone was standing near the boat, looking in her direction, and she was still lying like a fish on the floor of the boat under a blanket.

"Eva, are you okay?" asked Helene, as she brushed some hair away from Eva's tired eyes.

"Yes, Mother," Eva responded, pulling up to a sitting position. "I fell asleep, that's all."

Helene helped Eva out of the boat and Anton gave her some water. "Do you still feel sick?" he asked.

"I'm fine now," Eva said. "Thank you, Anton." She felt slightly embarrassed.

Inge and Helene helped Eva to a rock on the side of the river. They had arrived in Martelange, Belgium, on the banks of the Sauer.

Oskar offered Anton two diamonds for his help. He took the diamonds and shook their hands, "Good luck," he said to them.

Suddenly, car lights cut through the darkness and came toward them, flashing on and off. The car was accelerating hard. Seconds later, an old yellow Mercedes arrived with another smuggler who did not offer them his name. He had a thick, graying beard, bushy eyebrows, and a heavy figure that made him appear an older man.

The smuggler demanded payment up front before driving them to Antwerp, Belgium, almost 120 miles north of Martelange.

Oskar reached into his pocket and pulled out a wad of Reichsmarks.

"No, no," the smuggler said, shaking his head. "Diamonds...that is what I demand for my services."

Oskar looked at Helene, who nodded, in agreement. Oskar grabbed the leather pouch, hidden in his chest pocket. In his trembling hands, the pouch dropped to the ground. Several loose diamonds, like little suns, sparkled at them from the ground, and lying beside the stones was a beautiful diamond ring. Oskar quickly crouched down to pick up the jewelry. He shoved it all back in the pouch.

"I will take the ring," the snarky smuggler demanded.

"Take what they offer you," Anton said to the smuggler.

"Shut up!" the smuggler responded.

"The ring is out of question," Oskar said. Suddenly, a thought came to mind. "It's my daughter's ring. They are getting married." He pointed at Inge and Isaac. The smuggler looked in their direction.

Isaac quickly grabbed Inge's hand to make it look official.

"The ring or I drive away and leave you here," the smuggler requested.

"That is an impossible demand," Oskar said, trying to negotiate. "I am willing to give you two carats worth of diamonds and some money."

"Take it," added Anton.

"No!" the smuggler growled.

Before they could blink, the smuggler got into his car. The car cranked and drove away. Dust flew in the air. Tires screeched.

They stood there looking at each other in dismay.

"*Schwein*!" Anton exclaimed, kicking some gravel in the road.

"Know that man?" asked Max.

"No, never seen him before," said Anton.

"Now what?" Oskar asked.

"I have an idea," Anton spoke up. "Come this way."

They grabbed their belongings and followed Anton up a windy road.

In Martelange, the streets rose up and curled around valleys and hills. Enchanted forests, hundreds of leagues in length, formed a mysterious backdrop. They came upon a small, charming winegrower's village called Coeur de la Vallée. The village was an archetypal French-style winegrower's village, full of untilled arbors and sun-kissed vinery. Nothing stirred in Coeur de la Vallée. An occasional motorbike scurried by and the air was filled for a brief moment with dirty exhaust. A thin, stray dog walked along the road. Otherwise, silence rose in the night air. Quaint stone homes with Quercy roofs spilled down the hill to a stream. They sheltered those who most depended on the flourishing vineyards that stretched across the high plateau and woody valleys of the Belgium Ardennes. They grew and bottled Chardonnay, Riesling, Pinot Noir, and Merlot.

"How do you know of this place?" Eva looked at Anton. "It's magical."

"I once lost the oars to my boat and made my way on foot into Martelange and into this spectacular village," he said, with a smile. "It's amazing what you may find when you have lost your way."

"Come," Anton continued, leading them down a little cobblestone street. "Once upon a time, I met a wonderful human being. I know just the place to go."

In the darkness, they followed Anton down curvy, cobbled streets. With wide eyes, they stared at the charming village that surrounded them. Eva felt like a character in a fairytale story book. An old castle sat atop a conical hill, covered in vines.

They crossed an old bridge over a gentle stream, and at the edge of the village, they came upon a 200-year-old red-brick farmhouse. This house was not weather-beaten or neglected. An enticing and fragrant garden, bursting with fruit trees, surrounded the house amid four hectares of Riesling vines. Everything was neat and trim.

Anton wondered whether the old man was home. He stepped up to the front door, lifted the old-fashioned knocker, and knocked loudly. They waited in silence, staring at the door.

The old man sat up from a deep slumber. He thought he heard a knock at the door. Was he dreaming it? Another knock sounded, then silence. He put on his house shoes, forgetting his robe, and ran to the door. What time was it? Almost midnight, he thought.

After a lengthy pause, the door opened. The face of a giant in his pajamas appeared before them. He towered over them as he stared with piercing blue eyes, sharp eyes that twinkled from behind gold spectacles. The man, advanced in years, stroked his long, white beard. He could just make out the features of the family standing on his doorstep, shivering in the darkness.

"Hello, Roland," Anton finally said. "Remember me? I am sorry to bother you at this late hour. We had no other place to go."

Eva swallowed hard.

Roland gave them a blank look.

Now, Eva bit her lower lip. This was almost comical.

"You once helped...," Anton said. The old man cut him off.

"Ahhh...Anton!"

He grabbed Anton's hand and shook it.

Oskar and Helene had relief on their faces. Inge giggled.

Without any questions, he beckoned them inside.

Eva looked around, with some curiosity. Who was this man?

They entered the house through a living area with a large fireplace. The cozy room was filled with character—stone floors, yellow walls and wooden beams. It was rustic and warm, enrobed in a soft light from the fireplace. Uniquely woven, colored rugs covered the floor.

"Sit down, please," Roland said. "Make yourselves at home."

Helene, Inge, and Eva sat near the warm, crackling fireplace. Oskar, Max, and Isaac seated themselves on wooden chairs dispersed around the room. Eva noticed Anton took the old man aside for a chat. A few minutes later, Roland and Anton came back to the room.

"Are you hungry?" Roland scanned their faces.

They all nodded in agreement.

"It's been a long day," Oskar said.

"Thank you, sir," Helene said. "May we help you prepare some food?"

"Please call me Roland," the old man responded, with a broken accent. "I hate being called sir. It makes me feel old. I am not nearly a dignified enough man to be called sir. And thank you for offering, but I can prepare something to eat. Sit back and relax."

Eva smiled at his response.

"Anton, will you help me in the kitchen?" Roland asked.

They disappeared from the room. The family could hear the noise of clinking plates and cutlery.

They sat in silence, tired from the day, and enjoyed the warmness of the room. Helene put her arms around Eva and Inge. Eva noticed a quick smile pass between Inge and Isaac.

The wooden door to the kitchen creaked open. Anton popped his head out and said, "If anyone needs a lavatory, it's down that small hall to the left."

Eventually, Eva walked down the dark, stone hall toward the dim light of the washroom, the only room in the hallway that was lit by a candle. While there, she washed her hands and splashed her face with cold water. Soon, she felt human again. She suddenly heard a wooden door near the room creak open. Eva gasped when she saw the face of a little boy staring at her from behind the door that stood slightly ajar. They stood there for a moment looking at each other. She pulled open the door and crouched down so she was eye-level with the boy.

"Hello," he said in a whisper.

"Hello," Eva replied.

He was a sweet boy with big brown eyes, maybe six years old at the most. In the background, Eva heard another child coughing. She tried to look beyond the boy, but the room was very dark.

"That's Avi," said the boy. "He is having a terrible coughing fit."

She picked up on the boy's Polish accent.

"What's your name?"

"I am Solomon," he said.

"Is your friend ill?" Eva asked.

The boy nodded.

"Are you running from them?" he asked.

Eva stared at him in confusion. His eyes showed fear.

"Running from whom?"

"The evil men in the dark uniforms with the scary, big dogs," he said.

"Yes," she answered. "We all are, unfortunately. But we are safe now."

She smiled at the boy.

He forced a smile back.

She patted his back and told the boy to wait. He stood watching Eva as she walked down the hallway back to the living area. As she headed to the kitchen, she saw her mother and Inge look up at her.

"Something wrong, Eva?" Helene asked.

"Nothing, Mother," Eva responded. "I will return in a moment."

Eva told Roland about Solomon and the other boy who was coughing. He didn't say anything in response, but wiped his hands on a cloth and walked down the hallway.

"Is something the matter?" Anton asked.

"No, Anton," she smiled reassuringly. "All is well."

He smiled back at her.

A massive fireplace in the kitchen and beams encased in pine cladding caught Eva's attention; one can imagine the real house that was within. While they waited on Roland, they sat in the kitchen and hungrily ate potatoes, hearty soup, wholesome bread, and chocolate. They chased the food down with a fresh and vibrant Chardonnay.

Roland lit a candle, and he went cautiously down a wooden staircase leading into an old wine cellar, where he vinified his wines in the traditional way. The underground cave housed several French oak barrels that barricaded eight sleeping children in small cots, deep within the interior of the cellar. He lifted the coughing child out of his bed and grabbed Solomon's hand. He returned to the living area and sat them near the crackling fireplace. He went to fetch the sick child an elixir for his cough and a warm cup of milk for Solomon.

When they finished dinner, they returned to the living area and found Roland with two sleeping children in his arms. They all sat near him around the fireplace.

In a low voice, Roland began to speak.

"A university teacher, an old friend of mine, once saw an elderly Jewish man being beaten by a young gang of thugs. He was never the same after that. A well-known individual in his community, he was confronted by several Jewish families who asked for his help to hide their children. He came to me one day because he knew I had the means to help the children and I would not refuse. I have eight children, some from Poland and some from Germany, who I care for and hide from the Germans. The ones, who are old enough, wonder if they will ever see their parents again. The smaller ones were told they were going on an excursion to the country."

He then rose from his chair and carried the children one-by-one back to the wine cellar to their beds.

He returned.

"You are truly a wonderful man," Helene said. "What you are doing for those children is a blessing. Thank you for helping us. You have your hands full already."

"If we cannot save everyone, we must save the children at least," the old man said. "In Belgium, people are helping the Germans. I need to be very careful with these children. It's hard to know who is on your side. These days I try to stay to myself and not get involved in much mischief."

He paused to blow his nose with a handkerchief.

"You must be tired," Roland said. "It is very late. I know I am tired. I have a guest bedroom down the hall and I can provide blankets for the rest of you."

Helene told Eva and Inge to sleep in the bedroom, while everyone else curled up in blankets by the fireplace. The twins refused to let their parents sleep on the ground, but Oskar said he would be fine by the fireplace. Inge persuaded her mother to join them in the bedroom.

In the silence of the night and with relief that they had a comfortable place to rest, they drifted off to sleep under the shining stars of Coeur de la Vallée.

# chapter

# SIX

Just before dawn, Inge stirred as a burst of wind shook the bedroom window. She turned to face Eva and her mother, and could hear their soft breathing. Her eyes still heavy from exhaustion, she hoped sleep would take her. But sleep did not come. She grabbed the candle by her bedside, a blanket, and walked to the living area, where she found her father and Max wrapped in blankets, dozing soundly by the fireplace, while Anton and Isaac slept on wooden chairs.

Inge decided she needed some air and quietly opened the front door to the house. After a few minutes standing on the porch, she became aware of someone standing behind her. It was Isaac.

They started to speak at the same time, he apologizing for the intrusion.

"It's okay," she said, looking down at her hands.

For a second, he stared at her in adoration. He then cautiously draped a blanket over her shoulders.

"Thank you," she said, softly.

A moment of awkward silence ensued.

"Did you sleep well?" he finally asked.

"I did, up until about an hour ago," Inge said. "The wind woke me."

"Your father snores," he said. She burst out laughing. He laughed too. "I heard the front door open, so I jumped at the opportunity to escape," he replied.

"Did I wake you?" she asked.

"No," he said. "Sleeping on that chair was very uncomfortable. My neck is killing me."

They looked out in the distance as the village was beginning its day. An idyllic calm rested over the village. Many started their day early to cultivate the exceptional land with passion and dedication. The sky was golden as the early morning sun shined through the surrounding trees.

"Are you from Berlin?" Inge asked.

"Not originally," he said, folding his arms across his chest. "I was born in Nuremberg."

"Is your family there?" she asked, wanting to know more about him.

"Well...uhm...actually I am alone," he looked down. "I don't have anyone, any family... close by, that is."

"I am sorry," she said, touching his shoulder. "I didn't mean to intrude."

"No, it's quite alright, Inge," he said. "I don't mind telling you. I am actually an orphan. I grew up in a Jewish orphanage in Furth, a suburb of Nuremberg."

"Oh, I am sorry," Inge said, studying his face.

He shook his head, "No, it's fine. There's nothing to be sorry about." He cleared his throat.

"As a young child, my parents separated and my father disappeared, never to be seen or heard from again. I was an only child. My mother became unable to support me; she could barely take care of herself. Then one day, she left me in the care of the Jewish orphanage. I was six years old."

He paused. Inge kept her gaze fixed upon him, unsure if he could continue. Before she could say anything, Isaac continued. He took a deep breath.

"I remember standing on the front steps of the orphanage, holding a small suitcase, as I watched her sobbing in the car as she drove away. Tears slid down my cheeks, soaking my shirt collar. I didn't understand why my mother left me there, but I knew that she loved me. After several years, the letters from my mother became less frequent and I began to lose hope of her coming back for me. She had written in her letters that she had found love again and moved to Berlin. I grew up in that orphanage and came to understand why my mother had left me there. She wanted a better life for me, one that she could not provide. The heartache will never go away, but I somehow found the strength to live."

Tears welled up in Inge's eyes. She turned away, not wanting him to see.

"How did you make it to Berlin?" she asked.

"When I turned 17, I decided to leave the orphanage and find my mother. I arrived in Berlin with some money the orphanage had given me and a small bag with old clothes. I spent nights in railway stations and often fell asleep, while my stomach grumbled with hunger. I knew I was surrounded by the danger posed by the Nazi regime, and I needed to find work and get off the streets. I eventually found work at a Jewish butcher."

"I admire your strength, Isaac," she said. "That must have been very difficult. Did you ever find your mother?"

"No, I never found her," he said. "I've given up hope at this point. Now, I live my life for myself."

She wanted to reach out and hold his hand, and tell him he was safe. Instead, she surprised them both, and embraced Isaac in a strong hug.

Inge was luminous to Isaac, enveloped by a light that seemed to emanate from inside her, a gleaming halo wrapped around her entire body.

At that moment, the front door opened.

"Good morning!" The boom of Roland's voice filled the crisp morning air.

"Good morning," they replied, almost in unison.

Inge tore her gaze from the morning light that danced across the village.

"If you feel like some breakfast, help yourself in the kitchen," Roland smiled.

"Thank you, Roland," Inge said.

When they entered the house, chatter could be heard in the kitchen. They joined everyone as they feasted on breads, marmalades, jams, nut spreads, sliced meat, and cheese.

"Today was the first time in a long time that I woke up and felt safe," Helene said. "I am filled with hope that everything will be okay, that a new and better life is finally in front of us."

Oskar gathered Helene to him, and she laid her head against his chest. He petted her hair with even, calming strokes.

The roar of an engine sounded from outside. Moments later, a black Adler Standard 6 rolled into the street for the journey to Antwerp. Anton would be driving them the distance and then would return the car back to Roland.

"God speed," Roland said, as he handed over a basket he'd packed for the drive.

They squeezed into the automobile and were on their way to Antwerp, weaving through the picturesque streets of Coeur de la Vallée and onto the road leading to Antwerp.

They didn't talk much on the way. Inge fell asleep on Eva's shoulder. Max and Isaac were playing with a deck of cards. Helene and Oskar stared at the open road before them, wondering what the future holds.

# chapter

# SEVEN

*Antwerp, Belgium*

Jewish Antwerp became their new home, a neighborhood that had the feel of the old world, the shtetl. Upon arrival, they were struck by the omnipresence of Jewish life. Being a religious Jew in Antwerp was as natural as taking a breath. Black-hatted Chasidim hurried along narrow lanes, their curled sidelocks and long beards trailed in the wind. Children and adults cycled along Antwerp's extensive network of bike lanes. Along the Schupstraat, the pedestrian street in the Jewish quarter that was central for the global diamond trade, yarmulke-wearing men cut business deals with clientele from around the world. Religious or not, everyone spoke heimishe Yiddish. Agreements were sealed with a handshake, accompanied by an old religious well-wish—*masl un broche*—happiness and blessing. Mutual trust and respect was a pillar that never went unbroken.

Antwerp, located along the wide Scheldt River in Belgium, was one of the largest seaports in Europe and had been the center of the diamond trade for hundreds of years. By the mid-19$^{th}$ century, the diamond trade was flourishing and with the discovery of the South African Kimberley diamond fields in 1871, Antwerp became the powerhouse in the diamond market, known for its high quality and reliable stone cutting. Many of Antwerp's Jews were involved in the diamond trade.

The family quickly assimilated to life in Antwerp. Oskar became a member and dealer at the Diamond Bourse located on Pelikaanstraat, where all the jewelry shops were located. Where ostentation would be expected, the premier trading center had a laidback atmosphere. Standard business grey prevailed inside the diamond bourses, located in three well-protected streets, Hoveniersstraat, Schupstraat, and Rijfstraat. The cutting shops were filled with wooden work benches and well-used old machinery. This understated image was exactly how those in the diamond community wanted it. Locked doors and police sentries kept those without long-established relationships on the outside and provided a secure place for trading diamonds for only those with established ties. Those who knew the secrets of the trade could enter this world.

Oskar began his day in the diamond boiling shop, where brokers, traders, and cutters poured precious gems into seething pots. When the steam cleared and the gems were cleansed of dirt, the supervisor filtered the acidic liquid and dried the diamonds with a red cloth. Gems weren't weighed before they were boiled.

Everything was based on trust. With a friendly wave and 'thank you', Oskar slipped through the door to the boiling shop with diamonds wrapped in folded paper envelopes hidden away in his coat pocket.

At the Diamantkring, an exchange for uncut, rough diamonds, a floor-to-ceiling glass wall flooded the room with even sunlight. Oskar made his way past fellow diamond traders, cutters and dealers, an all-male, mostly Jewish population. At one of the wooden tables, a trader opened a newspaper as he waited for another trader. Oskar sat down at one of the wooden tables and awaited a young fellow named Carmen who was looking for a certain diamond. After a few minutes, Oskar noticed a nicely dressed, handsome young man enter the bourse. The man had a strong sense of purpose and duty, and he realized the man looking in his direction was Oskar.

The man slowly approached the table. "Are you Oskar?"

"Yes...hello."

They shook hands.

"I am Carmen," he said in a strong Polish accent. "Carmen Presel."

"Where are you from, Carmen?"

"Cracow," he said. "When the Nazis came to power, my family fled the city. We've been in Antwerp for four years."

"How do you like Antwerp?" Oskar asked. "Does your wife like it here?"

Realizing the small intrusion, Oskar let out a small laugh.

"I apologize," Oskar said. "I assumed you were married."

"Oh, no, I am not married," he replied, slightly blushing. "I came to Antwerp with my parents and my brother. It's slowly becoming home."

"Where are you from, Oskar?"

"Berlin," he said. "I have lived in Antwerp only for a few months. I have two daughters and a son. So far, life has been enjoyable here."

"I've never been to Berlin," Carmen said. "I'd like to hear more about it some time."

"Berlin is a wonderful place," Oskar said, as tears welled in his eyes. "Well, it *was* a wonderful place. It was my home for more than 40 years."

"Until the Nazis came?" Carmen gave a sympathetic glance.

"Yes," Oskar said. "Life changed so drastically..."

"It did," Carmen responded. "Life is very different now for all of us."

They sat in silence for a moment.

"It's probably time for some business, shall we?" Oskar asked, pulling out the small, origami-style folded paper from his coat pocket. He unfolded the paper and revealed three sparkling diamonds. A spirited exchange ensued as Carmen evaluated the diamonds through his loupe to see if they qualified for a place in his family's diamond firm Presel Diamonds.

After several minutes, Carmen set his sights on all three diamonds and made an initial offer for the gems. Oskar analyzed the diamonds with his golden loupe and eventually agreed on the initial offer. Sealed with a handshake and "*Mazel*", the deal was complete.

This inner circle of men conducted business with old-fashioned simplicity. Central to the traditions of the diamond business, each handshake and verbal agreement was based on a long tradition of cooperating with one another for the common good, within the framework of the bourse. Supply met demand in this simple way. There was no alternative. Being blacklisted in this tight-knit diamond community would mean the end of a career.

Now that the business side of things was completed, it was time to reveal the inner beauty of the diamond. Carmen's family business was located near the diamond bourses upstairs in an older building. The diamond cutter sorted the stones in artificial light and always in groups of three. That was how it was done in Antwerp. A deep look of concentration overtook the cutter's swarthy face as he cut the diamond with the skive, polishing one extraordinary facet at a time. Slowly, the cutter revealed the fire, radiance and light of the diamond. Eventually, the rough diamond became a flawless masterpiece, each one unique to the eye.

Shortly after their initial meeting, Oskar paid a visit to Carmen at his family business, Presel Diamonds Co. Carmen recounted to Oskar that he was born in Cracow, which was then part of Austria and in 1918, after World War I, was incorporated into the territory of Poland. He left Poland at the age of 12 for Brussels, Belgium, where he attended a private commercial school and obtained a bachelor's degree of commerce. Afterwards, he joined the family business and gained in-depth knowledge of the diamond trade, polishing, cutting, cleaving, and sawing.

Antwerp, in particular, welcomed Jews because Jews were productive members of the lucrative and promising diamond industry. Up until the 1930s, Amsterdam, Holland was the diamond capital of the world, but Antwerp enacted certain tax laws that were favorable to diamond cutters, hence shifting the world's diamond capital to Antwerp, Belgium.

As Oskar was trying to make a name for himself in the diamond center of Antwerp, the rest of the family tried to make a good life for themselves in a land that was changing and uncertain.

In 1939, Hitler invaded Poland and the war in Europe began. At first it was a cold war between patrols on the Siegfried Line and the border of France and Germany. At the same time, England declared war on Germany.

Eva decided to focus on things she enjoyed, small diversions from the horrors of war that could be read in the newspapers daily and heard on the radios. Her love for beautiful things led her to take a course by a doctor in beauty culture. While life around her started to crumble, this gave her some joy, a short escape from the harsh reality that surrounded her.

One evening, Oskar received a special invitation for an exclusive group of jewelers and diamond buyers to attend a unique diamond trade fair at the Antwerp Diamond Bourse – de Beurs voor Diamanthandel. As Oskar read the invitation, he knew just the person to accompany him. Eva grinned from ear-to-ear upon hearing that she would attend the fair with her father. Helene did not mind, and Inge's interests lay elsewhere – with Isaac.

It was a spectacle, a prestigious venue that neither Eva nor Oskar would ever forget. As they entered the bourse's heavily guarded trading floor, Eva and Oskar took in the crowd. Glamorous women dressed in elaborate, full-length evening dresses sipped cocktails while admiring each other and the dazzling diamonds that surrounded them. Oskar, dressed in a herringbone tweed suit and red patterned necktie, removed his bowler hat, placed it under his arm, and bent his arm for Eva to weave hers through. They walked together through the crowd.

Eva's silver gray satin evening gown, embellished with rich-colored sequins, flowed as she walked arm-in-arm with her father. The worldly crowd gathered at various sections of the trading floor as they admired beautiful models, dressed in magnificent evening gowns, showcasing dazzling jewelry. Champagne bubbled in flutes and diamond-shaped chocolate pralines appealed to those with a sweet-tooth. Here and there, they would stop and chat with fellow diamontaires, mainly Chassidic Jews prominent at the bourse.

"Hello again, Oskar," a familiar voice came from behind.

"Hello, Carmen," Oskar turned around and acknowledged the young man. "How do you do this evening?"

"What an exciting event," Carmen replied. "What an opportunity."

It was then that their eyes met. At first, Eva looked down, somewhat embarrassed.

"Carmen, I want you to meet my lovely daughter, Eva."

"Hello..." he said, putting out his hand. She shook it gently.

"Good evening," she responded with a smile. "It's nice to meet you."

Then, Oskar began chatting about diamonds and the fair.

Their eyes met a second and third time, and Eva felt a stirring inside, almost like a small burst of warm butterflies in her belly.

Carmen's hazel-brown eyes were flaked with gold. A quiet determination lay in those eyes as he stared straight into Eva's sky blue ones. His dark brown hair was neatly brushed back and framed his well-defined face, with a strong jaw, angular nose, and hollow cheek bones.

Eva had never believed in love at first sight. But he'd caught her breath. She hoped she had the same effect on him.

"Oskar, it was great to see you again," he said. "Enjoy your evening."

Then, Carmen grabbed her hand and kissed it. "It was a pleasure to meet you, Eva." He winked, and seconds later, he was lost among the crowd. She looked down at her hand, hoping he had left some mark, that his lips had touched her hand.

Her father smiled down at her and they continued their evening at the diamond fair.

Weeks passed and Eva wondered if she would see Carmen again. She kept herself busy, anything to take her mind off Carmen.

One Friday morning, Eva woke up late to the soul-pleasing scent of simmering chicken noodle soup. She found her mother cooking in the kitchen in preparation for the Sabbath.

"We are having guests tonight," Helene told Eva.

"Oh," Eva said. "Who, Mother?"

"Your father's client and his family."

"Carmen?" Eva asked, eagerly.

"Who is Carmen, darling?"

"Someone I met at the diamond fair," Eva responded. Helene's eyebrows perked up.

"Your father mentioned a name to me and it may have been Carmen," Helene said, smiling at her daughter. "Do you like this young gentleman?"

"He seems very nice," Eva said, blushing slightly. "May I help you with anything?"

To pass the time quickly, Eva helped her mother prepare dinner. Every time she thought about Carmen, her stomach flipped. She couldn't wait to see him.

Oskar came home early that day, and as the last minutes of the work week came to a close, he joined Helene in the kitchen, making sure the Shabbat meal was fully prepared. When the meal was ready, Oskar moved to a large wooden cabinet that revealed shelves filled with tablecloths, napkins, vases, and a beautiful pair of silver Sabbath candlesticks.

Then, eighteen minutes before the sunset, all became still as the hectic tension of the week fizzled. A sense of peace came over them as Helene, Eva and Inge lit the Shabbat candles, drew their hands toward themselves, closed their eyes over the flames, and brought the warmth of light within. They recited the blessing, commencing the arrival of the Sabbath.

Soon, thereafter, Eva found herself standing across the dinner table from Carmen as her father raised the Kiddush cup, closed his eyes, and chanted the prayer sanctifying the wine. Eva smiled from within as she traced the outline of Carmen's face with her eyes as he watched her father chant the prayer.

"Amen," they all pronounced.

As they enjoyed their dinner, Carmen and Eva shared similar thoughts about leaving their birthplaces so hurriedly to escape the Nazis.

"How did you flee Berlin?" Carmen asked.

Eva paused. Her face became serious. For a moment, she relived the sadness and fear she felt, and that uneasy feeling emerged in the pit of her stomach.

"If you don't want to talk about it, that's okay," he said, grabbing her hand for a brief moment. "I know it was very difficult."

She nodded and briefly their eyes met. Suddenly, the uneasiness disappeared. She noticed how his hand held onto hers with such care.

"We were very lucky," Eva said. "Max became involved in the underground movement. Through his connections, we were granted the necessary visas and smuggled out of Berlin. We were helped by great people who risked their lives for us."

"The kindness of strangers will never cease to amaze me—the people who helped us are rare, sensitive men and women," Carmen said. "They simply are altruistic and tolerant. But, it also seems that your brother was a miracle worker."

Eva smiled. She could now smile about it.

"Yes," she said. "He was our little miracle and showed amazing courage and foresight. He helped publish illegal newspapers, which were delivered to thousands of Jews awaiting information. We could not have escaped without him."

"What an incredible young man," Carmen said, looking at Max.

Eva adoringly looked at her brother.

"Leaving our home was terrible," Eva said. "We were suddenly homeless and without resources. Our home was everything and then we felt like we existed nowhere. The place where I thought I would live all my life was no longer the place where I could exist at all."

"Yes, I felt the same way about Cracow," he said. "I thought it would be my home forever."

"Even though, there was hardship and struggle, there were great miracles along the way," Eva said. "Inge met Isaac."

"Finding love is a miracle," he said, grinning at Eva.

"How did you and your family come to Antwerp?" she asked.

"Like you, with the help of wonderful people who risked everything," he said. "A Polish underground worker, an old friend of my mother's, obtained forged Aryan papers for my family. The woman helped us establish false identity as Catholics. We had to learn to stick firmly to our new identities, and then one day, we boarded a train to Antwerp. That woman was our hero."

"Carmen, do you think we are safe in Antwerp?"

"I hope so," he said. "I worry that Hitler will soon have his hands all over Europe. My main concern is my family's well-being and safety, no matter what happens."

"I have the same fears," she said. "I hope that we are safe in Antwerp, but I sense that it will not be home for very long."

"It's important to try to live in the present as best we can," Carmen said. "We will find a solution if things become dangerous."

As they shared the same fears, there was also a sense of ease and hope as they shared laughter as well.

Together, they tried to put the past behind them and discovered the uniqueness of Antwerp. They lazily strolled along the lively streets that were rich in architectural style and they talked for hours in the countless cafes. As the quiet canals reflected the moonlight, their friendship blossomed into something more. Standing at the edge of the old city of Antwerp, reflecting in the water of the canals, it wasn't long before Carmen kissed Eva. Eva didn't have time to get ready. He put both arms around her and pulled her towards him. His lips soft against hers, a kiss Eva would remember forever. The sweetness of his mouth and the warmth of his skin, everything about Carmen engulfed her.

They spent as much time as they could together. They would glide past the seductive aromas of warm and sweet chocolate at the nearby chocolate shops. Hand-in-hand, they stared at the neatly organized rows of glinting light brown, dark brown and creamy-white squares and oblong balls, some embossed in gold and others decorated with fancy swirls. Carmen often bought Eva as much chocolate as her heart desired. He loved the way she childishly and sweetly pointed to the ones she wanted as a white-gloved assistant popped them into a ballotin. He knew that she always picked one especially for him, his favorite *ganache*.

Then, after satisfying their chocolate cravings, they continued to stroll along the medieval streets of Antwerp. At every chance, Carmen pulled Eva into enclosed boulevards or silent alleys, drew her towards him and passionately kissed her.

As time went by, Eva quickly realized that she had met someone unique and special. There was no doubt in her mind. Carmen often spoke of his growing love for her, of their future together, and his gratefulness for finding Eva in such harsh, complicated times.

It warmed Eva's heart to know that Inge had found love, too, with Isaac. One night, Isaac proposed to Inge at the dinner table, on Shabbat, surrounded by her family. He first held her delicate hand, and then said to her that he loved her and that he had known for a while that she was the one for him. He proclaimed that when he looked at Inge, his heart skipped a beat and that when she laughed, he felt the problems of the world diminish, if only for mere seconds or minutes. He said he couldn't imagine life without her and that he truly began to live the day they met. And, as Isaac looked at Inge's family, smiling and crying tears of joy, he presented her with a ring as radiant as the stars in the night sky.

Eva and Inge often spoke about how right now was one of the happiest times of their lives, but also the most uncertain and unsettling. They had found love amidst a turbulent world, when the future of the Jews was terrifying and unknown. But, in life things happen for a reason, and for whatever reason, they were planted in each other's lives and in each other's hearts, for better or for worse.

There would be a wedding, even when the rise of Nazism left little cause to celebrate. The wedding gave them a sense of purpose and togetherness, a brief cushion against their fear.

It was mid-May, 1940. Springtime in Antwerp was the best time of the year, when the air was crisp and clean. The city was bathed in a warm sunlight and the countryside was fresh with new, colorful blooms.

It was the perfect time for a wedding that would take place in a walled secret garden in the back of an old, dilapidated church. The hidden treasure was the perfect spot as it was secluded and quiet, away from suspecting eyes.

The guests entered through a vine-covered arbor, surrounded by large trees, roses, daisies, and tulips. An elaborately decorated wedding canopy, *chuppah,* stood in the middle of the garden, under the stars, as a reminder of the blessing given by God to Abraham, that his children will be as numerous "as the stars of the heavens."

Dressed in his best suit, Isaac stood under the *chuppah* and waited for his beautiful bride. With her parents on either side of her, Inge weaved through the line of guests, dressed in a satin and organza wedding gown. Her eyes lit up when she saw her husband to be. When Inge approached Isaac, he smiled and whispered in her ear that she looked gorgeous. She gleamed with happiness as she walked around him seven times, symbolically invoking the creation of the earth in seven days.

The breathtaking bride and handsome groom stood side by side under the wedding canopy as the ceremony began. Inge felt like she was a princess in a dream. Her heart fluttered with joy. She tried to take in every moment of this special occasion and lock it away deep inside forever. Then, the moment came when Isaac broke the glass with his foot, in remembrance of a shattered Jerusalem, the home of the Jews. They embraced as husband

and wife. Tears of joy flowed down their cheeks as everyone wished them "Mazel Tov".

For some short-lived moments, they knew peace again.

Then, in an instant, it was broken—the peace, the happiness, the moment.

They heard the sound of a jeep coming down the street behind the garden. The rabbi hushed the crowd of guests. They stood frozen in silence. Inge held her new husband's hand, and Eva and Helene stood closely behind, their eyes still filled with tears of joy.

Carmen peered through a hole in the wall. He could only see a part of the dark olive Nazi military jeep as it stood empty on the roadside.

Then, they heard the sound of two men walking towards the back of the wall that surrounded the garden. The men began to relieve themselves.

"*Gestern habe ich Hunderte Juden ermordet,*" the one Nazi said. (Yesterday, I murdered hundreds of Jews.) "*Sie fielen in eine offene Grube.*" (They fell into an open pit.)

"*Sie können es zu Ihnen erhalten lassen nicht,*" the other said. (You can't let it get to you.) "*Es ist geschäfts. Wir sorgen für Geschäft.*" (It's business. We are taking care of business.)

"*Es sucht mich heim,*" he said. (It haunts me.)

"*Es sucht viele von dies heim, aber wir müssen dieses Land der Juden befreien,*" the other said. (It haunts many of us, but we must rid the land of the Jews.) "*Unser Gehorsam ist nach Deutschland und zum Fuhrer.*" (Our obedience is to Germany and the Fuhrer.)

Then, as quickly as they came, they left.

The joyous occasion quickly turned sour. Everyone stared at each other in disbelief, in sadness, and in horror.

The Germans had arrived.

# chapter

# EIGHT

The glamour and glitz was short-lived, only a façade in front of a changing and turbulent world. They began to see the writing on the wall, yet again. They would have to emigrate from Europe to save themselves from disaster.

On May 10, 1940, the Germans attacked Belgium and war came to their streets as well. The atmosphere—the silent streets and the presence of Nazis everywhere—was haunting. They were terrified by the bombardments, the Blitzkrieg, which happened at approximately 3 a.m. in the morning, every morning, at Antwerp Airport and the surrounding lands. But thankfully, no bombs fell on the city. German paratroopers left their mark, securing vital airfields and railroads.

One afternoon, Eva walked through the front door of her family's apartment in a Jewish neighborhood in the heart of the diamond district, and heard the phone ringing. As she dropped her leather satchel to the floor and ran towards the phone, the ringing stopped.

Eva instantly felt something terrible must have happened and after anxiously waiting, another call came through. Some inner voice told her something was wrong. Eva instantly picked up the receiver and she could hear Inge's faint voice.

"Inge, please speak louder," Eva said, repeatedly. "I am having a hard time hearing you. The connection is terrible."

Eva repeated again and again that she could not understand what Inge was saying, that the connection was bad, and for Inge to speak louder, but the only words Eva heard clearly transfer across the line were, "Please, please, you must come."

Eva quickly grabbed her satchel and ran down the street towards the little apartment that her sister shared with Isaac.

After her sobbing had subsided, Inge explained to Eva that Isaac was missing. He had left in the morning to run an errand and never returned.

Not knowing where Isaac was, they tried everything possible to figure out his whereabouts, even standing for hours at the Belgian authorities' headquarters, waiting to speak to someone, anyone. No one would speak to them. No one knew any information of Isaac's whereabouts.

As day turned to night several times over, they feared the worst. It was far too dangerous for Inge to stay in the apartment alone, so she stayed in her family's apartment. Isaac was still nowhere to be seen. Inge shook with terror and it took every ounce of her family's energy to console her on a daily basis. She slept her days away and barely ate. Devastated, Eva feared her only sister had possibly become a young widow. They waited day in and day out for news of Isaac—any news. Almost two weeks had passed and there was no news.

The rumors that spread within the community that Jews were being sent to concentration camps made the reality of Isaac's disappearance even more grim and unnerving. Oskar and Carmen spent little time at the diamond bourse out of fear that they would disappear as well.

ॐॐ

Isaac fell to the cement floor in the old, red-brick apartment building he shared with Inge. Out of breath and filled with exhaustion, he dug deep in his pockets to retrieve his apartment key, but there was no key to be found. He remembered securing the key in one of his pockets, hoping he would not lose it, but now his torn pockets lay empty.

His eyes scanned the floor of the building. He blinked, trying to clear his blurred vision. The dim lights flickered above him.

Where was Inge, he thought?

"Help me," he called out. No one answered.

He swallowed hard, desperately in need of water. It had been days since he had even a drop of water, let alone food. A wave of nausea hit him and a desperate cry escaped his lips. He leaned over and dry retched, his stomach heaving in turmoil. He placed his cheek to the cold cement floor. A short, somewhat refreshing chill spiraled through his tired and injured body. Exhaustion made his eyes heavy. He instantly drifted off to sleep, a tormented sleep that made him shiver from the inside out. His dream took him back to the place he would always fear, the place that would haunt him for the rest of his life.

Isaac was standing in the courtyard in the middle of a medieval fortress with walls built of huge blocks of stone, surrounded by a deep water-filled moat. He stood in silence, motionlessly facing the fortress wall, many men to his right and many to his left. His hands were stretched above his head and manacled. There, he stood for hours. He closed his eyes as he tried to drown out the yelling Nazi SS guards, and the terrifying sounds of gunshots as prisoners dropped to the ground.

Halfway between sleep and reality, he screamed out in pain. Quickly, sleep took over him again. He was back in the nightmare he would always know. This time, he was harnessed to an enormous wheel, forced to push it around for hours on end, drawing water up from the well.

Unable to open his eyes, he felt someone's presence upon him, stroking his hair and face, as tears wet his cheeks.

"Darling, Isaac, please wake up," he heard the familiar voice, the voice that always soothed him and warmed his heart.

Inge held Isaac in her arms and sobbed.

"Inge, I am alive," he said, with all the energy he could muster.

Isaac finally forced his eyes open.

Beaten, tortured, and almost killed, Inge cut the clothes off Isaac's bloodied body. He shuddered in pain as she washed him and bandaged his wounds. She fed him warm soup broth and bread, but he could barely keep any of it down. She let him sleep, waking him only to give him some food and water. After three days of sleep and barely moving, Isaac forced himself out of bed and sat with Inge at the table.

He held her hand.

Inge stroked his face. "Please tell me what happened."

Slowly, Isaac traced back the horrific events that almost ended his life.

He told Inge that he was rounded up the morning he left the apartment by the Belgian authorities because he was a German citizen. A Belgian registration card identified Isaac as a German national. Jewish or not, the authorities rounded up all German citizens and kept them at the military barracks outside Antwerp. He spent two days at the military barracks under the Belgian authorities. Then, a group of men, all Jews, were given over to the Nazis and driven in a truck to a concentration camp. Not knowing where they were, the prisoners eventually realized the Belgian authorities were Nazi collaborators and they were at a concentration camp named Breendonck, a fortress along the Antwerp-Brussels highway, 12 miles southwest of Antwerp. The camp was a waiting camp, designed to receive Jews and other prisoners before transport to Germany. There, torture, hangings and shootings were daily activities among the Nazis. The prisoners saw shootings every day. It was like a sport for the Nazis— merciless and macabre target practice.

One morning before dawn, Isaac and several other prisoners were led out of their cells. Walking in a single line at gun point, they were forced out of the fortress gates toward the railroad tracks. A sense of relief came over Isaac that he was leaving that awful place, but at the same time, he felt a sense of dread and fear of the unknown. Where were they going?

No fewer than 100 prisoners were forced into sealed cattle cars with enough room for only 40 people. They were packed in so tightly that they could not move and there was no room to sit down. They managed to sit by taking turns. A single bucket sat in the corner of the car for sanitation, but it would be too difficult to get to it if the urge arose. The air was stale, smelly and stifling. The light was faint. There was little conversation, a few whispers. Hours went by slowly and it became hard to determine time. People cried out; others sighed and grew impatient. Fear was visible in everyone's eyes, while prayer settled on their lips.

Suddenly, the train stopped. A German guard slid the door open and forced the prisoners out. They stood on an open field beneath a low-hanging, grey sky. The dark trees beyond were lashed by wind. The sun began to fade behind the dense clouds. A small, abandoned house stood several feet away and a fountain. "Water!" they exclaimed. They ran like animals towards the water.

After several short minutes, the Nazi guards pushed them back toward the train cars and threatened them with the butts of their guns. Moments later, the train departed again.

Hours followed hours, and darkness and cold filled the cattle car.

Swaying slightly, Isaac fell asleep in a standing position in the corner of the cattle car. He felt the rocking movement of the train under his feet. He tried to tune out everything that was happening around him and focused his thoughts on Inge—her long blonde hair and the gentleness of her calm, blue eyes like a clear blue sky.

Tears rolled down Inge's cheeks.

"I can't believe this happened to you, Isaac," she said. "I couldn't live without you."

"Inge," he said, stroking her hair. "I am here. It's okay."

Then, Isaac started to laugh. Inge looked at him in utter confusion. "Isaac, what's so funny? How can you laugh right now? This is all so terrible."

He continued to laugh hysterically.

She giggled, unsure how to respond to it all.

"You'll never believe what happened next," he said. "It's unbelievable!"

He patted her arm, trying to console her.

"Inge, by the will of God, I am here," he said. "There is something greater than us, Inge. A great power…something I never believed in before. When I was in Breendonck and in that train car, I hoped and prayed for a miracle. I never believed it would be possible. I wasn't sure if I would see you again."

He continued on with his story.

Suddenly, gunshots rang out and the acrid smell of gunpowder filled the train. Startled, Isaac opened his eyes from a brief sleep.

"What's happening?" someone in the train car exclaimed. Many in the car braced themselves and covered their ears.

"Silence!" another man yelled out.

They all looked at each other in panic. They heard shouts from SS officers. The train came to a screeching halt. Isaac remembered falling down and then trying to pick himself back up among many other fallen prisoners.

Moments of silence followed. The gunfire and screaming continued. A loud explosive boom shook the cattle car. Men fell to the ground again, one on top of the other.

"The explosions were deafening" said Isaac. "My heart was racing and pounding in my chest. Then, there were other loud sounds that we could not decipher."

All of a sudden, the air outside the cattle car was silent. Several of the prisoners tried to peer through the cracks in the car, but could only see grass and a small flutter of hurried footsteps. They stared at each other in shock. They stood in silence. Isaac thought the Nazi SS officers would open the cattle car doors at any moment and fill the train car with gunshots, killing them all instantly. Tiny beads of sweat fell down Isaac's cheeks. Time marched forward, twenty minutes, then maybe thirty, forty minutes. An hour went by and nothing happened. They continued to wait, not knowing if they should try to force open the door to the cattle car themselves.

After several more minutes passed, Flemish voices could be heard outside the train. Upon hearing the Flemish voices, several of the men in the cattle car cautiously forced open the doors. Cool air flooded into the crowded carriage, and then they heard the words, "You're free! The Germans are dead!"

They all jumped from the cattle car, tears of joy streaming down their faces. Plumes of flame from explosives could be seen across the railroad tracks that were ripped from the ground. Dazed survivors wandered quickly past the dead bodies of SS officers, killed by the resistance.

"The Belgian resistance saved your lives?" Inge said.

"Yes, my love," he said. "There's more..."

Fully-armed members of the Belgian resistance, disguised as members of the *SS-Totenkopfverbände,* directed the prisoners toward large trucks. They drove deep into the heavily- wooded Hurtgen forest. In the woods, the roads were very uneven and the trucks creaked and bounced from side to side. At one point the driving became treacherous, so they stopped and gave the prisoners some water and attended to some of the sick prisoners. The resistance members also supplied the prisoners with civilian clothes. In fear of being caught, the Belgian resistance could only take the men to the roadside and no further. A few of the prisoners needed immediate medical attention, and the other prisoners were picked up roadside and driven back to Antwerp where they could return to their homes and families. A few hours later, a car dropped Isaac several blocks from his home, and with the little bit of strength he had left, he made his way back to the front door of his home.

# chapter

# NINE

Belgium and the Netherlands surrendered in May. More than 300,000 French and British troops were evacuated from the beaches near Dunkirk across the English Channel to Great Britain. On May 13, 1940, Germany made a surprise entry into France through the Belgium Ardennes. The French troops were unable to put up a strong fight against Germany and the invasion of France was underway. Paris fell to the Germans on June 14, 1940. The German war machine was unstoppable. Germany's hands were all over Europe.

Late one night, sleep did not come easily for Eva. The safety of her family caused much angst in addition to the unnerving thought of never feeling secure. Eva quietly slipped out of bed and sat at a small desk in the corner of the room. She turned on the gold-toned table lamp and slid off her beautiful diamond ring. Eva held up the gleaming diamond engagement ring to the light. She found it amazing that she was wearing such an exquisite ring and that she had found love when the world was a frightening place and at war. She gazed at the way the diamond shined brightly, as if radiating hope onto her. She studied how the light refracted from one facet to another, then dispersed through to the top.

For a moment, her thoughts took her back to when Carmen proposed, a week prior.

Eva and Carmen were walking home after dark and it began to rain. Flustered at first, Eva scrambled to find shade, but there was no shade to be found. Carmen smiled as Eva stood in the pouring rain. The rain came down in buckets, drenching them in seconds. She grabbed his hand and pulled him so they could run home. But Carmen stood heavy-heeled on the wet street and would not budge. He burst out laughing and pulled her close against him. She caught him staring adoringly at her. She grinned back at him. Eva's sparkling blue eyes and that smile that would always be for him caused Carmen to smile in return.

"I love you, my gorgeous girl," he said.

Eva opened her mouth to say something, but Carmen's hands on her face and his lips on hers silenced her. As he deepened the kiss, the whole universe came to a stand-still. Nothing else in the world existed. At that moment, as the rain soaked the streets of Antwerp, it was like the rain was washing away all the sadness in the world, and that for that single moment as they shared a magical kiss, everything was perfect.

Carmen pulled back slightly and said, "There is no more perfect time than now."

He pulled out of his coat pocket a small velvet box and handed it to Eva.

She gasped as tears of joy flowed down her cheeks. Carmen got on one knee in the pouring rain. "Like a diamond, life has many facets, good and bad. But nothing in the world, no amount of rain, could ever take away our love for each other. It is a fire, a 'brilliance', which burns so brightly and so strong that nothing can ever diminish it. Eva, you are my diamond in the rough, you are my true love—will you do me the honor of becoming my wife?"

Eva now hoped as time moved forward, and as the world became more complex, that she would always remember that special, magical moment with vividness. She turned her attention back to the ring. It was mesmerizing.

She tiptoed out of her room to a small room in the apartment where Carmen slept. She knocked on his door, but not so loud that it would wake her parents.

"Carmen," she whispered.

He opened the door half asleep.

"Could you not sleep, my dear?" he said, holding her tight at the doorway.

"My mind is filled with thoughts," she said, softly. "I am afraid, Carmen. What will the future bring? When will we live in peace?"

He kissed her cheek and pulled her inside his room.

She sat on his bed and watched him grab a box from the closet. He came back to the bed with a small leather pouch. As he opened it, a glimmering emerald and two diamonds fell onto the sheets.

"Oh, Carmen, they are beautiful."

Then, sadness overcame her.

"What's the matter?" he asked, taking her hand.

"They remind me of the past," she said. "My mother used to wear a beautiful emerald and diamond pendant necklace when we lived in Berlin before the war. I loved it on her."

"They're the future," he whispered back, grabbing Eva's hand. She leaned down and kissed his hand. Carmen played with her blonde hair. "It will be alright," he said. In between gentle sobs, Eva asked, "Carmen, what if..." He cut her off, putting his finger to her lips.

"What happens in our lives is inescapable, yet somewhere amid what is happening around us, we can only hope that the future is full of wonderful surprises and holds promise," he said. "Eva, peace can sometimes be elusive, but together, our combined strength will enable us to find it."

"What if peace can never be attained, Carmen?" Eva asked as she lost control of her tears. "What do we hold onto?"

"Hope. Love. Family...and each other." Carmen embraced her warmly.

The next afternoon, Carmen and Eva came upon the synagogue they knew well. They entered the synagogue looking for answers and hope. An hour later, they left with a plan.

One Sunday afternoon, before the sun set, people began to arrive at the old synagogue. They did not arrive all at once, but discretely one by one so that nothing looked out of the ordinary. Once everyone had arrived, the doors were locked.

The synagogue looked different that day. Unlike the air that was growing cold and stale outside, an air of joy was alive in the synagogue. Candles that lined the aisles dimly lit the sanctuary. A beautifully decorated wedding canopy, *chuppah*, stood in front of the guests as a symbol of the home the couple will build together. Carmen waited for his bride at the front of the *chuppah*. As soft music rose into the air and with her parents on either side of her, Eva drifted down the aisle toward her groom, dressed in a lace wedding gown. She was overjoyed by the special moment and overwhelmed for what was to become.

When she approached Carmen, her features were shaded by a silk tulle embroidered lace wedding veil. She could see his hands trembling as she circled him seven times to demonstrate that he was now the center of her life. They joined the rabbi under the chuppah that was decorated with flowers. After the rabbi said the blessing over the wine, the rings were exchanged in their consecration to each other under the laws of Moses and Israel, and the Seven Blessings were sung. And, then Carmen shattered the glass with his foot. Eva lifted her veil and they became one.

As day became night, the candles in the synagogue no longer gave light. The guests no longer celebrated. The front door remained locked. Carmen and Eva, Helene and Oskar, Isaac and Inge, and Max exited the synagogue through a hidden back window. With precious and valuable gems hidden in their undergarments, they fled Antwerp and never looked back. Again, they were on the run, to attain peace, and to be free of Germany's stronghold.

# chapter

# TEN

Roland became a valuable friend and contact. He secured transportation for them to escape. Roland's friend, a countess named Alessandra, who despised the Nazi party and anyone associated with the Nazi party, picked them up by car from the synagogue. A high-profile member of society, Alessandra sipped champagne and ate caviar with the Nazis. She acquired useful information for the Jews.

"She looks familiar," Oskar said softly to Helene.

"How so?" Helene asked.

"I can't put my finger on it," he replied, as his eyes met Alessandra's soft brown eyes as she was getting into the driver's seat of the car.

They headed for La Panne, located along the North Sea coast of the Belgium province of West Flanders, on the border between Belgium and France.

Sitting next to Alessandra and with the others absorbed in their own conversations, Oskar attempted to find out more about the beauty who was helping them.

"Are you from Berlin?" he asked.

"Yes," she responded with a smile taking her eyes off the road for a moment. "I left Berlin two years ago. I couldn't stomach the place anymore. The German people are like robots, brainwashed by Hitler. I am different from them. I decided I had to get away from the center of the Nazi regime—Berlin. Not all Germans are Nazis. I left my husband, Count Fritz, as he rubbed elbows with the Nazis a little too closely. Let's just say, I had a strong sensitivity to suffering."

"It's wonderful what you are doing...for us," he said.

"I hate to see others suffer," she said. "I also hate to witness intolerance of any kind. That's why I decided to help in any way that I can."

"I have to tell you that you look familiar to me," Oskar said. "I cannot place it."

She turned to him and smiled.

"You don't remember?" she said, almost surprised. "I thought you would remember me quickly, Oskar."

"I'm sorry," he said, raising an eyebrow. "I never forget a face, especially one like yours."

"I purchased a lovely diamond and emerald necklace from you some years ago," she said.

There was a brief moment of silence before the memories all started flooding back to Oskar. He remembered draping the necklace around her long neck as she stared at it in the mirror in his diamond center. He could then hear her words, "It's stunning. I'll take it." Just like that, he thought. She had money to throw around.

"My God," he said, eyeing her. "Yes, I remember you now."

"I must ask you...why does a beautiful woman give up such a fine gem? Why was the necklace in the auction house?"

"I had seen you at the auction house many times," she said. "I went there often to buy unique pieces. When I left my husband, I wanted no ties to him, to that extravagant life—to the Nazi party. I put the jewel on auction, in hopes it would land in the right hands again. It seems like it did."

He smiled back at her.

"Yes, it did, but it's lost again," Oskar said. "The Nazis seized it before we left Berlin."

"Greedy bastards!" she stared at him compassionately. "I am so sorry. I know that piece represented so much. Why did you sell it?"

Oskar let out a sigh.

"Yes, it was a very valuable piece and hard to let go," he said. "I inherited the stones from my father, but eventually I needed to sell it. I made a large profit from it. I suppose it's gone forever now."

Silence ensued.

"I'm sorry," she said.

"Have you met Hitler?" Oskar asked with slight curiosity.

"Yes, once," she said. "I stood near him at a dinner party. I had accompanied my husband, who had been invited because he had done some business dealings with the Nazis. As I stood behind a luxuriously laden buffet table in a large function room, I watched the Fuhrer walk towards me. I must say my heart may have skipped a beat. There is something so menacing, evil, and complicated about him. He walked up to the buffet table, stood by and watched as his guests chose from the finest caviar, lobster, salmon and chicken, a smorgasbord that caterers had spent days preparing. I was amazed how he did not speak a word, but shook some hands, those who outstretched theirs for him to shake. As everyone sipped vintage French wine, he drank a tonic and only ate modest plates of salad and spinach, mainly delivered to his table by a personal steward. He never drank, not even for a toast. I do remember he was obsessed with a dark, bitter chocolate. Actually we all were, as they served it at these lavish dinners. What amazed me was this larger-than-life human being, who we saw yelling and spreading propaganda to crowds of thousands, was really smaller than I imagined and quite simple. Inside, I laughed at him, pitied him."

"Amazing...I would have thought he was a mad drunk," Oskar laughed.

Once they arrived in La Panne, Alessandra left them her car, some extra money and food, and said her goodbyes. Oskar wanted to somehow pay her for her help, but she refused outright any sort of payment on terms that she had plenty of diamonds and money to her name already.

"I am glad our paths crossed, Oskar," she said, shaking his hand.

"Indeed," he said. "It's been a pleasure. Thank you for your help. I hope our paths cross again one day."

"Yes, that would be nice," her eyes settled upon his face one last time.

In La Panne, they rented a small villa and paid rent for two months in advance. Unfortunately, the Belgian, French and English troops could not keep the Germans from advancing and after two nights spent in La Panne, they packed their things once again and left in a hurry towards the French frontier. As it was curfew, the frontier was already closed, and so they turned around and headed back to the villa. It took almost two hours to return to the villa as a constant stream of glassy-eyed refugees, fleeing the fighting front, clogged the roads of La Panne. The refugees walked, rode bicycles, pushed hand carts and traveled on horse-drawn carts, carrying whatever they could of their worldly possessions.

The next morning, they woke up to rain, but decided to drive south to Le Touquet (Paris-Plage) and from there to Bordeaux. The storm grew worse as the day progressed. Flooded streets forced them to stop overnight in the elegant French resort town Le Touquet. This unfortunate stopover was fatal as the Germans cut off this part of France and they could not proceed further south. They then traveled as far as Rouen, in northern France on the River Seine, but Rouen and its surrounding villages were ablaze from the attacks. They then tried the coastal route over Pont de St. Valery, but the area had also been raided and the route cut off, so they decided they had to return to Le Touquet. There was no other way. Civilian refugees stood blocked between immense columns of the French retreating army.

The distraught family came upon a large group of French soldiers with enormous guns, ready to fight the Germans. A French soldier warned them that danger was imminent, that the Germans were heading towards them. Frightened and insecure, planted between two warring countries, they quickly abandoned their car and cut across a huge pine forest through a little path that led to a small road.

Within minutes, they heard the sound of a horde of approaching German Luftwaffe planes, whose main target were the French soldiers. They quickly crumbled to the ground, screaming in fear. The German dive bombers—*Stukas*—filled the early morning sky above them. Bomber aircrafts dove from the sky directly at their targets, strafing the retreating civilians and soldiers with machine gun fire and bombs. The German war machine advanced unperturbed, pounding the French from above, sending defending troops and refugees reeling to their deaths in seconds. In an instant the world went dark. The sky turned a dark grey as if the sun had turned black. An acrid sting of smoke hit them. Human remains littered the streets and countryside. Destruction and debris were everywhere. Hitler's army continued to deliver punishing blows.

The noise deafened them. Their ears rang against the explosions. Their eyes stung from the smoke that hung heavily in the air. Terrified, they ran as quickly as their legs could carry them to a nearby dilapidated farmhouse, which stood empty. Panic-stricken, shaking with fear, they gathered together in the farmhouse, thinking that their last hour had come and that when they had to go, they would go together.

In those dark moments, under grave danger, Eva's thoughts, yet again, turned to God. As tears streamed down Eva's face, she buried her head in Carmen's jacket, and silently she started to say in Hebrew, "*Shema Yisrael Adonai Eloheinu Edonai Ehad*, [Hear, O Israel: the Lord our God, the Lord is one.]" In silence, she thought, "God, we face danger, grant us strength and courage."

The family waited several hours until all was quiet. Fortunately, they found their car unharmed. They decided to head back to Le Touquet, and they arrived in the evening just before the curfew and checked into the hotel where they had stayed the night before. Days later, they heard the sounds of guns and they hoped that the Allies were putting up a strong resistance and repelling the Germans from advancing any further. Unfortunately, being very close to Dunkirk, the gunfire was actually the final fight as the evacuation of British troops signaled the collapse of the Allied Army.

Le Touquet was declared a hospital city and the buildings that had been converted into hospitals had red crosses painted on the roofs. The largest building, a well-known hotel, consisted of three wings. The Germans, having no respect for the Red Cross, bombed the left wing, which actually housed wounded German soldiers. German troops entered the resort town and searched every house for hidden Allied troops. The reign of terror had overshadowed them completely.

Since Le Touquet was considered a Red Cross zone, the German army was not supposed to be in the city. Nevertheless, the greedy Germans occupied the most beautiful villas along the coast. The Germans also went after France's most valuable gem—wine. They raided wine cellars and labyrinths of limestone caves, where producers secreted away large amounts of wine and champagne. The Germans seized thousands of bottles and roamed around the town drunk, day after day. It was not pleasant to live in these conditions, but the family had no other choice, so they dealt with the situation for one long, exhausting month.

One warm morning, Carmen waited in line for several hours to buy bread, and Eva went to find him in the long queue to keep him company and bring him something to drink. She had suggested they take turns standing in line, but Carmen would not hear of this. On her way to find Carmen, she was walking along the sidewalk when a drunken German soldier approached her.

The German soldier cornered Eva, his sweaty face inches from hers. She turned away from his terrible breath that reeked of alcohol. He grabbed her cheek and turned her face toward him. Eva looked on with wide eyes and a racing heart. His body just inches from hers.

"*Was haben Sie gesagt?*" he said.

"I never said a word," Eva said in German, trying to sound not only polite, but as calm as she could. She wanted to spit in his face and tell him what she thought of him, but instead she found herself apologizing. She quickly put her trembling hands behind her so he would not see them.

"I am sorry, you must have thought I said something, but I didn't say a word," she managed to say, wishing Carmen was by her side.

Eva trembled as he laughed at her. He then peered at her with evil, icy blue eyes, his nostrils flaring, not saying a word. After several seconds, he touched her breasts and forced a wet, disgusting kiss upon her lips. She pulled away abruptly. He shoved Eva and walked off, looking back at her and laughing some more.

Some people walked by the scene, but didn't say a word out of fear.

Eva stood frozen, unable to catch her breath.

Finally, the soldier had disappeared down the street with several other soldiers. She took a deep breath and tried to console her shaking body. She wiped her mouth with her sleeve, straightened her dress and continued on walking until she finally found Carmen. There, Carmen stood, deep in the middle of the line, wiping sweat from his face with a handkerchief.

All Eva could do was hug him tightly and not say a word. Tears streamed down her cheeks.

"Eva, what is wrong?" Carmen asked. "Are you alright?"

"No..." was all she could muster.

He undid himself from the tight lock she had around him and put his hands on her shoulders. He stared lovingly into her eyes and said, "Eva, we'll be fine. You must be strong. We will be together, always." Then, Carmen hugged her again. Eva whispered gently in his ear what had happened on her way to find him. He let out a loud sigh, took her in his arms, and kissed her forehead. As the queue started to slowly move in front of them, Carmen and Eva shoulder-to-shoulder, hand-in-hand, pushed forth to get their small ration of bread.

After a long month, the order came from the German authorities that all refugees not living permanently in Le Touquet had to return to where they came from. Their car was hidden in an old, rundown garage and they had enough fuel to make their way back to Belgium. This time, the roads were not filled with fleeing refugees, but thousands of Allied prisoners, weary and battle-drugged. The soldiers walked in rags and staggered from hunger and exhaustion. When any one of the Allied prisoners fell down, he was beaten with batons and guns by German guards on motorcycles until he could pull himself up and start walking again. They looked like human wrecks, bloody, thirsty, hungry, and exhausted, and when on-looking traffic offered them food or water, they were threatened by German rifles. It was a constant and painful sight to witness human beings being cruel to other human beings.

Eventually, they arrived again in Antwerp, feeling completely defeated and saddened. They felt like they had taken one step forward and then had been forced back a thousand more steps. Their dream of freedom and peace seemed a distant, unreachable light.

Another blow hit them upon arrival at their apartment. They discovered that their apartment was occupied by German troops and no civilian could enter the building. German soldiers denied them entry, not even to collect some clothing. With no place to go, no home left to go back to, and with only the clothes on their backs and few belongings in their small suitcases, they walked to Inge's apartment in hopes it was not yet occupied. Luckily, it was vacant, so they all settled in there.

Life in Antwerp was unstable and dangerous. The city was occupied by German troops and the Gestapo. They could not go anywhere. At any time, they feared being caught by the Germans so they stayed in the apartment, kept the lights off and made little noise. At this point, they were used to living in fear, in darkness, and in silence. When they had to talk about the situation, they did not murmur a word, but wrote on paper their conversations to each other or they whispered in each other's ears. They had to be extremely careful as one never knew who was watching or listening, and at any minute the Gestapo could arrive at their door. The enemy could be anyone: a neighbor, a shop owner, someone walking in the street. The enemy was no farther than their doorstep. They lived as if those four walls were their only protection from the dangerous and chaotic world outside.

Helene and Oskar received a special permit from the German authorities to enter their apartment to collect some clothes. The apartment's caretaker, a German collaborator, told the Gestapo that they were at the apartment. They quickly gathered what they needed, but on their way out the door, the Gestapo stopped them. They were forced to show their papers and fortunately, they let them go. They were not on the transportation list, but if they had been on the list, they would have been beaten and placed in a camp awaiting transport to Auschwitz. They were so unnerved and sick over the experience that Carmen, Isaac, Max, and Oskar immediately started looking for a new way for them to escape.

Anton arrived in Antwerp immediately after and came to see them. He gave them the address of a candy shop in Brussels, which belonged to a Jew from North Africa. He passed along a password, *"Shalom"*, and instructed them to be careful upon whom they gave the password.

The next day, Carmen and Oskar went to Brussels and contacted the man in the candy shop. He gave them the telephone number of Mr. Bentz, a smuggler, who was living outside Brussels. As no one could be trusted, Carmen carried a gun when they went to see Mr. Bentz. Upon arriving at Mr. Bentz's villa, he told them of the arrangements to pick them up the next day, to take them to Brussels, stay in his villa overnight, and then proceed the next morning to France. When Carmen and Oskar returned to Antwerp to tell everyone the plan, Helene showed worry about the swiftness of the arrangements and if Mr. Bentz could be trusted. Oskar slouched back into a chair, crossed his arms and looked out the window off into the distance.

"We must move forward," Oskar told his family. "We cannot give up. There is no choice now, but leave as quickly as we can. We must go and we must go together. God will watch over us, and we will do our best to have faith that this time our escape will be more successful."

"Can we manage a deft escape, Oskar?" Helene asked with worry in her eyes. "Has our luck run out?"

"Helene, we cannot give up," Oskar responded. "I refuse for us to give up now and be transported to a concentration camp, only to face our deaths. We must keep trying. Danger faces us no matter what."

Everyone nodded in agreement. Silence filled the room.

Early the next morning before dawn, they left Brussels towards the Belgian Franco border at Mons, 35 miles south of Brussels. Their lives were constantly on the move. Peace was unattainable, unreachable. They had to remain constantly alert as they were continuously challenged. Exhaustion and hunger became the very least of their worries.

Arriving at the border town, the axle on Mr. Bentz's trailer cracked and they had to stop at a garage. In the meantime, they waited at a nearby restaurant.

Once again, fate stepped in. Max overheard a discussion between two old men who were seated at a table next to them. The one man told the other that the Gestapo was in full force at the border, arresting Jews who wanted to cross into France. Max quietly drank a cup of coffee and nibbled on eggs until they left the restaurant and it was safe to tell his family what he had discovered.

When they arrived at the border later in the day, they were surprised to find that the front was clear, but the Belgian and French Gendarmes would not let them pass as they feared German reprisals. After long negotiations, bribing the soldiers with Mr. Bentz's cigarettes and with promises that they would not divulge the place where they crossed, the soldiers let them through to the other side.

Along the way, they faced questions from other French Gendarmes, and so Carmen and Eva made up a story that they had to pick up their child, who was spending the summer with a cousin. Two French Gendarmes grew suspicious of the large group, consisting of Mr. Bentz and seven family members—Oskar, Helene, Max, Eva, Inge, Carmen and Isaac. Carmen told them it was urgent they pick up their child as she was ill, that they were traveling together to pick her up and continuing on for a short family holiday in France. Carmen handed the soldiers a pack of cigarettes and two small diamonds to appease them. Eventually, they let them pass.

Time was lost. They could not travel too far as it was already curfew. They found a small town nearby and their only option was to stop for the night in a dark street near a river and sleep in the car. Checking into a hotel would have been too dangerous.

The next morning, when the curfew was lifted, they proceeded onwards to unoccupied France and towards the demarcation line at Chalon sur Saone.

Upon arrival, they were again surprised to find the Gestapo. They told them the same story that their child was left behind on the other side with friends and they wanted to pick her up. They were told that they had to submit an application at the nearby German authorities. The application would then have to be sent to Berlin, and after a month or even two, permission may be granted. They told the Gestapo that they would go to the authorities and submit the application, but they never did. After a few hours, they came back to retrieve the trailer and drove away, but in their distress, they lost their way.

The exhausted family and Mr. Bentz pulled off to the side of the road to gather their bearings. They enjoyed a few minutes of shade near a meadow. Slight winds brought the fresh scent of sun-filled lavender fields to their senses. Eva and Inge tossed some lavender blossoms into their bags.

"Look everyone, someone is coming!" Max exclaimed, pointing toward the hill.

They peered in the hill's direction and watched as a young girl rode her bicycle down the hill slowly towards them. As she approached them, she stopped. Carmen greeted the friendly girl in French and asked her for directions. After a few minutes of cautious conversation, they discovered her name was Charlotte and she lived on the unoccupied side of France. She was visiting her grandparents in the occupied zone. She told them that she had to have a special permit to go to the occupied zone as the Germans did not allow anyone through without a permit.

Charlotte said there was only one German soldier guarding the road. She offered them some fresh baked bread from her grandmother. At first, they refused her sweet gesture, but she practically pushed the loaf in Carmen's hands.

"Please take it," Charlotte said. "I have plenty more."

With those words, they thanked her for the information, for the bread, and parted ways. They were starving, so after she left, they divided the loaf among them.

After a little break to enjoy the pleasant summer day and some sustenance from the bread, they decided they would take their chances once again. They made their way up the hilly road.

As they came around a bend in the road, a German soldier appeared from behind a tree, pointed his gun at them, and demanded them to stop. The family raised their hands in the air. The soldier whistled and within seconds, two more soldiers came into view and approached them, guns at the ready.

"What is your name?" asked the portly soldier, standing near Carmen.

"Carmen Presel."

"Are you a Jew?"

"No," Carmen replied, paralyzed with fear.

"Where are you going?"

"Our child is spending the summer with a cousin and we must pick her up as she has fallen ill," Eva chimed in.

"Who are they?" the other soldier pointed at the family.

"My family," Eva said to the man. "After we pick up our child, we plan to go on a short holiday in France."

She crossed her arms to hide her trembling hands.

"What is your child's name?" the soldier asked.

Eva eyed the soldier as her mind raced. She swallowed hard.

"Trudy," she said. It was the only name that Eva could think of at that very moment. "My daughter's name is Trudy and it is urgent that we see her as she is very ill. Please, let me go to her."

The podgy soldier gazed at the family.

The other soldiers stood there looking at each other.

Oskar stepped forward, only inches from the one soldier.

"We are in a hurry," he said. "I desperately want to see my granddaughter. Can we please pass through your checkpoint?"

After a brief discussion between the soldiers, one of them gave a strict warning: if they were seen going down the hill, they would be in danger of being shot by the patrols guarding the top of the hill.

Oskar slipped a thousand Mark note in the soldier's hand, which he refused. Then, they went as fast as their bodies could take them into the valley.

Not far away in the valley, on a gravel road, they were stopped by French Gendarmes. They told them that they were going back to Belgium, but they could not pass the demarcation line without a new permit and they had to arrange it at the next town. Whenever they were stopped, they had a different story to tell, which was much easier with the French authorities than with the German Gestapo. Eventually, they arrived at their next destination—Aix en Provence.

Aix en Provence was a small, classically Provencal town with winding narrow streets lined with 17th century buildings, hotels and stone plazas. They checked into a small hotel and while they were eating dinner, Carmen recognized a friend from Antwerp who also happened to be staying at the hotel. His friend had obtained Brazilian visas and advised them to do the same. He gave them the contact information of a man who was an intermediary between the Brazilian Consulate and themselves. Upon contacting the man, they soon learned that the Brazilian government was not handing out any more visas to Jews, so he also advised them to get baptismal certificates.

"If we are forced to pose as not Jewish for our survival, then that is what we must do," Oskar said to his family. "Do you agree?"

They all agreed, for their survival depended on it. Carmen, Isaac and Oskar visited the Roman Catholic priest in the town, but attaining the certificates for everyone was costly. Fortunately, their stash of diamonds and some money helped cover most of the cost, and with the assistance of the American Consulate, they received the baptismal certificates, which were accepted by the Brazilian Consulate. And, after paying the intermediary money and diamonds, they also received tourist visas for Brazil.

But it did not end there. They still needed Portuguese transit visas to leave France and cross Spain. After paying the intermediary, he told Oskar that it was possible to get visas "under the counter". The head of the consulate was issuing visas to Jews. But the visas came with strict regulations. The visas were available to baptized Jews only. Using their new baptismal certificates, the family was able to prove their baptism, and after queuing at the consulate for many days, they finally received Portuguese transit visas. It was a gratifying moment!

With all the necessary papers in place, the next challenge was how to pass the frontier between France and Spain, which was almost impossible by train as the immigration authorities in Spain did not let anyone through of military age. They managed to get Carmen's passport to read that he was 40 years old, instead of 29, and his premature balding was helpful in this matter. Isaac was over 30, so there was not much of a worry. Max became a concern as lying on his passport would have been too obvious. He was young and strong, and most importantly, he was the right age to enter the military.

They took the chance and traveled from Aix en Provence to Perpignan, in southern France, by train. It was an easier journey than they had thought. An overnight train journey led them to Perpignan by daybreak.

As the family strolled through the streets, they realized Perpignan was no scruffy border town. The city was more Spanish than French, and narrow medieval streets gave way to packed outdoor market stalls. They relaxed in the market and tasted local sausage, olives, cheese, and bread. They stayed the night in a small, rundown hotel and prepared themselves for the challenge that lay ahead.

The next day after they arrived in Perpignan, the family set out to the rugged foothills of the dazzling Pyrenees Mountains. They hired a knowledgeable mountain guide to take them across the Pyrenees to Spain.

Upon meeting the guide, they realized how unprepared they were for the journey. The friendly guide noticed the family's distress and gave them some water and fruit before their departure. He told them not to worry, that he carried in a back pack some extra food, a compass and warm clothes.

At around 8 p.m., they walked toward the edge of the mountain. The guide told them to be as quiet as possible and to follow each other's footsteps. Their stomachs were in knots and nerves on edge, but they knew they had to be strong and brave. They had to continue moving forward to reach their goal. This was just another challenge to overcome in their quest for freedom.

Their first task was to scale the high retaining wall that stood tall in front of them. The steep terrain made the ascent very strenuous, but the grandeur of the magnificent mountain left an unforgettable impression on their minds and reminded them that there was still beauty in the world. The path was covered with large patches of ice and snow, and all they could do was trust their feet on the dark patches of grass. After extreme exertion, they reached level ground on the mountain and stopped there to rest. Soon, they continued over frozen streams and rugged valleys. Their pace was slow and everyone was tired. Helene kept sitting down as she begged for more rest.

"We must keep going," Oskar said, trying to catch his breath.

"Please, I need a few more minutes," Helene begged as she began to limp.

"Mother, are you okay?" Inge asked.

"I am okay," she said. Her eyes were filled with fear and worry. "My feet are very sore."

The guide gave Helene an extra pair of thick socks that she quickly put on.

"Better?" he asked.

"Yes, I think so," she said. "Thank you."

They rested a few more minutes as he passed around some water. Before continuing, the guide encouraged them, showing them that the pass was close. They were warned by the guide that the passage was watched by the Germans, who would unleash vicious dogs upon hearing any noise at all. They walked quickly, but cautiously, as any slight misstep would ruffle some leaves or cause one of them to trip over a rock or uneven ground. After a few terrifying hours of walking along the escape route, hearing in the distance barking dogs and in total fear of being caught, they realized they had reached the peak of the mountain, the border between France and Spain.

The guide, sensing their exhaustion from the intense few hours, told them to sit for a moment and gather their strength. He gave them some bread and leftover cheese. Suddenly, a male Alpine Accentor flew towards them, his bill full of insects. He landed close to where they were resting. Then, he began to climb upwards. No one moved as he was about to reveal his nest. With a final hop, a chorus of chirps erupted.

Upon hearing the sweet sound of birds chirping, the guide then did something they would never forget. He bent down, picked up a branch in the darkness and threw it about a yard further.

"There is Spain," the guide said.

It was that simple, that real. They were speechless. Tears fell down Eva and Inge's cheeks as their husbands grabbed their hands. Oskar and Helene embraced Max in a hug.

They thanked the guide and signed a promissory note, as they had deposited his payment with a third party in Perpignan. Just before parting ways, the guide directed them not to follow the path any more as they could land back in France. Their only choice was to slide down the mountain on the other side. The kind-hearted guide left them shortly thereafter, and in the shadows of the Nazis, they sat discretely along a dark and mostly invisible mountain route surrounded by some trees and bushes until the early morning hours. Hungry, tired, cold, and frightened, they huddled together, and in the early hours of the morning, they followed the guide's instructions to slide down the mountain on the other end.

About halfway down the mountain, they heard the sound of some-one chopping wood. They came upon a kind Spanish woman who directed them down the mountain by a shortcut; otherwise, it would have taken hours to reach the road.

Isaac knew a few words in Spanish so he was able to understand the Spanish woman's directions to the customs and immigration stop. By the time they arrived at customs and immigration, they paused for a moment and looked at each other's dirty clothes, and scrapes and wounds. Helene realized she had lost the heel of her shoe and Eva stroked her ripped stockings and scrapes on her legs. Inge also noticed her legs were covered in blood from the thorny bushes on the mountain, as if the mountain was cursed. Isaac sat her down upon a rock and took his handkerchief out to wipe away some of the blood—their injury and pain a profound reminder of the suffering they had faced. Inge kissed his hand, not caring that it was covered in dirt and blood.

"Freedom is near," Carmen whispered, grabbing Eva hands.

"Is it?" she asked. "It's so hard to believe now that we are here."

"We've gotten this far," Carmen said. "We can do anything together. We are true survivors."

Carmen pulled her up to a standing position.

"Come, we are close now," he said. "Continue to be brave and strong for me."

The Spanish authorities gave them a basin filled with hot water and some towels to clean their wounds. After all the formalities, they were allowed to proceed. The authorities directed the refugees to specific routes. Some could go via Valencia direct to Portugal, while others had to go via Barcelona, Madrid and Badajos, the frontier between Spain and Portugal.

They checked into a hotel for much needed rest and decided to proceed from Barcelona to Madrid and then to Badajos where they would change trains to Lisbon. They arrived in Lisbon late in the evening a few days later and stayed nearly a month, eventually securing passage on a ship called the Equinox to Rio de Janeiro.

Rio was a viable destination due to restrictions and quotas imposed by other countries, and it was seen as a country of immigrants that saw widespread economic growth. It also seemed to be the right place for Carmen and Oskar to launch their diamond business since Rio was a source of rough diamonds.

# chapter

# ELEVEN

Portuguese naval captain Capelo peered into the night as he stood in the crow's nest of the 5,000-ton transport ship Equinox. He stroked his graying beard and puffed on his pipe, as the smoke momentarily fogged his view. The cloudless sky blazed with stars. He stood alone and with slight worry. Not only were the high seas unkind as he knew from many years at sea, but the world was at war and the enemy hid in the dark depths of the sea.

This was the seventh night of the voyage to Rio de Janiero. So far, so good, Capelo thought. He had seen worse. Captain Capelo paced the deck as he had done a thousand times before. He listened to the steady rhythm of the engines.

Meanwhile, in the dining saloon, many feasted and enjoyed conversation among passengers. People played cards, sang songs, and clinked wine glasses, toasting a bright future—a stark contrast to the suffering that continued to unfold in Europe among the Jews and others.

Eva sat amongst her family as they ate dinner. She felt tired and queasy from the tossing seas. She retired to the cabin she shared with Carmen, Inge and Isaac. Max and her parents shared another cabin.

As she started to undress for the night, Carmen entered the cabin and sat on the edge of the bed. He put a hand on her wrist and drew her towards him. He kissed Eva. Held her. Kissed her again. First her mouth, then her neck. She kissed him back and unbuttoned his shirt, touching his chest. He touched her firm belly and kissed her navel, then her breasts. For a few moments, she felt her queasiness disappear and heat grow inside her. She unbuttoned his pants and they fell to his ankles. For a few pleasurable moments, they made love, and afterward, she lay cradled on his chest. They laughed then, thinking what would have happened if Inge and Isaac had walked in on them.

Suddenly, Carmen and Eva could hear chaos in the hallways. A frantic officer knocked on their door and ordered them on deck. Not knowing what was happening; they quickly dressed and left the cabin. They had no idea where the rest of their family was and did what they were instructed, they headed towards the ship's deck.

On deck, they learned that a German U-boat had intercepted their ship and was threatening to sink it. Eva frantically looked around the crowded deck in search of her family, but chaos and hundreds of people blocked anyone from view. The German U-boat captain ordered all passengers into lifeboats. Crewmembers threw lifejackets at the passengers and lined them up.

One yelled, "Women and children first!"

The women and children were helped into lifeboats. As fast as the boats were filled, they were lowered into the sea and rowed off a short distance from the ship. Eva held Carmen's hand tightly, unwilling to let him go, but an officer pushed her into the line to get into a lifeboat.

"Carmen, please don't leave me!" Eva cried as she helplessly stood in line with the other women and children.

"I am right here, Eva," Carmen responded, waving to her from another line of men. He blew her a kiss.

As her lifeboat pulled away, tears streamed down Eva's cheeks. Her eyes never left Carmen's face as he stood in the line, but she lost sight of him when his boat merged in the water with the other lifeboats. She looked around her to find Inge, Isaac, Max, and her parents. They were nowhere in sight. Several lifeboats floated nearby, but darkness made it difficult to decipher any faces. The darkness and the rough seas brought great uncertainty as did the fog that suddenly encompassed them. The night was opaque. Eva could only see the people in the boat with her, and little else.

One woman, frantic with worry, asked one of the sailors in the lifeboat what was happening.

"We've been intercepted by a German U-boat and the captain has threatened to sink the ship," he said. "I don't know any more. Please remain calm."

But no woman in that lifeboat was calm. Their eyes never left the sea around them as they searched desperately for their loved ones. Some called out family member's names. Eva sat in silence as she quietly sobbed. Her stomach was in knots. Panic gripped her tight around the ribs, making it hard to breath. She wanted to yell out the names of her family, but instead she sat staring into the blackness beyond as the waves broke gently around them.

Another lifeboat appeared from behind a thick curtain of fog. Eva perked up, looking about the boat for any signs of her family.

"Eva!" she heard her name being called.

"Inge!" she yelled back at the familiar voice.

As the boat came closer, Eva saw her sister. She moved frantically to the other side of the boat as Inge outstretched her arm towards her sister.

"Sir, may I please join my sister?"

He shook his head. "Sit down," he said.

"Please, sir," Eva stared at the sailor. "I beg you!"

"Fine," he finally said, as he gestured to the other sailor. They moved the boats close together as Eva was helped onboard into the other lifeboat.

The sisters hugged.

"Sit down, ladies," the sailor said. "I don't want anyone falling overboard."

On board the ship, Capelo spoke with the stern German U-boat commander, Wilhelm Schonder. Capelo demanded that the German commander seek permission from Berlin before sinking the ship. He outright refused and paced the ship's lower deck as German officers searched the ship. One officer approached the commander and told him something in German. The Portuguese captain remained calm. He would not let his guard down in front of the cowardly German commander.

"Are there men of military age aboard this ship, Captain?" Schonder asked.

Capelo hesitated briefly before answering as if he was weighing his options.

"Yes, a few young men, who are too ill to fight or injured," he responded.

"Identify the men at once or I will sink this ship immediately!" the German commander ordered.

"Very well," Capelo answered, walking off towards one of his sailors.

The young sailor ran off and returned ten minutes later with three men. One walked with crutches. The other wore an eye patch. And the third man, the weariest of the three, carried a bucket as seasickness had overcome him.

Schonder studied the three men for a few minutes. He finally let out a small laugh.

"These men wouldn't last three minutes on a battlefield, now would they?"

"No, commander," Capelo answered him. "They would not. They are quite weak in their own right."

"Take them away," Schonder directed the sailor. "I can't stand looking at the imbeciles."

As time marched forward and as his passengers floated in the sea, Capelo felt a strong surge of anxiety as to what was to become of the situation. Capelo wanted answers.

"What will be the fate of my ship, Commander?"

Schonder only let out a big sigh. He turned toward the sea and stared at the many lifeboats floating aimlessly.

"Delays are dangerous in war...we will await word from Berlin," the German commander said.

"Yes, commander," Capelo answered, almost sneering at the German commander.

They waited and stood on deck almost two hours more. Capelo's patience began to grow thin. He couldn't stand to look at the German's face any longer and feared the safety of his passengers out at sea.

A German naval officer appeared before them and told the commander that word had come from Berlin. The direct orders: *Do not sink the ship*.

The German commander gave a snide grin, stormed off, and boarded the U-boat. All lifeboats were ordered back to the ship.

As the U-boat left and headed toward the open sea, out of nowhere, a British bomber appeared in the dark sky above, charged the U-boat and fired her guns. What lasted merely seconds was deafening. Suffering some damage, the U-boat quickly dove into the deep waters, evading the attack. The aircraft circled the area and disappeared into the night.

Several of the passengers cheered as they boarded the ship. Many shook in fear and panic. Others were sick from hours of uncertainty in rocky seas.

Chaos now filled the deck as everyone tried to find their loved ones. Eva and Inge pushed their way through the crowded deck.

"Carmen!" Eva yelled. "Where are you, Carmen?"

"Max! Isaac!" Inge yelled.

Others yelled names at the same time, so it became useless even trying. They continued to roam the deck. Eva felt cold and exhausted. She sat down on a chair for a few moments as she continued to scan the deck. Inge stood above her, peering out into the jam-packed crowd.

Then, amid the bedlam, Eva noticed them. People several yards away were floating on the water's surface. Eva ran to one of the ship's crew, pointed toward the people, and yelled to help them. Most had lifejackets, and some did not as they swam towards the ship. Several crewmembers jumped into a lifeboat and as it hit the water, they rowed the boat toward the weary passengers, pulling them into the lifeboat, one-by-one.

Eva and Inge anxiously waited as crewmembers rescued the passengers. Carmen suddenly appeared from the crowd and joined the twins as they watched the scene unfold. They waited several minutes before they recognized Isaac and Oskar. Something was wrong. Her father looked deathly pale and lay flat in the boat. A sailor was attending to him. Eva gasped. Inge began to cry. Suddenly, they heard someone yelling their names. It was Max and their mother walking towards them. They hugged each other and then Eva told them about the others.

Once they were all reunited, they learned that Oskar almost drowned as their lifeboat sprung a leak and began letting in water. As the boat quickly filled with water, everyone panicked, and they realized they had no choice but to jump into the dark sea. But Oskar did not know how to swim. Isaac had secured a lifejacket around Oskar and forced him into the cold water with him. As Isaac tread water and held onto his father-in-law, he struggled to keep Oskar's head above the pounding waves. Oskar swallowed lots of seawater and began to choke. With all the might left in him, Isaac pushed Oskar onto his back. Eventually, help arrived and they were rescued.

# chapter

# TWELVE

*Rio de Janiero, Brazil*

As the ship approached, Rio de Janiero harbor unfolded in unforgettable splendor. It was as if they were sailing into the mouth of a river from the massive Atlantic Ocean. The ocean jutted into the land, opening itself to the bay that connected two gigantic mountains. The mountains stood tall, protecting the entire bay and the wondrous land that prevailed before them. Eva and Inge tried to count the many ships and yachts in the bustling bay, but there were so many traveling in and out that they lost count. Tired passengers stared at the spectacular mountains and peaks, the surrounding city and sandy beaches. Rio looked inviting, yet mystical, a land unlike where they came from.

They had arrived in a new country with little money, but thankfully, with some diamonds to help them start a bright future: diamonds that would become their lifeblood. They were excited to be far from Europe, far from danger, and ready to begin a new life. Small boats welcomed them as they disembarked the ship.

"Oskar!" They heard someone calling. They continued walking from the port with their suitcases, thinking the person must be calling for another Oskar. Again, they heard, "Oskar!"

Who did they know in this part of the world?

Oskar stopped walking and looked behind him. All he could see was a large crowd of people. He shook his head in slight annoyance, weary from the long journey.

"Who is calling my name?" he asked in a frustrated tone, glancing at faces in the crowd.

He looked at Helene. She shrugged her shoulders.

"I don't know, Oskar," she replied, setting down her bag for a brief moment.

Then again, they heard his name being called, this time not as faint as before. They saw a man appear from the crowd, flagging Oskar down. They all looked at each other wondering who the man was and what he wanted.

The man waved and finally approached them, with a woman in tow.

They all stared at the man. He appeared to have a shaved head or was bald. The man looked to be in his fifties and was sweating through his blue shirt.

"Oskar from Berlin?" he asked.

"Yes, may I help you?" Oskar asked, suspiciously eyeing the man from head to toe.

The man took off his hat and grabbed Oskar's hand to shake it.

"Well, it's wonderful to meet you…this is my wife Sylvia and I'm Barry Goldschmidt. We're from Berlin as well, and your friend Roland suggested we meet you here."

"Ah…Roland," Oskar said. "I see…it's very kind of you to meet us here. It's hard to arrive in a foreign land and not know a soul."

Oskar smiled.

"Sylvia and I have been in Rio for three years now. Enough about that, can we help you with your bags?"

"Honestly, we'd appreciate the help, but we don't know where we are going yet," Oskar responded, picking up his suitcase. "We still have sea legs. Everything is so new and unfamiliar, and we're exhausted."

"You're in luck, my friend," Barry said, grabbing Helene's bags. "We've booked you some rooms at a boarding house. It's not luxury, but will get you by for a few days as you settle in."

"Thank you!" Oskar said. "We are very grateful."

Oskar then noticed his family staring at him.

"Forgive me for being so rude," Oskar said, turning toward his family. "Let me introduce my lovely family—my wife, Helene; my daughters, Inge and Eva; my son, Max; my sons-in-law, Isaac and Carmen."

Barry tipped his hat, "Pleasure to meet you. What a beautiful family."

"Thank you," Oskar said.

On the way to Copacabana, a popular beach neighborhood, a sight of lights greeted them.

When they arrived at the residential building, they were overjoyed to see a room brightened with exquisite flowers and baskets filled to the brim with fruit and candy. They shared two rooms and while it was not luxury, they awoke to an amazing view of Rio and the green-blue waves crashing on the shore. Eva and Inge opened the window immediately upon awakening so that they could smell the sea air. They had only seen the ocean once before on a trip to the south of France.

When the Goldschmidts came to visit, Barry urged Oskar and Carmen to sign a contract to work for him as he was in the process of organizing a diamond polishing factory. He offered them a substantial salary and promised to arrange an apartment for each. Oskar and Carmen signed the contract and began work immediately. The timing worked well as they had to leave the boarding house because the owners took money from all the refugees and left them in a lurch after a couple of days.

As Oskar and Carmen often worked 12-hour days polishing and cutting diamonds in an old building that lacked air conditioning, they discovered their new boss led a secretive diamond operation in the state of Minas Gerais, Brazil.

Barry disappeared for weeks at a time. He occupied a small villa in the valley of the Jequitinhonha River that flows through the state of Minas Gerais. Closeby, he managed a small team of miners who busied themselves in the banks of the river. He kept a watchful eye against thieving as his workers kept the contents of their trough in constant motion until the mud was washed away and the water was quite clear. Then the workers took the sand and fine gravel in their hands and searched for diamonds.

Barry never took his eyes off his workers. He sat in a canoe deep in thought, chain-smoking, facing his workers. He would wipe his sweaty brow with a white handkerchief every few minutes. Sometimes hours went by and nothing was found. He would then grab a heavy metal flask, take a sip, and then grimaced at his workers. But many times, he received the signal that a diamond was discovered. Barry took a cloth and rubbed the stone clean. He held it to the sunlight, squinted, and ensured his workers that it was in fact a diamond. Then, days later, the discovered diamonds were sent back to Rio where Carmen and Oskar cut and polished them into beautiful gems to be sold.

As time wore on, Brazil did not feel like home. Eva and Inge disliked the humidity and hot climate. Oskar and Carmen felt like slaves as they dripped with sweat cutting diamonds all day long. Even Max didn't feel quite himself in Rio. He struggled to make friends and didn't feel a strong connection to the Jewish community. Helene often spent hours at a time alone in the apartment with no human contact. Isaac became distressed because he could not find work.

꽁∾ᕥ

Peering out the window of the apartment, Helene couldn't take her eyes off of the favela shantytowns on the hillside above the Copacabana. She had never seen such a sight before. Nothing like it existed in Berlin. The irregular settlements looked somber; a reminder of the disparity in wealth, yet Helene noticed the vibrant shades of colors of some of the outer walls of the poor homes, adding a glimpse of lightness to such darkness. As the favelas faced the city's prosperous seaside neighborhoods, they were juxtaposed with the luxurious apartment buildings and mansions of Rio's elite.

As Helene studied the favelas, her heart ached, for she knew she could not live forever in their small, musty apartment that looked out on the shanty settlements, housing the poorest of the poor. She longed for the life she once knew, the good old days in Berlin before the war—days that were bright and joyful, and that held promise were now lost in a distant past. All a fading memory now—life was wonderful back then. Would they ever find that peace, that joy, again?

A knock at the door broke Helene's concentration. She opened the door. It was Eva.

"Hello, darling," Helene said, as Eva kissed her mother's cheek.

"Hello, Mother," Eva said. "How are you?"

Eva walked towards a chair and sat down.

"Fine, Eva," Helene responded, sitting down near her daughter. "I'm hoping that your father will arrive home at a decent hour this evening."

"I hope so, too," Eva said. "Carmen has been getting home late as well. Is Father happy here, working for Barry?"

"It is not ideal, Eva," Helene responded, shifting her eyes to the floor. "Your father is doing what he can at the moment. He feels a little like he's gone backwards, not forward."

"What about Carmen?" Helene glanced at her daughter.

"Carmen will make do," Eva said. "He isn't crazy about the work, but will do anything to make a living."

Helene nodded.

"Things will get better, Eva," Helene said, touching her daughter's hand.

"Darling, would you like a cup of tea?" Helene rose from the chair.

"No, thanks, Mother," Eva said. "It's too warm today for tea."

"You look pale and thin, Eva," Helene said, brushing back her daughter's hair from her face. "Can I make you something to eat?"

"No, thanks," Eva said. "I'm not very hungry. I am just tired, that's all."

Helene hugged her daughter.

Eva wanted to desperately tell her mother the good news. She was not showing yet, but she would soon. She would wait to share the news of her pregnancy when her family was all together.

As she sat down with her cup of tea, Helene told Eva that her father felt Rio wasn't the right place for them. "Something was missing," she said.

"Where will we find happiness, Mother?"

"We will figure it out, Eva," Helene said. "If we leave, we all leave together. Your father refuses to break up this family. If Hitler couldn't tear us apart, nothing will."

Eva nodded and smiled at her mother.

"Where will we go?" Eva asked. "Where do you want to go, Mother?"

"We will discuss it together as a family on Friday night," Helene replied.

&#8766;

As Carmen was trying to build a new life, he was constantly distracted and worried about the lack of news from his family. Until 1942, Carmen still was receiving news through the Red Cross from his parents and brother. They were living in Antwerp. They corresponded often and Carmen even sent them food parcels. Then, as time went on, all news ceased and they eventually learned from cousins who survived the war in Poland, under false papers as Christians, that Carmen's parents and brother were deported on Rosh Hashanah in 1942 to the extermination camp of Belscz, located along the Lublin-Lvov railway line in Poland.

Carmen was hit hard with the news. He felt guilty about leaving his family in Antwerp. His father's words still rang loudly in his mind, "Go

Carmen. Begin a new life for yourself. We will soon follow." But they never did follow. He made his father promise that he would leave Europe, but his father said the world was too unsettled for promises. They struggled to secure the right papers and leaving became impossible.

One evening as the family ate dinner and discussed the possibility of leaving Rio, Carmen and Eva eyed each other for the right moment. In a moment of silence as the family enjoyed their dinner, Carmen stood from the table. Everyone looked on, unsure as to what was happening. Oskar took a sip of his wine. Eva stood, too, and took her husband's hand.

"Sometimes the most beautiful things happen at the hardest of times," Carmen said, looking into Eva's eyes. "The beauty of this moment is that we are all together and we are safe. We are alive, we are healthy, and a land of possibilities stands before us. There have been moments when I wasn't sure if I could bring a child into this world, this complex world at war. But I soon realized that the bonds of family can never be broken. I couldn't be prouder at this moment to tell you that we are having a baby."

Eva's eyes flooded with tears of joy. Inge and Helene rose from their chairs and hugged Eva. Oskar stared at his daughter from across the table, tears flowing down his cheeks. She finally went to him and kissed her father on the cheek. Max, who now towered over his sister, hugged her tightly.

"I can't wait to be an uncle," Max told Eva. She smiled back at him, pinching his dimpled cheek.

Isaac and Carmen shook each other's hands.

Now there was a baby on the way. And, once again, finding that peace, that place they would call home became urgent.

At first thought, they decided to move to New York. The American consul allowed Eva to proceed to America, but because Carmen was born in Poland, the quota was full and he was not allowed into America. Carmen told the Consul that he was not prepared to split up his family during the war, so why should he do it now?

After almost two years in Rio, they decided to immigrate to South Africa. The year was 1944 and the initial attraction was diamonds.

In 1866, a teenage boy, Erasmus Jacobs found the first diamond in South Africa. He discovered the stone on the banks of the Orange River near Hopetown in the Northern Cape. The farmer on whose land it was discovered, Schalk van Niekerk, sent it to Grahamstown where it was identified by a geologist, Dr. W. G. Atherstone, as a diamond worth about R100 000 today. The 21.25 carat stone was named the Eureka, which means "I have found it".

Between 1870 and 1891, no less than six kimberlite pipes—a type of rock that occurs in the zone of the Earth's crust in vertical structures and is a source of diamonds—were discovered in Kimberley. The biggest pipe in South Africa was discovered at Cullinan, near Pretoria, in 1902. The world's largest gem diamond, a 3,106-carat stone, was found there in 1905. The discovery of diamonds at Kimberley in 1870 and the discovery of large gold deposits in the Witwatersrand region of the Transvaal in 1886 caused an influx of European immigration and investment.

The discovery of diamonds in South Africa made the country attractive, especially to Oskar and Carmen. That and the fact that they were still looking for the perfect place to call home, a place that would provide economic security away from political oppression. South Africa was the land of opportunity and a magnetic force for Carmen and Oskar—men with skills, vision, energy, and the spirit of enterprise.

Once again, the family packed their belongings and boarded the 900-passenger ship Ruys to set sail for Cape Town. This time their journey was less adventurous, and the only thing they contended with were the rough open seas. A pregnant Eva slept more than she was awake. And when she was awake, she sat on deck, breathing in the sea air to try to calm her nausea. She couldn't stand the motion of the ship. Inge would sit by her side, as she also couldn't stand the choppy sea. Together, they suffered and when they felt well, they walked arm-in-arm around the deck of the ship. Helene and Max played cards for hours. Occasionally, Isaac would join them whenever he was not devouring pages of books. Oskar and Carmen stared at the horizon and talked of their future plans in the diamond business.

As their journey came to an end, weary passengers emerged from every corner of the ship. As the ship sailed into beautiful Table Bay Harbour, passengers gazed at the breathtaking and majestic flat-topped Table Mountain that kept a watchful eye under her descending slopes on Cape Town and Table Bay, which dominated the rocky cape Peninsula.

The sun was shining and the weather was beautiful. As the mountain basked in the afternoon sun, a "table cloth" layer of soft clouds covered its flat top. It was a sight to behold.

As they stared in awe, Isaac broke the silence.

"Do you know the legend of Table Mountain?" he asked, still staring at the mountain.

Eva and Inge shook their heads.

"Van Hunks was a Dutch pirate who lived a life of villainy, sailing the high seas before he retired in the Cape," Isaac began. "One of his favorite pastimes was to sit under an ancient tree on Table Mountain and smoke his pipe. One day he was approached by a cloaked stranger, who challenged him to a smoking competition. Proud and confident of his pipe-smoking abilities, Van Hunks accepted, and ended up defeating the man. The stranger took off his hood, revealing himself to be the Devil, and the two vanished in a puff of smoke. Legend has it that to this day, the Devil of Devil's Peak and Van Hunks continue their challenge, each time obscuring the top of Table Mountain with their pipe smoke as they try to out-do one another."

Sea-legged immigrants traversed wooden gangplanks as they stepped off the ship. The family walked away from the ship, ready to start fresh in a new land. With their suitcases in tow, they exchanged smiles as they took in the splendid surroundings of Table Bay. As Oskar walked alongside his family, a sense of relief and peace came over him. For once, he could breathe. The panic that lay in the pit of his stomach for so long was gone. He felt like he had just walked out of a long nightmare. Oskar grabbed Helene's hand. She squeezed his hand back and he knew that they were finally headed in the right direction, thousands of miles away from the danger they had faced in Europe.

# chapter

# THIRTEEN

*1944, Ravensbruck, Germany*

Trudy eyed the new female prisoners as they arrived at this special hell for women, located alongside Lake Schwedt, 50 miles north of Berlin. Ravensbruck was a mini city of low gray barracks surrounded by concrete walls on which guard towers rose at intervals.

She carried a plaited whip in one hand as she watched the women being processed into the camp. This particular group were all Jewish women, identified by the yellow triangles they would wear on their striped prisoner garb, but sometimes unlike the other prisoners, they wore a second triangle for the other categories or for "Race Defilement". She could already tell who would be shot, worked to death or subjected to torturous medical experiments.

Trudy was still not used to this new life of hers, and like the prisoners, she wished she could be anywhere but there. She had been appointed *Aufseherin*, overseer, but she was inexperienced and she knew that she was not mentally capable of handling the role. And then there was the stench. She still choked at the pungent, revolting stench that filled the air in the camp. Fresh air became a luxury as did other simple things—food, clothes, soap, water, and even sleep. She closed her eyes briefly and remembered her father's words, "that this would be an honorable job for her country and for the longevity of the Third Reich."

Trudy placed her hand on her whip and even after two months in this place, she struggled to use it. The other female *Aufseherinnen* used their whips with such ease, as if the prisoners were not human, but animals.

Then, one day Trudy was truly tested. Ravensbruck was also a place where female students were trained to be sadistic guards. The head training overseer, a woman who wore heavy boots and carried a plaited whip and pistol, showed the women the finer points of malicious pleasure. She called Trudy before a group of five prisoners and demanded that Trudy pick an inmate and beat her.

Trudy stared at the prisoners. She noticed their weak, feeble bodies that hung limply under striped prisoner uniforms. Their hollow, pale faces pointed toward the cold, concrete floor.

Trudy only shook her head at the guard.

"*Wählen!*" The guard yelled at Trudy.

"*Nein*," Trudy said, eyeing the brutal head guard. "*Ich kann nicht.*"

The head overseer grabbed her whip and as Trudy watched, she struck the prisoners. Trudy flinched and turned her head, unable to bear the harsh treatment in front of her. As the Jewish prisoners lay on the ground, bloody, beaten and bruised, her thoughts flashed back to Eva. Her sublime image came to mind. Trudy wondered where Eva was. Was she safe? Since Trudy arrived at Ravensbruck, she studied each prisoner's face—to make sure that none of the prisoners were *them*. She did not know what she would do if Eva, Inge or Helene had arrived at such a place. She would not be able to watch them endure such anguish, such hell.

The snap of the whip brought her back to reality. Trudy turned her eyes to the floor thinking she was next. But the whipping stopped.

"You will be removed of your duties immediately," the stern punisher said. "You are incapable of carrying out any obedience towards these prisoners. You are a disgrace to your country. What happened to your loyalty—loyalty to the Fuhrer? For that, you will be punished."

The words rang in Trudy's head...*a disgrace to your country.*

As fear gripped her, Trudy felt her heart beat rapidly.

What sort of punishment, she thought.

"You will be transported to a sub-camp of Buchenwald to clean the camp commandant's home," the head overseer said. "The camp commandant's wife needs someone, and instead of sending a worthless Jew, I am sending you. You will leave immediately."

Trudy smiled inside. It didn't sound like a punishment. Anywhere would be better than this hell.

⁂

The commandant's two-story villa stood just outside the prison compound, perched on a foot hill of the rugged Harz Mountains in Germany. It was nestled amid a dense forest. A fairytale garden in front of the home acted as a strange diversion to what stood only yards away. The main camp of Buchenwald was surrounded by an electrified barbed-wire fence, watchtowers, and a chain of sentries outfitted with automatically activated machine guns.

Trudy knocked on the door, but no one answered. She noticed the door was unlocked. As she entered the home, the commandant was coming down the stairs.

"Who are you?" he asked.

He was tall and wore an impressively pressed uniform and shiny black boots.

"I am Trudy," she said. "I am the Aufseherin from Ravensbruck, sent to clean your home."

His face screwed up in confusion. He laughed.

"What did you do to cause you to land up here?" he asked. "Ach, it doesn't matter actually. Where is the Jew I asked for?"

"I was sent, sir," she said.

He paused briefly before answering.

"Clean the house today, but by tomorrow I shall find a prisoner to replace you," he said. "When she arrives, make sure you watch her at all times. I will never trust a Jew as long as I live. This house must be spotless. My wife doesn't care for mess. Is that clear?"

"Yes," Trudy said.

Seconds later, he was gone.

Trudy walked around the home. It was cozy and quaint. The three bedrooms were finely furnished. The two bathrooms displayed pristine white tiles. She strolled into the kitchen and noticed everything was neat and tidy. She helped herself to a golden apple lying in a fruit basket. She eventually found a mop and began to clean. Hours went by and there was no sign of the commandant's wife or the prisoner to do the cleaning.

Suddenly, she heard sounds coming from the kitchen, as well as a slew of workmen in the back of the house banging and clanking. She heard running water from the kitchen faucet and the clank of pots and pans. When Trudy appeared in the kitchen, she found a prisoner cutting carrots and onions.

"Hello," Trudy said.

Startled, the prisoner looked up from her work.

"Sorry, I didn't know anyone was here," she said.

"I'm Trudy," she said. "I'm here to clean the house."

The prisoner cracked a small smile. Her lips were severely chapped. Her teeth yellow and her skin pale.

"I am Elsa," she said. "I come every day to cook dinner."

"Nice to meet you," Trudy said.

"Same," Elsa said.

"Would you care for an apple?" Trudy asked. "I had one earlier and it was delicious."

The prisoner stared back at her with a horrified look. Then, her eyes shifted to the fruit that lay in the basket.

"No," she said. "If I ate the apple, I would be shot."

Just then the commandant's wife appeared. She wore a midnight blue dress and a three-strand pearl necklace in yellow gold. Her long red hair sat upon her shoulders in waves. She eyed the two of them.

"Are you working on the stew?" she inquired, pointing at the big pot.

"Yes," Elsa said.

"The commandant will be very hungry when he returns," she said. "We must eat promptly at 6 o'clock. We have a party to attend this evening."

"Yes," Elsa answered in German. "The food will be ready."

"Who are you?" she asked, looking up and down at Trudy.

"I am here to clean your house," Trudy said. "I'm Trudy."

"Where is your prisoner uniform?" the woman snapped back.

"I was sent from Ravensbruck," Trudy said. "I was an Aufseherin there."

"Are you serious?" The commandant's wife chuckled.

"Well, you're obviously weak and I suppose you were released from your duties," she taunted. "It's a shame to be German and pathetic like you. Germans are strong people."

She walked around Trudy, examining every inch of her.

"You have good looks, but little else," she said. "Make sure my home is spotless. I don't like dirt...or germs. And make certain my house does not smell like them."

She pointed at Elsa.

"Yes," Trudy said. Her eyes darted to the floor. She swallowed hard.

The woman eyed the prisoner, swept by Trudy and walked upstairs.

Trudy went about her cleaning and Elsa went about her cooking.

When evening settled in, Trudy was upstairs folding clean clothes and she noticed the door ajar to the master bedroom. As she walked by, she caught sight of the commandant placing a ravishing diamond and emerald necklace upon his wife's neck. She stood by out of view and watched as they exchanged a passionate kiss.

Trudy froze. Could it be? She took a quick glimpse. She had seen that necklace before. It was unique, one-of-a-kind. That necklace was not the commandant's, it was Oskar's! She recalled the very night she was with Eva and Inge when their parents were leaving for a dinner party. She had always envied the beautiful necklace that was exquisitely draped around Helene's neck. Her eyes returned to the commandant and his wife.

"What's the matter, Dietrich," the woman asked.

"It seems the clasp is broken," the commandant said.

"Oh, what a shame," she said. "I was so looking forward to showing if off tonight."

"I am sorry, darling," he said. "I don't want to risk it. It may fall off during the evening."

"That is a pity," she said.

"Wear your other diamond necklace," he said. "I will have the jeweler collect it tomorrow to be fixed. Leave it on the dresser."

Trudy quietly slid into the nearest bedroom.

After the commandant and his wife left for the evening, the house was eerily quiet. Trudy retired to the sparse servant's quarters, separated from the rest of the villa, down a narrow hallway near the kitchen. The commandant had left a pair of his muddy boots near the doorway of her bedroom. She would need to polish them before bed.

The tiny room was plain, similar to a jail cell. A small cot lay in the corner, a single wooden chair beside it, and a narrow window just above it.

Dampness and cold fogged up the window. Trudy wiped it with her sleeve. Faintly, she could make out the electrified fence to Buchenwald. SS patrol with guard dogs walked the perimeter of the fence. Beyond the fence stood a large city of brick buildings and wooden prisoner barracks. A main watch tower enveloped three Nazi guards with machine guns, one of many guard towers around the concentration camp.

In the early morning hours at five, Trudy woke to the sounds of barking dogs and guards yelling *"Schnell!"* She noticed that the room was freezing cold.

She began to shiver as she gazed out the window. She could see hundreds of prisoners lined up in the well-lit square. It was roll-call time, where the prisoners were counted morning and evening. She jumped at the sounds of gunshots.

After a little while, Trudy heard *"Schnell!"* again as the prisoners marched through the main gate to work in the quarry. A camp orchestra played melodies from Viennese operas.

Shivering, she got back into bed, but could not sleep. From that moment, she hated who she was and what she had become. It didn't matter that she could not whip those prisoners. She was still a Nazi. She had watched prisoners enter Ravensbruck day after day and had even watched them starve to death and die. A pang of guilt attacked her heart.

Trudy tried to fall asleep, but all she could think about was the diamond and emerald necklace. She knew she could not leave the villa without it.

When sunshine came softly through the window, Trudy got up, washed in the small bathroom across from the bedroom and dressed. She packed her bag and put it aside. Today would be a busy day, she told herself. Her stomach grumbled with hunger. She needed some food.

Trudy entered the kitchen and found the commandant's wife making coffee and toast.

*"Guten Morgen,"* Trudy said.

*"Haben Kaffee und Toast fertig in den frühen Morgen,"* (Have coffee and toast ready in the mornings) the woman said in a cold manner.

*"Ja,"* Trudy said. *"Ich entschuldige mich."* (I apologize.)

The commandant's wife put her breakfast on a tray and disappeared up the stairs. Hesitant at first and light-headed from hunger, Trudy cut two pieces of *Schwarzbrot* (black bread) and smeared the pieces with red raspberry preserves. She poured herself a small cup of coffee.

She ate quickly and when she was finished eating, she cut some extra pieces of bread and hid them away in the kitchen.

Trudy noticed that the prisoner the commandant had promised her had never arrived to clean the home. She grabbed the commandant's boots and cleaned and polished them. She disinfected the bathrooms and vacuumed the dining room. Eventually, in the early afternoon, the commandant's wife, elegantly dressed once again, came downstairs and left the villa. Where was she going? Trudy wondered.

Now was her chance, she thought. She went upstairs and found the pendant necklace still lying on the dresser. Trudy grabbed it, hid it in a black sock in her bag and continued with her duties.

Lost in thought and in her work, Trudy jumped when she heard the front door open. It was Elsa arriving for her duties, accompanied by an agitated SS guard. The guard stood watch in the kitchen as Elsa began to make dinner. Trudy went upstairs. About an hour later, she heard the guard leave.

Trudy found Elsa in the same spot as before, cutting up vegetables. She noticed Elsa looked extremely weak and upset.

"Are you okay, Elsa?"

Elsa shook her head. A single tear ran down her cheek.

"I didn't see my husband this morning," she said. "I usually see him at roll call."

"Maybe you just missed him," Trudy said.

"No, I know where he usually stands," Elsa said. "I think something has happened to him. I may never see him again."

"Sorry, Elsa," she said. "I am sure he is okay."

Trudy noticed Elsa fighting back her tears.

"I can't be certain," she said. "People disappear all the time, never to be seen again. It happens in an instant here."

Trudy put her arm around the prisoner. At first, Elsa pulled away, surprised that a German would want to be that close to her.

"Elsa, I want you to eat something," she said.

"I cannot," Elsa said. "If they find out, I will be killed."

"They won't find out," Trudy said.

Trudy grabbed the bread she had hidden away and put a piece in front of Elsa.

"Eat," Trudy said in a gentle voice.

Not used to eating much or any food at all, Elsa broke off small pieces of the bread and ate slowly. She smiled weakly at Trudy.

"You must try to eat when you are here," Trudy said. "You must stay alive."

The prisoner nibbled on bits of bread.

Trudy gave her a cup of water.

Nervous that someone would catch her; Elsa quickly ate more bread and drank only a sip or two of water. She disposed of the food and then went back to work.

As Trudy was dusting the entry hall chandelier, the commandant returned home early from the camp.

"Did the jeweler come?" he asked.

Trudy froze. Her palms began to sweat.

"The jeweler?" she questioned. "Oh, yes…he did. He came this morning."

"Did you give him the necklace?" he asked.

Trudy held his gaze, weighing her options.

"Yes," she said. "I wasn't certain why he was here, but eventually we found the piece of jewelry."

"Very well," he said. "I will check in with him."

"No," she said.

He eyed her. "No?"

"The jeweler said the clasp will be fixed in two days," she said. "He will deliver it then."

"Fine," he said and walked away.

Trudy held her breath until he was out of sight. Nerves overtook her. Several minutes later, Trudy lifted the receiver to the black telephone.

"I am ready," she spoke into the phone in a quiet voice. "Please come immediately."

After she finished her duties, Trudy went back to the servant's quarters. She put on a black sweater. She heard footsteps coming towards the bedroom. She kicked her bag under the bed.

The commandant was standing at the doorway. His eyes were bloodshot.

"Going somewhere?" he asked.

"No," she said. "Felt cold, that's all."

Her pulse quickened. She could feel her heart thumping in her chest. Her eyes moved to his flat cap displaying the death's head insignia of Hitler's SS.

"Are my boots polished?" he asked.

"Yes, I put them by your bedroom this morning," she said. "Did you not see them there?"

He shook his head.

"Thank you," he said. He continued to stand at the doorway.

"I haven't found a prisoner yet to clean the villa," he said. "No one seems right...no one as good as you."

The commandant then came closer within a foot of the cot she was sitting on and stood like a giant above her. Trudy suddenly felt as though she couldn't breathe and the walls were closing in on her.

"You're very beautiful, you know," he said.

"Thank you," she said, nervously.

He then stroked her blonde hair.

"A piece of lint in your hair," he said. "There, it's gone now."

Then, he leaned down, lifted her face and planted a wet kiss upon her lips. A second later, she turned her face away from him.

"Sorry," he said. "I couldn't resist."

Trudy stared at the bare concrete floor of the bedroom.

"You must have a boyfriend somewhere. A husband, perhaps?" he questioned her.

She nodded her head, anything to get him to go away.

"Yes," she said.

Just then, they heard the commandant's wife.

"Dietrich! Where are you, Dietrich?"

The commandant stroked Trudy's face and immediately left the room.

Trudy closed her eyes, trying to calm herself down. All she could think about was how to leave, swiftly. She sighed. Her mind moved a million miles per second. Then, it came to her. She remembered there was a side door close to the kitchen.

Trudy grabbed her bag and tiptoed towards the kitchen. She heard footsteps in a nearby room and then the sound of someone opening envelopes. She froze against the wall. After a few minutes, the noise softened and the person disappeared up the stairs.

Trudy quietly opened the kitchen door, scanned the ground, and sprinted as fast as she could towards the front of the house and across the deserted road. Moments later, a dense forest of beech trees surrounded her. Breathing hard, eventually she was in the clear as she rested between the tall trees. The air in the forest was heavy with humidity. She glanced upwards, noting the full moon. Trudy smiled to herself. She remembered not to get disorientated by the maze of the thick forest and grabbed a compass from her bag, a gift from her father that she always carried with her so she never lost her way. She continued to walk until she reached the shoulder of a small, gravel road. Trudy waited behind a tree staring at the dark road beyond. As headlights came towards her, she didn't move until she was certain she recognized the car. An old, red Mercedes pulled to the side of the road and flashed its lights.

Trudy ran towards the car, opened the passenger door, and slid into the seat. She embraced her mother in a tight hug.

"*Hallo, mutter!*"

"*Sie sind in ordnung?*" her mother asked. (Are you alright?)

"*Ja, Mutter, fahren Sie einfach,*" Trudy said. (Yes, mother, just drive.)

The car sped down the pitch-black road. She noticed dark circles under her mother's eyes.

"*Haben Sie schon einmal vom Vater?*" Trudy asked. (Have you heard from Father?)

"*Nein,*" she sighed. "*Nichts.*"

Trudy stared out the window. She wondered where her father was or if she would see him again. He ran off and left her mother a year ago. The last time they heard from him, he told them that he was somewhere in Poland, working as an SS officer at a camp, and that he now belonged to the Fuhrer first and foremost and his family came second.

When they arrived at their apartment in Berlin, Trudy noticed a leaflet lying on the ground in the hallway. The words "Africa" caught her eye. She had always wanted to go to Africa. She pushed back her hair and glanced at the words on the paper:

*Attention German Nationals: Teach English in Africa! How well do you speak English? If you are fluent in English, don't miss this exciting, never-to-be-forgotten adventure into different cultures of South Africa. This once-in-a-lifetime opportunity should not be missed! Perfect your English, aid communities, and help develop the world! Get paid! Call today!*

"Attractive opportunity," Trudy said, handing the leaflet to her mother.

"You speak English so well," her mother said. "That would be great for you."

"It would be nice to get away from Germany and experience a new world," Trudy said.

Germany had nothing left to offer her.

What if Germany lost the war? What would become of Trudy and her mother?

Russian forces were advancing from the East and the Allies were pushing from the West. Every day the news portrayed how the Allies were pushing more and more troops into the war, and the Axis powers were rapidly losing ground and resources. The Germans were virtually surrounded in Europe and blockaded by the British. The Russians, invading from the East, were eliminating the German army. It was becoming clear that Germany might lose the war.

# chapter

# FOURTEEN

Eva waddled into the kitchen where she found Carmen dunking buttermilk rusks, a hard, crunchy snack with the texture of cake or bread, into coffee. She kissed him on his forehead.

"Your child is kicking me a lot this morning," she commented. Eva was now seven-months pregnant.

"Well, maybe you deserve it," he said, with a laugh.

She grinned back, making herself some Rooibos tea, a mineral-rich herbal red bush tea.

She pulled out a jar of Marmite, a nutritious savory spread, to put on her toast. She was told she would either love or hate the powerful flavor, but she now couldn't get enough of it. She really loved it.

Eva sat down next to Carmen and sipped her tea.

"I don't know why you like that salty spread so much," he said. "I can't bear the taste. Wouldn't you prefer a rusk?" he asked.

"Please," she said, grabbing one from the tin box where they were stored and added it to her plate next to her toast. "I love rusks, too."

Carmen shook his head and laughed.

"What a delicious combination!" he exclaimed, kissing her on the mouth.

They were enjoying life in Cape Town and had fallen in love with its beauty. They had a charming little home they shared with Isaac and Inge in the residential suburb of Cape Town called Rondebosch. Oskar, Helene and Max lived a few streets away in an elegant 19th century style Victorian house. The family found instant tranquility in Rondebosch, one of Cape Town's oldest suburbs. Their homes were nestled in a leafy neighborhood, abundant with oak trees and playful squirrels, in the shadow of iconic Table Mountain.

Carmen and Oskar opened a diamond center called PristineHaus in the historic center of Rondebosch. It was a perfect spot, a bustling suburb center near the landmark Rondebosch Fountain, where flower sellers sold fresh flowers every day. Many would buy flowers and then admire the stunning diamonds displayed in the window at PristineHaus. The diamond cutters were also a spectacle as many peered through the center's window to watch the craftsman transform a raw diamond into a glistening gem.

⊱⊰

As immigrants to a new country, success did not come easy. Oskar and Carmen had to re-establish themselves in a thriving, but competitive diamond industry. The few remaining diamonds smuggled from Berlin were used to finance their homes in Rondebosch.

Once they settled in, it was Oskar who came upon the vacant store in Rondebosch's historic city center. They barely could cover the costs to acquire it. But the store was in a prime location, and the property manager, a Dutch Jewish immigrant, understood the challenge and agreed to work with Oskar. A cutting, polishing, and diamond store would thrive well in the vacant space and the property manager didn't have any better prospects. Oskar gave the property manager a small diamond pendant for his wife in exchange that he promised to hold the store for two months until Oskar had the necessary funds.

Carmen and Oskar knew the quickest way to make the money they needed was at the diamond fields of Kimberley, Northern Cape, largely owned and operated by De Beers. It meant being away from the family for a short amount of time, but in Carmen and Oskar's eyes, a small sacrifice for success. The family was not in full approval, especially since Eva was pregnant, but the two men knew in their hearts that they had to go to Kimberley.

Dressed in a white starched collared shirt, dark tie, carrying a long frock coat in one hand and a small suitcase in the other, Carmen and Oskar stepped foot in Kimberley. It was June 1945. They looked forward to forging new friendships and establishing close ties with the big wigs in Kimberley, that of the well-known Oppenheimer family of De Beers. Ernest Oppenheimer, a diamond and gold mining pioneer came from a large German Jewish family, and controlled the De Beers Empire.

It all began when a Boer, a farmer, named De Beer sold his farm. The soil upon this farm was vastly rich, for millions of pounds of diamonds lay beneath the dry earth. It only took one large discovery for a rush of miners, businessmen, and others to try their luck at the land. Two men stood out from the crowd, Cecil John Rhodes and Barney Barnato, who owned most of the claims on the land and combined their fortune to create a massive diamond enterprise. Then, in 1927, Ernest Oppenheimer took control of the De Beers Empire.

Their first stop, a place Oskar desired to see for many years, was Kimberley's Big Hole. Carmen and Oskar walked along zigzagging, dusty streets until they hit the abyss. They stood on the high platform in amazement, peering at the gigantic hole, deep below the earth's surface that yielded over three tons of diamonds before it closed in 1914, which resulted in a global network of diamond distribution and sales.

"It's breathtaking," Carmen said. "I can't believe thousands of miners dug the hole with only picks and shovels. It's truly amazing."

"It took almost 30 years!" Oskar responded as they continued to stare in awe at the hole.

It was then that they were greeted by Edward Roberts, a young mining supervisor who was born and bred in the Kimberley area.

"Welcome," he said. "It's great to have you both."

"We are delighted to be here," Oskar said to the man.

Edward then handed them a steel helmet with a built-in lantern. "As a safety regulation, we require you to wear one at all times," he said.

Oskar had already done his homework. He knew the lay of the land. He could immediately see the whites had supervisory positions at the mines, while the black mine workers came from places like Lesotho and lived in the area, trying to support themselves and their families on meager weekly salaries.

They came upon a jeep and Edward motioned them inside.

"Let's take a look at Wesselton, shall we?" Edward looked at Oskar and Carmen.

Carmen and Oskar nodded. On the way, Edward pointed out the sea of squatter camps where thousands of workers lived in tiny shanties of corrugated iron. Oskar was suddenly overwhelmed by the magnitude of poverty; the only happiness being the workers' children playing in clouds of dust.

The Wesselton mine, located a mile from downtown Kimberley, was one of the deepest mines.

When they arrived at the mine shaft, Edward stepped boldly into the steel cage and told them to follow. Edward pressed a red button, and with a sudden jolt and a loud creak, they whizzed down the mine shaft. Carmen hated the motion and closed his eyes. Edward just laughed at him. Oskar looked upward and noticed far in the distance, a small patch of sunlight. No more than two minutes later, they had reached the mining level, approximately 2,500 feet below the surface.

"Here we are, gentlemen!" Edward announced and opened the cage door. As they stepped out of the steel cage, it was as if they had stopped into a new world, below the earth's surface. They found themselves in a large chamber with a well-lit road running through it. Large trucks drove by and hundreds of men bustled through the chamber, hard at work.

They followed Edward down the road. As they walked, he talked. He explained that a shaft was drilled in the bedrock that encased the volcanic pipe. Many tunnels ran parallel to the surface. The kimberlite, a type of volcanic rock that contains diamonds, loosened by dynamite, poured into the tunnels.

Edward looked at his watch.

"Get ready, gentleman!"

There was a loud crash, followed by several other explosions. Thunderous echoes reverberated through the passages.

Carmen jumped with fright. Oskar held his chest and put his hand over his nose as burnt sulphur wafted in the air.

"Dynamite!" Edward exclaimed. "The miners are blasting in this area."

"Could you have possibly warned us?" Carmen asked Edward in an agitated tone.

"Sorry, I am so used to the noise and I forget how deafening it can be," he said, with an apologetic smile.

Carmen was not certain he liked Edward.

As they continued on, they witnessed the intricate process at work. Bulldozers scraped kimberlite ore through a hole in the tunnel. The ore poured into hopper cars on the level below. Then, the ore was dumped into the shaft and brought to the surface.

The next day, their real work began. Carmen and Oskar's wealth of knowledge and skills would be most valuable in the sorter's office, where diamonds from the mines in Africa were graded according to size, shape, color, and quality. They possessed the right instincts and knowledge to be proficient and trusted sorters, analyzing large quantities of the newly discovered gems on a daily basis. In the sorting room, they used their knowledge to help determine the special characteristics of the many rough diamonds they inspected and the profitability of the production. The men sat for hours on end and sorted a mixed quality of rough diamonds, all with an assortment of color, quality and sizes. They identified the white or colorless diamonds, which were more valuable and rare, as well as those with inclusions or flaws. They sorted the rough stones into thousands of categories. Divided first by size, then shape, clarity and color, the stones were further subcategorized by thousands of different criteria. They took copious notes and passed them onto the supervisors.

Once the goods have been sorted, the comprehensive method began that determined which goods to supply to sight-holders (diamond manufacturers) during sight week. Sight-holders aimed to collect their goods as fast as possible. When the sight opened on the first day, brokers were gathered in lieu of their clients to pick up the hard, black briefcase-like "boxes" with a yellow stamp on the front. Inside were sealed bags of rough diamonds. Oskar recalled a time he had collected his goods in Antwerp from a sight-holder and remembered he never got enough or what he needed. De Beers (DTC) set the price of each box in advance and determined the quantity and quality that each site-holder will receive.

Oskar squinted under the fluorescent lights. He blinked a few times to regain his focus. He pushed aside some flawed stones into his so-called "rubbish" pile. He scrutinized several other stones and then he saw it.

Oskar picked up the glimmering gemstone with his tweezers to catch the natural light from the high windows above his worktable. He pushed a jeweller's loupe to his eye and gazed at the stone through his eyepiece. He turned it this way and that, and noticed how a prism of color dazzled upon the diamond.

"So beautiful," he said.

This one was close to flawless. Almost perfect, except for the small feather, a slight imperfection in the stone, Oskar thought. The cutters would know just the right way to cut through the tiny cracks, creating two perfect diamonds from the stone, each possibly three carats. He held up the stone between thumb and forefinger. Satisfied, he laid the diamond aside with the other chosen few, ready to be distributed to the cutters and polishers.

Each evening before retiring to bed, they chased away the exhaustion of the day with a tumbler of whiskey in the old tavern, The Star of the West, where hordes of thirsty miners took solace. Carmen and Oskar mostly kept to themselves and they sometimes battled fixed stares from miners wondering who the well-dressed men were and where they had come from. They did not want to get into diluted conversations or fuel more curiosity, so they spent most evenings at a small table in the corner of the tavern. They sipped their whiskey, usually satisfied their hunger with Kimberley Street chicken or fish, and listened to the joyful tunes from the honky-tonk piano. Carmen missed Eva tremendously and after several weeks of hard work and long days in Kimberley, Oskar fought to keep Carmen's spirits up. "Just two more weeks is all we need and then we will return to Cape Town," he would tell his son-in-law, while patting his arm.

ॐৡ

Meanwhile, in Cape Town, Eva's belly was swollen, making her feel big and clumsy. She craved a strange combination, Marmite and tomatoes, even pickled tomatoes. She couldn't get enough and constantly munched on tomatoes and toast with Marmite until the rush of cravings that hit her several times a day, like a tidal wave, diminished.

Eva disliked being stuck inside and enjoyed exploring beautiful Cape Town. The city boasted natural, divine beauty, which led Eva to a new-found interest in photography. She often got lost in pursuit of a perfect photograph. Many times, drivers hooted at her, but she ignored them and hoped they would pass her.

One afternoon with more than an hour to spare before meeting her mother and sister for tea, Eva followed the De Waal Drive around the lower slopes of Devil's Peak Mountain. Before she reached the University of Cape Town, she swung off the road and drove up through the pine forests and oak groves until she reached the car park behind the Cecil Rhodes Memorial. She left the car, grabbed her camera, and strolled down to the semi-circular terrace below the 49 stone steps (one for each year of Rhode's life) flanked with eight bronze lions. Eva lifted her camera towards the bronze statue of a noble horseman, with one hand lifted to shade his eyes as he gazed over the city.

She marched back up the stone steps that led to the granite pillars reminiscent of a Greek temple. She paused for a moment to catch her breath and saw a single fallow deer on an afternoon stroll. She quickly tried to get a clear shot of him, but he noticed her motion, and took off into the forest. Eva then found a pleasant spot just up the slope from the Memorial, a small forest plush with striking evergreen trees. She hugged herself about the shoulders as the wind whipped through her sweater. It was then that Eva heard the soft cry of a woman close by.

At first, Eva hesitated. She did not want to involve herself, but the cries continued. She walked toward the sobs and saw a coloured woman sitting on the steps near the Memorial. No one else was in sight, only them. Eva stood a few feet away, still wrangling with her emotions. Stay or go? She could leave now without the woman seeing her, she thought. The coloured lady was between 30 and 40 years old. She wore a blue cotton housedress and black laced work shoes with thick heels. She held her head in her hands. Eva could hear her sniffles in between sobs.

"Hello...Are you okay?" Eva approached the woman.

The woman lifted her head, wiped her eyes, and stared for a second at Eva.

She nodded. The woman had a pleasant, plump round face with eyes as dark as night; eyes that seemed to have lost its sparkle amid the uneven road of life.

"Can I help you?" Eva asked.

"No, madam," the woman said.

She held her head in her hands again.

"Did someone hurt you?" Eva asked.

"No," the woman replied.

There was a moment of silence. Eva didn't know what else to do and began to walk away.

Then the woman said to her, "The man I worked for, for 15 years, died today."

Eva turned toward the woman.

"I've no work now," the woman said. "I don't know what to do. I have nothing. I cannot face telling my daughter, Zola."

Eva sat on the step next to the woman.

"I'm sorry," Eva said. "May I ask your name?"

"Zoe," the woman answered.

"Zoe, that is a lovely name," Eva tried to console her. "I am Eva."

"Where do you live, Zoe?"

129

"District Six."

"Ah," Eva said, "I am not so familiar with it. I'm new to town, so please forgive me."

"I live there with my daughter, Zola," she said.

By now, the tears that wet her cheeks had dried up.

"How old is your daughter?" Eva asked.

"She is 13, madam," Zoe said.

"What a wonderful age," Eva said, as she glanced at her watch and realized she was running late to meet her mother and sister.

"Well, Zoe, I could use some help, if you're interested," Eva said, with a smile. "Why don't you come by my house at 9:00 o'clock tomorrow morning?"

Eva wrote down her address for the woman.

"Yes, madam," the woman said, smiling back. "Thank you."

"Goodbye for now," Eva said.

"Goodbye," Zoe said.

Eva hurried off to meet Helene and Inge at the tea garden near the Memorial.

The adorable room was decorated like a charming English tea room with a sun-dappled courtyard. The tables were set with fine china, silver and white linens. The walls were adorned with antique pictures and decor. Soft music played in the background.

Eva kissed her mother's forehead and placed a soft kiss on her sister's nose. They smiled at one another.

"Sorry, I'm late," Eva sat down at the table.

"This place is lovely," Eva said, looking about her. "Good choice, Inge."

"Where have you been?" Inge asked. "We were so worried."

"Darling, I don't like you driving around aimlessly looking for a place to photograph," Helene set her eyes on her daughter. "I don't think it's safe. You don't know Cape Town well enough yet. And, you're pregnant. Anything can happen."

"Don't worry, Mother," Eva said. "I went to see the Cecil Rhodes Memorial—such a beautiful place. And it looks like I may have found a maid!"

"Really?" Inge asked, focusing on her sister.

"Yes," Eva said. "A coloured woman...she will be coming to the house tomorrow morning."

"Where did you find her?" Helene questioned, crossing her arms.

"At the Memorial," Eva responded. "The person she worked for died recently and she has no work. I found her crying on the steps at the Memorial. She was so upset and helpless. She has a small daughter. I had to help her somehow."

"Where does she live?" Inge asked.

"I couldn't understand what she said," Eva said. "I am sure we will find out soon enough."

"Make sure you know everything about her before you let her roam around the house freely," Helene said. "I've heard stories about maids stealing and far worse. Please make sure Isaac is home when she arrives."

"There will always be stories, Mother," Eva said. "Not all maids steal. Some are worth everything you pay them and probably more."

Helene fell silent from her daughter's response. Inge grinned at her sister.

They sipped a variety of teas, Darjeeling, Ceylon, Assam, and Kenya. They savoured delicious food, served on ornate tiers that were decorated with fresh flowers from the garden. Freshly baked scones were served with clotted cream and preserves. They tried for the first time the South African milk tarts, *melktert* locally, which was a sweet, creamy custard tart with a sprinkle of cinnamon. They nibbled on delicate finger sandwiches that looked too pretty to eat, smoked salmon, egg mayonnaise, and cucumber. They ended it all with a delectable chocolate cake.

They discussed how South Africa was unlike anything they had envisioned. It was primitive, yet industrial. The immense beauty and vast landscapes created a home for many difference races and ethnicities. It was slowly becoming their new home.

The next morning, Inge stirred at the sound of someone working outside. She opened her eyes and realized it was Charlie, their gardener. She turned over and gave Isaac a peck on the cheek. Then, she glanced at the clock and jolted out of bed.

She ran down the hall to Eva's room and threw open the door.

"Eva!"

"Eva, wake up!"

"It's almost 8:30!"

"What!" Eva exclaimed. "I overslept. I am exhausted and can hardly move. My belly is getting so big."

"It's okay," Inge said. "We all overslept. Isaac starts his new job at the University of Cape Town in an hour!"

"He does!" Eva responded. "That is wonderful. You never told me."

"Sorry, Eva, I forgot all about it with everything going on," Inge said.

Eva pulled herself out of bed and dressed for the day. Zoe would be coming to meet them soon.

When she arrived, Zoe walked through the front door of their house with a newfound confidence. It was as if she was another person, not the person perched on a stone step, crying with her head in her hands.

Zoe was taller than Eva imagined. She was tender-hearted and soft spoken. She wore a faded blue skirt, a light pink blouse, and her hair was piled up in a bun, with a mix-and-match *doekie* upon her head. She smelled like soap.

"Inge, this is Zoe," Eva introduced her sister.

"Hello," Inge said.

"Hello," Zoe said, looking from Eva to Inge and from Inge to Eva. "You are so alike. I can't tell the difference. Twins?"

"Yes, Zoe, Inge and I are mirror-image twins," Eva said, grabbing her sister's arm. "We've gone our whole lives confusing people. People always struggle to tell us apart. We are used to it by now."

The women let out a laugh.

"You are both beautiful," Zoe said, staring at them briefly.

"Thank you," the twins said, in unison.

Inge instantly saw the sweet nature that Zoe possessed, but the reality of her life was evident in the roughness of her hands and chipped fingernails.

They walked Zoe through their home and reviewed her chores: make beds, clean toilets, scrub floors, vacuum, wash and iron clothes, prepare dinner, and sometimes buy groceries. And, any additional chores that needed to be done. They would pay her 22 pounds per month, from 9 a.m. to 4 p.m. daily.

Zoe decided she would take a chance and ask for more money. She knew it was a risk in a society where many maids would have worked for that price. She had heard the awful stories of maids asking their employers for more money, only to be turned down, called stupid, and locked out of their employer's homes, forbidden to ever return. She knew she wasn't getting younger and her joints hurt from years of housework. But she also knew that she had to continue to work to support herself and her family. She needed a little more to make ends meet. After all these years, Zoe was used to the long hours of work and low pay.

Zoe was born in rural South Africa and migrated to Cape Town at the age of 14 to help support her family. At 14, she was employed as a maid. Zoe only had a sixth grade education.

Now, she hoped her new employers had a sense of gratitude.

"Madam, could you pay me more?" Zoe asked. Her eyes stuck on Eva for her reaction.

Eva was caught off guard. She had never hired a maid before, let alone negotiated wages. Eva thought she should consult with Carmen, but as black desperate eyes stared back at her, she couldn't say anything, but "yes". They agreed on 25 pounds per month.

"Zoe, tell me again where you live," Eva crossed her arms. "I only remember something about a district."

"District Six," Zoe said. There was a brief silence. "It's not somewhere you would want to know or even be. It's all I know and I don't know that I will ever know any different."

Zoe looked down at the floor.

"I understand," Eva replied.

"No, madam," Zoe said. "You couldn't possibly understand. No white person could ever understand."

They stared at each other briefly without saying a word.

# chapter

# FIFTEEN

Situated in the city bowl of Cape Town, at the foot of Table Mountain, and within sight of the docks, District Six was an inner-city, lively community made up of former slaves, artisans, merchants, priests, fisherman, teachers, midwives, and other immigrants, as well as Muslims brought to South Africa by the Dutch East India Company during its administration of the Cape Colony. A microcosm of clogged streets, filled with butcher shops and bakeries, churches and mosques, Victorian houses, markets, and bars. While it was home to a mostly coloured community, it was also comprised a large Jewish population.

The community of people came from all over the world and different corners of South Africa, and together created a rich mix of distinctive cultures, all living in harmony. But a blighted area existed among this community. The slum was dangerous, rife with gangsters and drug abuse. This den of vices was full of immoral activities, like gambling, drinking, and prostitution, and residents were prone to social ills, poverty and alienation.

Zoe and her daughter Zola lived in the slum in a corrugated iron shack. That was all they could afford and the shacks they lived among almost touched each other. Each shack was not just made from plain sheets of metal, they were adorned with colorful rope and plastic bags, anything the residents could get their hands on to personalize their homes.

Homemade shops, barbershops and salons, and car repair shops, housed in tiny tin huts, were also vibrantly decorated. And the secrets of the community were hidden in their walls. People socialized at the busy shebeens, illegal bars run out of sterile matchbox houses, and at the spaza—small, informal shops that operated out of homes—that sold cigarettes, soft drinks, sorghum beer and milk stout, as well as necessities, like maize meal, bread and sugar.

Life was lived on the streets, but the street they lived on was not really a street. It was an unpaved, dirt road, marked by blood, sweat and tears. It breathed in the sadness and hopelessness from the heavy footsteps of the residents.

Every day Zoe thanked God they were alive. In the warm summer months, their tin shed was like an oven. In the damp, cold winters, they froze and rain water flooded into their home. They shared a dirty toilet with a few other families, and there were no showers. Instead, they washed with water from a standpipe poured into a plastic bucket.

An old chair and a few abandoned crates comprised their makeshift furniture. Torn, ragged blankets were their only warmth. Zoe and Zola shared an old, small bed at night, otherwise when it became uncomfortable, Zoe slept on the hard, dirt floor with a blanket. But, even still, they considered themselves one of the lucky ones. Some shared a shack with other families. Their shack was their own.

An old, rusty green pickup truck stood abandoned by their shack. No one could move it as the wheels were stolen from it. A cracked windscreen from a bullet was a daily reminder of the crime the residents faced. Chickens scratched in the rubbish, sprawled around the township. Rain from the night before pushed sewage and rubbish through the gravel streets. Dogs lazed everywhere, while children dashed around and played.

Like many families living in the townships, employment was very unstable. Many took jobs in whatever they could find and work was meager. Food was a luxury, not a necessity. Some days, Zoe and Zola would not eat at all. Zoe hated herself on those days...the days when she could not feed her child.

Each morning as Zola dressed for school, Zoe joined other women at the standpipe where they washed clothes in buckets. She saw the old coloured man every day as she walked to the standpipe. He would wave at her and she would wave back.

The man lived five shacks down from theirs. At dawn, he emerged from his rundown shack and watched as the others began their day. He stood slightly slumped, leaned on a gnarled stick, and waved at everyone as they passed by. Some thought he was crazy, but everyone knew he was wise. At 95, they knew he had seen it all. His dark eyes showed pain and fear, but at the same time, a hint of happiness.

In the afternoons, he sat on an old plastic chair, drank *umqombothi*, a frothy African beer, and smoked a *zol*, a homemade cigarette. Sometimes he talked to himself as if he was fighting off old demons. Other times, some of the older men would join him. They didn't talk much; they watched and listened, letting time slip away, like they had given up a long time ago. They didn't possess the strength in themselves any more. Occasionally, the old men would laugh, exposing toothless grins.

The man was not just an ordinary *ou balie* (old man). While his body was old and weary, his magical hands healed. He was the township's *sangoma* (witch doctor). In a community that believed in superstition and witchcraft, the witch doctor blended ointments and medicines using an array of unique ingredients, like wild herbs, baboon, snakeskin, and sheep's hoof. Beyond the cascading waterfall of herbs and plants that hung in his doorway, his dark shack hid a collection of small bones, seeds and shells, each significant to human life. He carried the power to throw the bones and see into the future. Some feared him, but many sought his magical healing powers.

"*Heita!*" The women greeted each other each day, in the early dawn hours.

As Zoe leaned over her bucket of water, she overheard an older woman giving a younger woman an earful.

"It's *dom* to go out looking like that after nightfall because of the *skollies* (criminals)," the woman said, as she reprimanded a younger woman. "You know what happens…Don't be *mamparra* (cheeky)! You *kak* pretty. You will get yourself into trouble with the *skollies*."

"*Ag man*," the younger woman replied. "Sorry, *antie* (older female authority)."

"And lay off the *dagga* (marijuana)!" The older woman now looked at Zoe.

"Howzit, Zoe!"

"Heita," Zoe replied. "Howzit!"

They smiled at one another. Zoe avoided much conversation and worked quickly so she could eat breakfast with Zola before she left for her new job.

When she was done washing the clothes, she carried it to the line near their shack and hung the washing upon it.

When Zoe returned, Zola had made some *melie pap* (porridge made from maize flour).

She told her daughter about her new job.

Zola hugged her mother.

"I'm proud of you, mama," Zola said. "We will be okay."

Zoe held her daughter's face in her hands, "I will always be a maid, Zola, but you can be more."

Zola stared into her mother's eyes, but she only saw a glint of happiness. She saw mostly pain in her eyes, which were full of love for her.

"Zola, you're smarter than I am," Zoe said. "You must push yourself; you must not give up on your dreams. I want a better life for you, if that's possible in this place, in this country."

Zola nodded. "I will try mama...I will try my very best."

"You must try, Zola," Zoe said. "You must never give up. We can only dream of what we know, what is in our reach, Zola. But, in this harsh world, where we dare to dream, I have many dreams for you. I wish I could inspire you to do more, but how, my sweet daughter? How? When I work as a maid, and I come home with calloused hands, broken fingernails, hungry and tired— how can I inspire you? Each morning, you see groups of our people huddled together along the roadside outside of the township, hoping to get work of any kind that day. Most walk away, after hours of standing, in disappointment. I want you to dream and I hope your dreams come true. Promise me that you will keep up your school work and be inspired to learn."

"Yes, mama," Zola answered. "I promise."

They sat in silence in their tin shack and ate their *melie pap*.

As Zola made her way to school, Zoe rode in an old bus to a nearby bus station. Eventually, she arrived at Eva's home.

"Morning, Madam," she said, as Eva opened the front door.

"Morning, Zoe!"

After Eva showed Zoe a few things around the house, she began her housework. As Zoe changed the bed sheets, she saw him for the first time. He waved as he trimmed the bushes. She waved back. He was like her...a coloured man.

Charlie was from a nearby township. Like Zoe, he came by bus every day to care for the garden and do the heavy work in the house. He was also an uncle, a brother and a father, working as hard as he could under the circumstances he lived, while trying to earn hard-earned money to care for his struggling family. He had never known proper freedom, and hoped that one day he would. His education was minimal and he would never be given the chance to get a good job. All because of white immigrants, who came to South Africa long ago and used blacks as their slaves, planting the roots of great prejudices and injustices that would last a few hundred years to come.

❧

It poked through the soil as Charlie raked some leaves. At first, he did not notice it and kept the rake in motion until the metal object hit his shoes.

He stopped and picked it up from the ground. He turned it this way and that way. He cleaned it off on his blue overalls. Puzzled about the object, Charlie stared at the inverted triangular-shaped, enameled metal badge with a black camel thorn bough or Dreidorn, with a Swastika at its bottom point.

Charlie ran inside.

"Madam, come quickly!" Charlie yelled at Eva.

"What's the matter?" Eva asked, as she walked into the kitchen.

"Madam, look what I found in the yard," he said, placing the metal badge in her hand.

She stared at it with wide eyes, instantly noticing the Swastika. She wasn't sure what it was, as the badge did not look like any she had seen before.

"Thank you, Charlie," she said, looking up at him. "It just seems to be an old memento from the past, that's all."

"Yes, madam," he nodded and walked outside.

Eva sat down at the table. She smoothed away some of the soil on the badge with her fingers. She sighed. Panic began to churn in her stomach. She swallowed hard, trying to push the feeling away. Eva never wanted to feel that way again. And here she was in another country, staring at a badge with a Swastika.

Eva placed the badge on the table and wondered if her family could ever escape their past.

"What's that, Madam?" Zoe asked, picking up the badge from the table.

"It's just an old badge, Zoe," Eva said. "Don't worry about it."

Eva turned to face the window. A tear drifted down her cheek.

"Are you crying?" Zoe put a hand upon her boss's shoulder.

Eva wiped a tear from her cheek.

"It takes me back to another place," Eva sniffled. "It opens old wounds."

"What place? What wounds?"

Eva turned to face Zoe.

"Do you recognize my accent, Zoe?"

"I'm not sure, madam...could it be German?"

"Yes," Eva answered. "I am a Jew. My family escaped from Germany and Europe. That badge shows a Swastika, a Nazi symbol. I know what it's like to be hated, to feel inferior, Zoe."

The South African coloured woman and the German Jew had one thing in common: They were victims.

"If I ever look at you like 'they' do, remind me of what I just told you," Eva grabbed her maid's hand.

"Yes, but while you are a Jew, in this country you have nothing to fear," Zoe said. "Your skin is white. You may be hated by some, but their focus is not on you, it's on me, a coloured woman, and everyone else with a skin color unlike yours."

Eva now knew she was on the "other" side, where Anti-Semitism might lie just under the surface, buried away, but the focus was not on her any longer, but on those of color, who were feared to outnumber the whites.

Inge entered the kitchen with a bag of groceries. Immediately, she could tell something was wrong.

"Morning, Inge," Zoe grabbed the bag from Inge and laid it on the counter. She began unpacking the groceries.

"What's the matter, Eva?"

"It's nothing really," Eva replied. "Charlie found this in the garden." She walked over to Inge and placed the badge in her hand.

Inge's eyes widened.

"*Gott schrecklich!*" She yelled. "*Was ist los? Was willst du*? I thought we had left this all behind us?"

"We did leave it behind, but it seems to be everywhere," Eva said. "Anti-Semitism lives and it seems to live just about everywhere."

Inge peered at the badge.

"I know just the person and place to shed more light for us," Inge said.

Later that day, Eva and Inge arrived at the magnificent campus of the University of Cape Town along the slopes of Devil's Peak and Table Mountain. They trekked across the campus, on the beautiful Rhodes estate, to Isaac's office. Isaac had landed a job as a humanities professor.

They entered the building and climbed the stairs to the small, dark office on the third floor. When they arrived, Isaac was surprised to see them. Inge bought him a plant for his office, which desperately needed some brightening up. With no windows, the office lacked any light, any decor. Isaac peered down at his work under the artificial light of an old lamp.

"Thanks, my love," Isaac said, hugging Inge and then Eva. "Welcome to my new home."

Isaac spread his arms wide almost touching the walls of his office. "It's small, but cozy."

"How is work going?" Inge smiled.

"Very well," he replied, crossing his arms. "I met some of the other professors in the department and start teaching next week."

"That is great!" Eva said. "This job seems to suit you well."

Eva pulled the Swastika badge from her purse. Isaac analyzed it from under his lamp.

"Charlie found it in the garden this morning," Inge said.

"Other than the Swastika, I don't know what it means," Isaac said. "It's different to what the Nazis in Europe wore. Wait here a moment."

He left the office and returned ten minutes later with another professor, a very distinguished older gentleman.

"Eva and Inge, this is Professor Henry Lutz."

"Nice to meet you," they said, shaking his hand.

"My knowledge of this badge is not very extensive," Henry explained. "I do know that during the Weimar-period in Südwest-Afrika, groups of boy scouts were formed, known as Deutsche Pfadfinderschaft. In 1928, they combined and chose a flag and a uniform. The uniform was copied from the uniform der Deutschen Schutztruppe. The insignia is known as the 'Dreidorn'. It was worn in an embroidered form (left upper arm) as well as in enameled metal upon the tie or left breast pocket. In the summer of 1934, the group was abolished by the government. But, in 1935, the boy scouts were allowed to form again and were then known as Deutsche Pfadfinder von Südwestafrika. The group was dissolved once again by the South African administration in 1939 on the outbreak of World War II."

"Are there a lot of groups sympathetic to Nazism in South Africa?" Isaac asked.

"Unfortunately, some exist," Henry said. "*Greyshirts* or Gryshemde was a name given to a South African Nazi movement that existed during the 1930s and even now as we speak. However, the Greyshirts have struggled to maintain unity and spawned a number of minor splinter groups. As you are well aware, Jewish immigration from Nazi Germany to South Africa grew significantly during the 1930s and the Greyshirts launched campaigns calling for an end to the immigration of Jews. Relations between the National Party and the Greyshirts actually improved, initially as a result of a 1937 letter from Frans Erasmus, at the time Secretary of the National Party, praising the Greyshirts for bringing the so called 'Jewish problem' to the forefront and culminating a number of leading Greyshirts to hold National Party membership."

"We face this challenge again," Inge said. "This is very disturbing, Professor Lutz."

"Yes, I am quite sure it is," Henry sighed. "You will find people who hate Jews in South Africa, but the intensity of it is nothing like what you once faced. Less significant forms of Hitler exist, but you are not the biggest problem in South Africa—the non-whites are the problem. I am not saying that history doesn't repeat itself, but that new histories will be written. In this country, Jews are not the number one problem. The war will soon come to an end, and then new wars and new challenges will begin. There is always someone to blame."

Eva's thoughts quickly turned to her new maid, Zoe. She touched her very pregnant belly and thought about the future and her unborn child.

Eva and Inge left the University and drove home mostly in silence.

"Eva, let's keep this to ourselves," Inge told her sister. "Let's not show it to Father, Mother, and even Max. You know how Max is, he will become malcontent."

"Yes, you're right," Eva replied. "What should we do with it?"

"We should have left it with Isaac at the University," Inge said. "Maybe we should bury it where Charlie found it."

"Not on our property, Inge!"

"Where then?" Inge asked.

"I will find a place," Eva said.

When they arrived home, Charlie and Zoe had left for the day. The house was quiet and looked so neat and tidy.

"Zoe is great, isn't she?" Eva looked at her sister.

"Yes, she is wonderful," Inge said. "You found a treasure."

"Funny, I just smelled a whiff of Carmen's cologne in the air," Eva said. "So strange...I miss him so much, Inge."

As Eva was about to ask her sister about dinner, she caught Inge smiling while looking at the doorway.

Eva turned around to find Carmen standing in the living room.

Tears streamed down Eva's face as she ran towards him.

"Eva, my darling!" He laughed. "I am home!"

Eva flew into his arms. Carmen smiled and pulled her into a tight embrace. She put her arms around his neck and kissed him.

That night, they dined as a family again. Helene cooked a delicious *bobotie*, South African dish consisting of spiced minced meat baked with an egg-based topping. She served it with chutney, a sweet sauce, and they enjoyed Malva pudding with custard for dessert.

Carmen and Oskar told stories of the diamond mines of Kimberley, how they spent lonely nights in the tavern listening to music, and how the Big Hole produced riches and amazement. "I looked down at the gaping pit below and I saw such hope and promise," Oskar said. Little creases around his eyes revealed hard work and exhaustion.

"Everyone was sick with diamond fever, and their minds were filled with visions and dreams," he said. "Kimberley is a city of limitless opportunity."

They also toasted to Isaac's future at the University.

"Max will be joining you as a student," Oskar said in between bites of food.

"I thought I would join you, Father," Max said, placing his fork on his plate. He gave his father a sour look.

"No, Max, you need to create your own path in life," Oskar said.

Max looked at his mother for her reaction.

"Your father is right," Helene chimed in. "You must go to school, Max, and get an education of some kind. The world is changing and unstable. You need to infuse your future with some promise. An education is the best way...the only way, I'm afraid."

"The diamond industry is not for you, Max," Oskar continued. "It would bore you and drain your creative energy. You are destined for other things. You have a strong passion for certain causes; maybe your future lies in humanities or even law."

"Max, stop by my office tomorrow and we will figure out what needs to be done for you to enroll," Isaac said.

Eva ruffled her brother's wavy hair. "Don't be so glum, brother!" Eva exclaimed. "They're right."

She grabbed her brother's hands.

"These are not the hands to cut diamonds," Eva said. "Those are not the eyes to examine gems under a loop. Those are the hands to rally people for special causes with a keen insight and good judgment to discern good from evil."

Max smiled fondly at his sister.

# chapter

# SIXTEEN

As a soft rain dripped from the night sky, Inge couldn't sleep. Her mind ran a marathon of thoughts as her body lay exhausted next to Isaac. As he slept soundly, she stroked his soft face. She rose from the bed and walked to the kitchen. She turned on the stove to heat some milk. She tilted her head towards the window and the darkness beyond as she watched rain drops slide down the window.

Without any notice, a sudden sharp pain radiated through Inge's abdomen. She shut her eyes and clutched at her stomach. It must just be a cramp, she thought. The pain disappeared as quickly as it came.

Inge stirred the milk as it warmed. Again, a pain shot through her abdomen. She gasped, laid down the spoon, and quickly turned off the stove. She sat down at the kitchen table and massaged her stomach. Strange, she thought. Maybe it was something she had eaten. The pain weakened once again. She stood, walked to the stove, and poured the milk into a cup. Inge sipped the warm, silky milk. She could feel the smooth liquid warm her insides. She noticed the clock read 12:30 a.m. She left the mug in the sink and walked back to her bedroom. She finally felt her eyes grow heavy with tiredness.

Inge heard the door to Carmen and Eva's room click open. She stopped, turned and eyed the door.

"Inge, your sister is in labor!" Carmen excitedly stepped into the hallway. "Please sit with her while I call the doctor and gather her things."

A wave of emotions flooded Inge. She felt nervous, excited, and every emotion in between. Her sister was having a baby. It was a monumental, surreal moment.

She entered the bedroom and found Eva sitting on the floor against her bed propped up on a pillow. Eva's water had broken in her bed, leaving the sheets stained and soaked. Pearls of sweat emerged on Eva's forehead. Inge sat down on the floor close to her sister and wiped her forehead with a damp cloth.

"I am so proud of you," Inge said.

"I can't believe this moment has come," Eva grabbed her sister's hand. Just then a sharp pain struck Eva. She breathed deeply and pursed her lips to exhale.

"Relax, Eva," Inge said. "Take some deep breaths."

"Carmen caught me in the hallway as I was coming from the kitchen," Inge said. "I couldn't sleep, was making some hot milk, and then out of nowhere I felt these ghastly stomach pains. Now, I realize God was trying to tell me something."

Inge looked at her sister. Eva let out a burst of laughter. "The horrors of being a twin," Eva said. "You're going through this with me."

"It seems so," Inge said. "You know that I would go through any amount of pain for you."

Carmen entered the room and helped Eva from the floor.

When they reached the car, Eva stopped.

"What about Isaac?" she asked.

"Ach, don't worry about him," Inge said. "You have more important things to worry about. We will let him sleep. He can sleep through a war."

They headed towards Table Mountain and where the road rose steeply, the car traversed toward Groot Schuur Hospital.

As they entered the hospital, a nun sitting behind the front desk responded quickly upon seeing Eva. She called for a wheelchair. Within minutes, another nun arrived with a wheelchair to take Eva down the hall.

"Please, can my husband accompany me?" Eva asked the stoic-faced nun standing before her.

"I am sorry," she replied. "We will prep you and when you begin pushing, we will let your husband in."

Inge kissed her sister's forehead and Carmen grabbed Eva's hand and squeezed it tightly.

"You will be okay, my love," Carmen said. "I will see you shortly."

As the nun wheeled Eva down the hallway, Eva's nerves began to overwhelm her. She bit her lip and shifted her eyes to the sterile-looking floor. She suddenly felt afraid, afraid of the unknown, and overwhelmed to become a mother. She hoped her child saw brighter times than her own. The nuns didn't lend much comfort. They were simply going through the motions without any emotion or connection to their patients.

She gasped as another bout of pain shot through her. The pain grew more intense with each passing minute.

"Don't forget to breathe," the nun said.

When they arrived in the room, the nun instructed Eva to change out of her clothes into the hospital garment.

"Is this your first child?" the nun asked.

"Yes."

"Your age?"

"Twenty-five."

"Any health conditions we should know about?"

"No."

"Someone will be with you shortly," the phlegmatic nun left the room.

Eva let out a deep breath. The stoic nun unnerved her and so did the sterile and cold room. There was a first time for everything. No one told Eva this is how it would happen. But she knew that the end result was well worth it.

Then, it all happened so quickly. They shaved her pubic area. They gave her an enema. They made Eva walk around the room. They gave her a shot. The pain was unbreakable and constant. Eva gripped the sheets of her hospital bed, closed her eyes, and imagined she was lying on the beach, the warm sun hitting her face. She perspired through her garment. She was given a little whiff of gas to relax her. She slipped in and out of consciousness. When her eyes opened, Eva noticed Carmen was at her side, holding her hand once again.

"You're so beautiful," he said, brushing away strands of damp hair from her face.

When the effects of the gas started to wear off, she heard them say "push". Like a programmed robot, she did it. She pushed in a complete daze, in complete exhaustion. She kept pushing and pushing on cue, not matter how severe the pain was that shot through her body. Exhausted and out of breath, her head hit the pillow when they told her to relax.

"One last push, Eva," she heard the doctor declare. "You can do it."

Suddenly, she pushed hard and as she did, she forgot all about the pain. Eva heard the most beautiful sound—her child's low-pitch first cry. Tears streamed down Eva's cheeks. She had brought life into this world. Eva looked at her husband. Carmen looked so proud, so calm, and incredibly happy.

"It's a girl!" The doctor proclaimed. "A healthy girl."

For a brief moment and for the first time, Eva held her baby in her arms.

"She's so lovely and tiny," Eva said.

The baby had not yet opened her eyes. Eva gently touched her little hands. The baby extended her tiny, pink tongue. Her skin was translucent and delicate.

"Isabella," Eva said. "My little Isabella, it's so wonderful to finally meet you." She kissed the baby's forehead.

"I must take her now," the nun took the baby from Eva's arms. "You can see her again soon."

As Eva slept in her hospital room with Carmen relaxing in a chair nearby, a nun entered.

"She is hungry," the nun said to Eva.

Eva pushed herself up against her pillow and the nun bent over and placed the baby in her arms.

She wore a pink cotton cap and little white socks. Her soft cry quietened as she lay in Eva's arms.

"Look at her," Eva said, pulling the blanket away from her daughter's adorable little face. Eva held her tiny wrists as she gazed adoringly at her child.

Eva smiled as she saw the baby had her same blue eyes and Carmen's nose. "Our daughter, Carmen," she said. "Can you believe it? She's a beautiful mix of the two of us." Carmen stood over them proudly.

Eva unbuttoned her white nightgown, turned the baby's face toward her breast and began to nurse.

After a few days in the hospital, they returned home, a home filled with flowers, food and gifts. Oskar and Helene fell in love with their first grandchild and wanted to see her every second. Helene was instrumental in showing her daughter how to tend to the baby, from how to pin a diaper to how to calm the baby's many gripes. Inge would watch as her mother showed her sister how to care for the baby.

"Watch and learn for when your turn comes, darling," Helene would say to Inge.

Those days their sole focus was on Isabella and satisfying her every need. Slowly, Eva learned to understand the baby's cries, and once her needs were met, she fell instantly asleep. Isabella, sporting a woolly hat, pouted in her sleep. Carmen and Eva spent lots of time admiring their baby, her eyes that were like Eva's, her nose like Carmen's, and dimples like Max's.

When Isabella was only two weeks old, as Eva put Isabella down for a nap, she realized Zoe had not arrived. Maybe she was running late, she thought? Maybe she had missed the bus? She asked Charlie, but he did not know. She knew Zoe was dependable and loyal, and began to worry. As morning turned to noon, Zoe had still not arrived. Eva knew that all she could do was wait since she had no way of contacting Zoe.

That afternoon, Eva poured her parents cups of rooibos tea along with rusks and milk tart. They had come to visit their granddaughter.

"Lovely, thank you, Eva," Oskar said, as she handed her father a porcelain hand-painted cup and saucer with scalloped rims.

"Sugar and milk?" she asked her father.

"A little of both," he replied.

"Where is Zoe, darling?" Helene asked as she bit into her rusk.

"She never showed up today," Eva said, pouring herself a cup of tea.

"I hope she is trustworthy and not taking advantage of you," Oskar said.

"Zoe is trustworthy, Father," Inge said, noticing her sister's growing frustration. "She has been very helpful so far and she is very kind."

"I agree with Inge," Eva added. "I can't complain. She works very hard for so little."

"What are you paying her?" Oskar inquired.

"25 pounds per month," Eva said.

Oskar gave Helene a look.

"What's the matter, Father?" Inge asked.

"Ach…you girls should know better," he said. "You should have first made her prove herself before paying her that kind of wage."

"She has already taken advantage of you, I'm afraid," Helene responded.

"Zoe has so few pleasures in life and we have so many," Inge said, stirring some sugar into her tea. "Her life is so difficult compared to ours."

"I feel guilty that she works so hard and earns so little," Eva said. "That is why we decided to give her a little more money. And I think she is worth the amount we pay her and more."

"You can't think that way, girls," Oskar retorted. "I warn you—she will take advantage of you, time and time again."

"Well, I don't want to be like so many people here who bark orders at their maids and don't treat them with an ounce of respect," Eva said.

"I just want you to be more aware," Oskar said. "That's all."

"They are not all bad, you know," Eva said. "Some can be trusted."

"Perhaps," stated Helene. "We would just hate for you to have to deal with a bad situation, like we did."

"I think your first maid was a bad egg, that's all," Inge said. "Not all of them steal and hold up a kitchen knife when you fire them."

"You need to set some boundaries with your maid," Oskar said. "I now have to lock all my cupboards and keep the keys on me at all times. I think most servants are thieves. I haven't met one who isn't. They take sugar, chocolate, even liquor and wine. So, just be careful, that's all I am saying."

"Zoe is not a thief," Inge said.

The discussion ended quickly when they heard Isabella crying.

"Eva, let me see to her," Inge said. "You relax this afternoon."

"Thank you," Eva gave her sister a grateful hug.

❦

It was going to be a nice evening, Zoe thought, as she stepped brightly down the unpaved, potholed road towards the spaza shop to purchase some chocolate and Coke for Zola. Now that she had a new job, she decided to splurge a little. As she stepped into the store, she carried her purse in one hand and a bag in her other hand, packed with some table scraps of chicken and rice from Eva. She picked out two chocolate bars and a Coke, and paid for the purchase. Zoe then headed home as the warmth of the day had disappeared and a slight chill appeared in the evening sky.

Zoe paused in front of her shack and noticed that an old plastic crate she had used as a chair lay smashed to pieces on the ground. "Heita, Zola!" Zoe yelled as she entered the home. "What happened outside, my girl?"

No response, only silence.

Immediately, as she entered her home, Zoe dropped her purse and the bag carrying the food, and ran over to her daughter who was lying curled up in a fetal position in the corner of their tin shack. She knelt beside

Zola and heard her cries of pain and desperation. She noticed her face was bruised and bloodied. Her skirt was ripped and her legs were stained with blood. Without saying a word, Zoe knew what had happened to her daughter. She held Zola in her arms as she sobbed.

"I am sorry, Mama," she murmured.

"Shhhh...Zola," Zoe said softly, stroking her daughter's face. "You must not say 'I am sorry'. Don't ever think this was your fault. It's going to be okay. You will be okay. I am so sorry this has happened to you, my angel."

The very thing she feared the most had happened...her daughter had been raped. White-hot anger began to seethe within her. A deep ache in the pit of her belly made her heart grow heavy. Her daughter had been robbed of her very essence, her purity. Zoe grabbed a blanket and placed it over her daughter. She then picked Zola up and carried her to the tin shack with herbs and plants hanging from its doors.

"Zulu!" Zoe screamed. "Please help us!"

The old man opened the door. He eyed Zoe holding her daughter in her arms with desperation on her face.

"Please, can you help us?" Zoe pleaded with the sangoma.

"Yes," he said, motioning them into his secret shrine. Candles lit the dark room. Zulu pointed to an area plush with blankets and pillows. His eyes turned toward Zola's lifeless eyes. Her listless body abused and drained. Without saying a word, he knew why the girl was in his home, needing his help. He had seen this happen time and time again.

He touched Zoe's arm to calm her and pointed to a chair.

"I will make you tea just now," he said.

He knelt next to Zola and then threw bones and shells onto the dirt floor to help him diagnose any other health conditions. He clapped and chanted a song invoking the ancestors. After a few minutes, he stopped and sat in silence.

He then said, "It is the ancestor who is providing the information. The sangoma is the messenger."

Zoe nodded in amazement.

Zulu turned his attention to the pile of bones and shells on the floor.

"The bones represent the forces that affect any human being anywhere," he said.

He then studied the pattern they formed. He took a wooden stick and pushed the bones and shells this way and that way.

"She will be okay," he said in a whisper. "Time will heal the wounds, the mind, and the heart. No broken bones, just bruises and pain, deep emotional pain."

Zoe nodded again at the wise man.

As the old, emaciated figure emerged on his knees over Zola, bone jewelry hung around his neck. Beside him, water boiled in a kettle. He inspected her wounds up close and placed a soothing hand on her stomach. As soon as a loud whistle sound surrounded the room and raging steam emerged from the kettle's spout, he grabbed a towel and poured some hot water over it. He added a mysterious white ointment from a glass jar to the towel and began to clean her wounds. First, he gently cleaned Zola's delicate face and then her thighs and legs. He added more hot water and ointment to the towel and handed it to Zoe, instructing her to clean her daughter's private areas. Zola's breathing calmed.

Zulu selected a pungent herb from his stacks of jars and burned it until the aroma filled the tiny home, all the time muttering incantations to the spirits of the ancestors, who many Africans believe watch over the living, like angels or saints.

As Zola drifted off to sleep, he then made Zoe a cup of strong tea.

"I see lots of worry in your eyes," the sangoma looked at Zoe, as he passed her a cup of herbal tea.

"I am very worried," she said. "What if she is pregnant?"

He paused before answering her.

"I don't see that she is," he said. "The bones don't say that. It is too early to tell, but that is the least of your worries. Disease is my worry. Take one day at a time. Everything will be okay."

He smiled toothlessly at Zoe. She forced a smile back.

When Zoe finished the last drop of her soothing tea, she thanked Zulu for his help and carried her sleeping daughter back to their home. Zoe laid Zola on the bed, removed her torn clothes and placed a blanket over her body. She curled up next to her daughter for the few remaining hours of the night. Instead of sleeping, she was filled with worry as she watched her daughter sleep. One of her worst nightmares had come true.

When the sun seeped through the cracks in their tin home, Zoe opened her eyes and sprung to her feet. She dressed and grabbed Zola's ripped clothes. Today, she didn't walk towards the water spout, but to a secluded area of the township. While no one was watching, she made a small fire and threw the clothes into the smoldering flames. She watched as Zola's clothes quickly turned to ash. In the distance, she could hear the barking of dogs and the sputtering of old car engines. Rickety buses tooted their horns to alert those who needed transport to the white world for work.

As she stood facing the edge of the township, she wished she could take her daughter's hand and lead them away to a place different from this one, a place where hatred and crime was non-existent, if such a place even existed. The reality was there was no escaping this world. When the fire weakened, she walked towards her home with one top priority on her mind, the well-being of her daughter.

Zola slept another hour and when she opened her doleful eyes, she found her mother's gaze upon her.

Zoe grabbed her daughter's hand.

"How's my sunshine?"

"Mama," Zola squeezed her mother's hand. Zola opened her eyes, one bruised, half open.

"Did you sleep okay?" Zoe asked.

"I can't get the image out of my mind," Zola said.

"I wish I could take it all away, Zola," Zoe gave her daughter a sympathetic look.

"When he was on top of me, I screamed and fought him, but he was too strong and held me down. I couldn't move. I couldn't breathe. I closed my eyes and imagined I was somewhere else. I wish I could have drowned into the earth below me."

Then, Zola sobbed.

"This will haunt me for the rest of my life," she looked at her mother.

Zoe swallowed her tears. She had to be strong for her daughter. "It's over now. You will never forget this, but time will heal the pain. We will get through this together. Zola, you must tell me one thing. Who did this to you?"

"I can't tell you, Mama," she answered. "I swore I wouldn't."

Zoe hugged her daughter.

"You must not feel any shame," Zoe stared into her daughter's eyes. "You must tell me. It's the only way I can protect you from this ever happening again, you hear? Please, tell me. Please, sunshine. It will give us some closure, some peace of mind."

Zola whispered the boy's name to her mother.

Zoe did not respond when she heard the name. These boys have no role models; no one to teach them right from wrong, she thought.

"Now, you must try to eat and drink something," Zoe said.

Zoe rose from the bed to make her child some *pap 'n vleis* (porridge and meat).

"Will you eat with me, Mama?"

"I want you to have a proper meal today, Zola," Zoe said. "I don't think there is enough for both of us. Don't worry about your old mama. I won't go hungry, my child."

While her child ate, Zoe dressed for the day. She then tended to her daughter's bruised face and swollen eye.

"Go to the sangoma today so he can tend to your wounds," she instructed her daughter. With no proper medical care available to people in the township, the sangoma was the best medical treatment Zola would receive.

"Yes, mama," she said.

"Rest as much as you can," Zoe said.

She picked up the Coke and candy bars that still lay in a bag on the ground.

"I bought you a treat last night," she handed the bag to her daughter.

Zola smiled when she saw the Coke and candy bars.

"Drink some Coke," Zoe said. "It will make you feel better and give you some energy."

Zoe hugged her daughter, grabbed her bag and left their tin shack.

She stopped in front of the neighbor's shack.

"Rachel! Please come out...I must have a word with you." Zoe waited, tapping her foot until she saw the woman emerge from her shack.

"Heita, Zoe!" Rachel said as she stood eye-level with Zoe.

As Zoe stood face-to-face with her neighbor, she gazed into Rachel's black eyes as she explained what had happened.

"That was not my boy...no, Zoe. Not my Baruti."

"Yes! Your boy! My daughter has eyes. It was him on top of her."

"We must keep this quiet then," Rachel said, holding her wide hips. "No one can know. What would people say if they knew my son did such an awful thing. Let's rather we shut up about it."

"You owe me then, Rachel."

Rachel knew that she couldn't fight. She did owe them. It was standard to pay some sort of damages, a compromise of sorts.

"I can't pay you, Zoe. I have no money to give you."

Rachel walked around Zoe in thought. She clutched at her apron.

"For now, I can repay you with eggs. That's all I have that's worth anything. It's food on your table, something that will feed your hunger, soothe your souls. Anytime I have extra eggs, I will give them to you."

Just like that, they had come to some understanding.

"Rachel, there's one more thing before you go about your day. Make sure your son knows what he did was wrong and that if he ever lays a hand on my daughter again, I will kill him. Understand? We have to teach them somehow, Rachel."

Tears ran down Rachel's cheeks. She looked down at the dirt road.

"It will do no good," she said. "He never listens to me. I sometimes don't even know where he is. Sometimes he doesn't come home. He won't just stop at one girl, Zoe. They never do."

"Well, if you do see him, you let him know what I told you," Zoe said.

As Zoe began to walk away, she realized she had forgotten something and stopped. "Oh, before I forget, we'd like two eggs for supper, hey."

Rachel nodded.

Zoe walked down the dusty, unpaved road toward the bus stop. The strength she had shown her daughter the past couple of hours was now lost to her. Tears poured down her cheeks.

Why did this happen to my daughter, she thought. She felt exhausted and hopeless. Crime was everywhere. She always thought that it was never if, but when, she or Zola would become a victim. She was scared. She no longer felt free, but imprisoned by her own people, her own destiny. She no longer trusted anyone and hated the world around her. Zoe wanted Zola to have some normalcy in this world, if that was even possible. She had always been resilient and faithful, but what happened to Zola had broken her heart.

When Zoe arrived back in the white world of fancy homes, sparkling jewelry and designer clothes, she felt ashamed. She would have to explain her absence and she wasn't certain of how accepting her new boss would be.

As she opened the front door to the home, the first thing she heard was Isabella's cry. She knew enough about babies to know what that cry meant. The baby was in need of nourishment, her morning feed.

She stepped into the kitchen and found Inge rocking Isabella in her arms.

"Hi," she announced.

"Hi Zoe," Inge said. "We've been so worried. Are you okay?"

Monique Roy

"Yes, I am very sorry I was not at work yesterday," she looked Inge in the eye. "My daughter..." She paused briefly. "My daughter was ill."

"Sorry, Zoe," Inge said with concern. "Is your daughter feeling well now?"

Before she could answer, Eva walked into the kitchen.

"I am so sorry, madam, for my absence yesterday," Zoe said, turning towards her.

"Don't worry, Zoe," Eva said. "Is everything okay?"

"Yes, madam, everything is just fine. My daughter, Zola, felt unwell. That's all."

"I see," Eva replied. "I am sorry to hear that. Is she better today?"

"Yes, she's better now," Zoe said. "It won't happen again...that I am absent from work."

She became stiff, unsure how her boss would react.

"Ach...please," Eva said, waving her hand in the air. "It happens... we're just glad everything is fine."

Eva took Isabella from Inge.

Zoe felt a pang of relief. She had heard stories of other maids in the township who missed work for one reason or another. When they returned to work, they were yelled at and even fired on the spot.

"She is so sweet," Zoe said to Eva, touching the baby's tiny fingers.

"Thank you," Eva said as she kissed her daughter. "We think so, too. She is a good baby. Zoe, could you please give her a bath this morning?"

"Yes, madam," Zoe replied. "Also, what would you like for dinner tonight? I want to make sure we have everything we need."

"Beef stew?" Eva asked, looking at her sister for approval. Inge smiled back. "I know Carmen and Isaac would enjoy that very much. They work so hard these days."

"Yes, madam," Zoe said.

"Speaking of food, did you enjoy the chicken?" Eva smiled.

Zoe hesitated. Chicken...she forgot all about the leftover chicken that Eva had given her for dinner, the chicken that lay on the dirty ground of their shack. The chicken that would have soothed their hunger that evening, but now was rotting away. Zoe hoped that Zola had seen the chicken and thrown it away.

"Yes, very much," Zoe said. "Zola enjoyed it most. It's not always easy to scrounge up a full meal for my child."

156

"While you work under my roof, Zoe, I never want you or your child to go hungry," Eva said. "Do you understand? Please take food home when you need it."

"Yes, thank you, madam," Zoe said, smiling. "You are so kind, hey. There are many nights that we go to bed hungry."

"That's horrible," Eva said. "Why don't you bring Zola one day so we can meet her? Tomorrow evening may be perfect as I will need you to work a bit longer, for extra pay, of course. It's Shabbat and my family is coming for dinner. I'd like to prepare something special. Maybe your daughter can help you and eat a proper meal here."

"It may be difficult for her to get here," Zoe said, trying to make plausible excuses. "Let me talk to her this evening. Thank you for asking."

"No excuses, Zoe," Eva said. "I will give you money for the extra bus fare. You can always go home earlier and bring her back in the evening after dinner is prepared."

"Yes, madam," Zoe said. She turned away from Eva. How would she explain what had happened? She really needed the extra money.

"I will be here tomorrow evening, but Zola has been ill. She should stay home and rest."

"Well, if she feels better, we would love to meet her," Eva said. "If not, you can pack up some supper for her. Okay?"

"Yes, thanks madam. Would you like a *Kitke* (challah bread in South Africa) for tomorrow night, and maybe matzo ball soup and brisket, hey?"

Eva's eyes brightened. She smiled at Zoe.

"Zoe, that sounds wonderful. Where did you learn to make matzo ball soup and *Kitke*?"

"I was taught years ago when I worked for a Jewish family," Zoe said. "I can also make chopped herring, chopped liver, and gefilte fish."

"That is so amazing," Eva said, with a newfound respect for her maid.

"I often had to prepare lots of food for many guests over the Jewish high holidays," Zoe said, proudly.

As work filled her day, Zoe struggled whether she should tell Eva about Zola's rape. She felt embarrassed and ashamed. The right moment never came.

Eva and her family lived the kind of life Zoe could only dream of. She didn't want Eva to think Zola was raped for any reason other than because of the culture she lived in and the crime that was rampant in her community.

Eva and Inge arrived home that afternoon with just enough time to change for supper.

They stopped in their tracks. The dining room table was immaculately decorated with a beautiful lace tablecloth, candles, and fresh flowers as a centerpiece. The cutlery was nicely polished and the wine glasses glistened in the candlelight.

"Zoe, the table looks fabulous," Inge said.

"Just beautiful," Eva responded.

"Thank you, madam," Zoe said, with a big grin.

After Eva bathed Isabella, gave her a bottle, and rocked her to sleep, she dressed for the evening. Then, she went to the kitchen to check on things.

"The only time I want to see you come into the dining room is to serve the food," Eva instructed. "I will let you know when to serve each course. I will ring a little bell. Okay, Zoe?"

"Yes, madam," Zoe said.

"If you hear me scream, please come in!" Eva said, trying to be amusing. "Having the whole family for dinner can be stressful."

Carmen entered the kitchen.

"Hello, Zoe," he smiled.

"Hello, master," she responded, wiping her hands on her apron.

"The food smells good," he said.

"Are we serving wine tonight, Eva?"

"Yes, Carmen," she pointed to two bottles lying on the counter, one red and one white.

Just then, Isaac walked into the kitchen.

"Do we have Scotch for your father?" he asked.

Eva threw one hand up in the air.

"Let the women take care of the food and the men take care of the drinks," she said.

Zoe chuckled.

"Yes, there should be some left in the bar," Carmen said.

Then, Inge dressed in a classic black dress appeared in the kitchen.

"Zoe, I can't wait to try your *Kitke*!"

Isaac stepped toward her and gave her a peck on the cheek.

"You look lovely," he said to her.

Inge winked back at him.

When she heard her parents and Max arrive, Eva said to Zoe, "Make sure you have some food as well."

"Yes, madam," Zoe said.

"I wish you had brought your daughter so we could meet her," Eva said, before exiting the kitchen.

"You will meet her soon," Zoe said, reluctantly.

❧

After she served the family their first course, a delicious matzo ball soup with fluffy egg noodles, Zoe sat in silence in the kitchen, lost in her own thoughts.

As the family emptied their wine glasses and refilled them several times over, and as laughter and conversation filled the air, she could not help but think that she would never have the opportunity to dine at an elegantly set table, adorned with crystal wine glasses, fine China plates, and fresh flowers at the table's center.

Zoe stared at the large pot that held the nourishing matzo ball soup. She then looked at the old plate and bowl that Eva had set aside for her. As they ate on expensive China, she ate from old plates and bowls. As they passed around bottles of wine and Scotch, she drank from a cup with only water. Zoe eventually took the soup ladle and filled her bowl with soup, but only halfway. She wasn't comfortable filling the entire bowl. In silence, she ate the warm soup. When she had finished the soup in her bowl, her stomach was still not nourished, yet she washed the bowl clean and set it aside. It was not the first time she felt hungry. She checked on the rest of the dinner and then she heard the little bell ring.

Zoe walked into the dining room and began to clear the soup bowls from the table.

"Accolades to the chef," Oskar said to Zoe. "The soup was delicious. It reminded me of my old bubbe's matzo ball soup."

"Thank you, sir," she said.

"The *Kitke* is very nice," Helene chimed in. "I've never tasted one like it."

"Thank you, madam," Zoe smiled.

"We're very happy with Zoe's cooking and baking skills," Inge said. "We are so well fed."

Zoe served the salad and the main dish, a beef brisket, along with roasted potatoes and a colorful bowl full of steamed vegetables.

As she began to clean the soup bowls, she heard the conversation shift. There was much to celebrate that evening. The end of the war had come.

Monique Roy

A great downfall had occurred a week prior, on April 30, 1945. Berlin was a shattered, flaming inferno. With the Soviet ground forces nearby, the end was near. Hitler and his new wife, Eva Braun, ended their lives in the Führerbunker, located 50 feet below the Chancellery buildings in Berlin. The Third Reich ceased to exist. Germany had finally succumbed to the overwhelming power of its enemies.

"Wasn't that an amazing parade the other evening?" Max said. "Thousands of people crowded the streets, celebrating VE-Day. There was such a grand spirit in the air. You should have been there, Father."

"Ach, no," Oskar said. "You know I hate crowds, Max."

"It was a good-natured celebration, that's all," Max said.

Max recalled the friendly crowds who moved about the decorated streets. Some revelers were more joyful than others; they sang in the streets and popped champagne corks. Others took in the news of the end of the war more solemnly. Crowded cinemas depicted highlights from the war.

"I wanted to listen in peace to Mr. Churchill's announcement that the war was over and of the cease fire," Oskar said, his eyes slightly tearing. "It was an emotional moment after all these years. I was so happy to hear Admiral Doenitz announce to the German people that the Nazi Party had disappeared and the foundations on which the Reich was built had dissipated. With the occupation of Germany, power has passed to the hands of occupying troops. I especially wanted to hear the King's speech to the Empire, which was of solemn thanksgiving and a complete and crushing victory. It's been a hard six years for everyone."

"An unprecedented moment for all of us, and for all who suffered across the world," Isaac raised his glass. "War has a unique way of distinguishing between things that matter and things that don't."

"Cheers," they said, clinking their glasses.

"Thank God for peace," Carmen said. "South Africa has special reason for gratitude. The land is unscathed. The sacrifices of its people were far less than other countries. South Africa contributed far more than they hoped they could, bringing a deepened sense of nationalism."

"That's true, Carmen," Isaac said. "Hopefully, the many sacrifices of the war lead to lasting peace."

"We should be very thankful that we fled Europe when we did," Oskar said, looking about at his family. "When I think what could have happened to us, I am so grateful. When the Allies entered Bergen-Belsen concentration camp, they found piles of naked bodies. The shame of the camps has finally been revealed, and the Nazis were gruesome murderers."

# chapter

# SEVENTEEN

Three months passed before Zoe took her daughter's hand and lead her into Cape Town's "white world". Zola was in better spirits, her wounds healed, and Zoe could no longer provide Eva with constant excuses for her daughter's absence.

They walked down the unpaved road leading to the end of the township and rode in a loud and crowded bus that transported them from one reality to another. Zoe smiled at her daughter and put a consoling arm around her.

As they stepped off the bus, Zola finally understood what it was like to be in the white suburbs of South Africa. The roads were nicely paved. Shops with glass displays showed off beautiful things. People were nicely dressed and refined.

White South Africa lived in the big, modern city. It was the place where dreams were made. As Zola walked the same streets, she felt a tinge of humiliation and her mind was a disjointed, dark chamber flooded with thoughts—the festering memories of her rape and the harsh realities of her life and the world she lived in. But the air was the same air "they" breathed, she thought. Maybe in this world, in white South Africa, she could dream.

When they came upon the street, Zola stopped dead in her tracks. Her wiry body turned a complete circle as she breathed in the grandeur that surrounded her. Her wide eyes stared at the manicured and sprawling lawns and gardens. Not only did the street look different to what she was familiar with, but also it smelled different, a sweet vibrant smell.

The scent of oranges drifted their way. Zola looked up at the ripe fruit that hung from the branches of a fruit tree along the side of the road. Zola couldn't help herself. She sprung in the air and quickly plucked a small orange from the tree, admiring it as if it was golden. As they walked, she carefully peeled back the thick skin of the orange and popped slices of the juicy fruit into her mouth.

Zola knew her mother was treated well, but she questioned herself if they, white South Africans, were really as sinister as she had been taught.

The path that led to the home stood before them. A well-manicured border of colors spilled onto the path, the assortment of flowers welcoming them. They followed it to some steps that led to a *stoep* or covered veranda. As Zola entered the home, she felt the opposite of what she had expected to feel. There was nothing cold and sinister about it. Eva and Inge greeted her with warm, welcoming smiles. They told her that she was beautiful, grown up beyond her years and sweet. Only her mother had told her those things before, and no one else.

They took Zola on a tour of the home. She felt as though she was floating through a castle. Every room was more impressive than the next. The house was filled with so many things and Zola had never seen more stuff in her life.

Then, Inge and Eva did something unexpected. They presented Zola with a large gift bag. When Zola opened the bag, she discovered fancy clothes and books. She only owned four outfits, plus her school uniform. The bag held more clothes than she had ever owned or ever dreamed to own.

"We hope that the clothes fit you," said Inge.

"We had some help from your mother," Eva said. "Enjoy it all."

"Thank you!" Zola gave the women a hug.

Zola felt as though it was her birthday. She had never had a birthday quite like this before.

Usually Zoe would buy her something she really needed for her birthday, such as socks or maybe a magazine or book. Today began just an ordinary day like any other and Zola received more than she could ever imagine.

They sat together in the kitchen. As Zola enjoyed a delicious bowl of linguine with beef Bolognese sauce and parmesan cheese sprinkled on top, the women enjoyed a lighter fare, tea and scones.

Zoe became uncomfortable sitting for more than a couple of minutes, not attending to her duties, so she eventually rose from the table and began to prepare dinner.

"What are you making tonight, Zoe?" Eva asked.

"Dover sole, madam," she said.

"Sounds delicious, Zoe," Eva said. "How do you prepare it?"

Eva needed to learn to be more domesticated. She barely knew her way around a kitchen.

"You first make sure the head has been removed, hey," Zoe said. "If not, you can ask the fish monger to prepare the fish. You take a little olive oil and kosher salt. And some black pepper. Take a large saucepan and rub the oil, salt and pepper around the fish. Roast in the oven for 15 minutes."

"At what temperature?"

"400, madam."

"Is that it?" Eva asked.

"No," Zoe shook her head. "Then, you must make a sauce with butter, capers and lemon."

"Butter, capers, lemon..." Eva repeated. "How is that done?"

"Over medium heat...when the butter browns a bit, you add capers and lemon. Voila!"

Zoe and Zola laughed.

"Sounds simple enough, hey," Inge said.

"Easy," Zoe smiled. "It should be easy enough."

"Zola, remember I told you that Eva, Inge and their family came from far away?"

"Yes, mama," Zola said. "I remember. You're from Germany, right?"

"Yes, Germany," Eva said. It was sometimes so hard to speak about Germany.

"I would love to go there one day," Zola said. "It sounds so interesting...the mountains and castles."

"Well, it can be," Eva said. "I hope that when you go to Germany one day that it will be a better, happier place."

"What do you mean?" Zola asked.

"Zola, don't ask so many questions," Zoe said, chopping an onion.

"No, it's okay," Eva said. "A horrible, evil man came to power and we were forced to leave for a better future. He destroyed the Germany we once knew and loved."

"You understand?" Eva asked the young girl.

"Yes, are you talking about Hitler?" Zola questioned.

"How do you know about Hitler?" Zoe asked her daughter.

"School…the radio, the newspapers…Hitler is everywhere," the girl answered. "We may live in a tiny shack, mama, but we still live in this crazy world."

She meant the old, busted radio they owned that could barely pick up sound, and when it did, it was Hitler's voice they heard, his screams pouring through the radio as he dictated to the masses. Or, of the scraps of newspaper that blew around the township that depicted the stories of war.

Zola gave Inge and Eva a compassionate smile. She was young, but she understood much about the world today. They were victims in another land and they fled in search of peace. Sometimes Zola wished they could do the same.

Zola looked on as her mother worked steadily to prepare dinner. For a moment, her mother seemed old and worn, her life filled with hard, mundane work, and nothing more. Zola wondered if she was staring her fate in the eye; that one day she would be standing in a kitchen in the same white suburbs cooking, cleaning, ironing, and caring for small children.

❧

Zoe and Zola awoke one morning to something new. They had just spent their first night in their new home, a tiny whitewashed room nestled in the corner of the family's backyard. It was connected to a small bathroom with only cold running water. There, they shared an iron bed that stood under a single window. No longer did they have to sleep on a dirt floor. It was not luxury, but far better than living in the crime-ridden, poverty-stricken township that had been the only home they had ever known.

It was plain and simple, but it was theirs, for now. The floor was covered with an old rug. Two wooden chairs stood in the corner with a small table. Even though they were prisoners in the 'white world', they somehow felt lucky.

Then, on May 26, 1948, they were not just prisoners trapped in the white suburbs. Their already lowly status in society worsened before their eyes when they became subjected to harsh and severe 'apartheid' laws. At that moment, on that day, no one knew what a turning point it would be, for the country, for history, for people of colour and people of non-colour. Radical change loomed over them.

The people of South Africa pointed fingers and they pointed them at Prime Minister Jan Christiaan Smuts and his cabinet. South Africa faced hardships following its participation in World War II. There were better alternatives to Smuts' tired regime.

Smuts was ousted by the Reunited National Party, led by Dr. D.F. Malan. His party realized that many white South Africans felt threatened by black political aspirations. After Malan led the National Party in the first campaign that centered on white unity, the Party held to its promise that if elected it would make permanent the fundamental principles of separation. They labeled the new system of government 'apartheid', which was a rigid policy of segregation of the non-white population.

The harshness of apartheid quickly filled the air and raced along every street and every narrow lane. No longer could black and white mix, not in public and not in private, not on a park bench, nor at a beach, or a public restroom. Everything was marked accordingly—*'whites only'*—all to ensure the survival of the white race and to keep the different races separate on every level of society and in every facet of life.

"Doesn't this all seem so familiar?" Carmen asked Eva one evening.

"It's like another nightmare has descended upon us, but this time we are not on the receiving end," she said. "But we are bystanders, spectators…just like the Germans were when the Nazis rose to power."

"It's really an outgrowth of the same ideals as Nazi Germany, an ideology the Afrikaneers accepted because of the affinity they felt towards Germans," Carmen said.

"It does resemble Nazism," Eva said. "I don't know that I can sit back and watch it all unravel. It breaks my heart to see people discriminated against because they are different. I need to help in some way, Carmen."

"You must be careful, Eva. I mean, what are you really going to do? Form an army? We also need to protect ourselves, our family. Remember, if you helped the Jews, you were sought and killed. Who knows what they would do here if they knew you were helping the blacks or the coloureds."

"I know, Carmen…I know."

She grabbed Carmen's hand, kissed his lips, looked at him and said: "I just want peace and happiness."

He cupped her face in his hands and kissed Eva some more.

"We'll create our own little world filled with an abundance of peace and happiness," he said.

Monique Roy

She laughed. He pulled her into his arms and held her tightly.

"Your father seems to think it might be the right thing," Carmen said. "Blacks and whites should live separately. He thinks it's better for our well-being, our future."

"My father must have forgotten how quickly the tables turn, that once he was discriminated against, and that it was best to get rid of the Jews to purify the German race. The Germans had all kinds of problems with the Jews, as South Africans do now with the blacks and coloureds."

"Yes, you're right, darling."

"It's much better for Zola and Zoe to live here on our property...it's safer for them, don't you think?" Eva asked.

"Yes, as long as they do as their told and they don't run amuck beyond our streets, if you know what I mean," Carmen grinned.

"They are not slaves, Carmen," Eva looked squarely at her husband. "They are human beings, like you and me. They are good people. Zoe is very hard working and trustworthy. We have never had an issue."

"Not yet..." Carmen said. "I fear how that young woman will turn out when she grows up. All she has ever known is crime, poverty, and lowly things."

Sleep did not come easy that night for Zoe. As Zola slept peacefully beside her, all her fears combined like chains in the pit of her stomach. She hoped Zola's dreams were peaceful, unlike her own dreams—dark and haunting. She suddenly felt claustrophobic as if the four white walls would close in around them and swallow them whole. She inhaled deeply and shut her tired eyes, but all she could see was blackness, the very same blackness before a storm.

When the morning sun streamed through the window above their bed, Zoe knew it was time to face the day. It was a new day, a new era, under the apartheid laws. They would be stepping into a new world, a world filled with hatred—a world where the color of their skin defined their status, a status that was barely human. But still the sun did shine and from that there was hope.

Zola stirred from her deep sleep and hugged her mother.

Zoe handed her daughter an apple and a banana that she grabbed from the kitchen the night before. She was grateful to Eva to be able to take extra food for their home.

"What are you going to do today?"

"Read, mama."

"That's good, baby...Maybe one day you can teach your mama to read, hey?"

"Yes," Zola smiled.

"If you need me, just knock on the side door near the kitchen," Zoe told her daughter.

"Yes, mama."

"And Zola, do not leave this house, child," Zoe stressed with sternness. "It's dangerous...the police are everywhere. Whenever we leave this house, you must help me to remember to carry my passbook."

"Yes, mama," Zola answered.

"It's important that I have it," Zoe emphasized. "I will be arrested without it."

Zola knew what her mother meant. The heavily armed police force maintained law and order, and cracked down on non-whites who did not have a legitimate reason to be in the white cities and towns.

Zoe started her day that morning attending to Isabella. She changed the baby out of her pajamas, fed her some apple sauce, and gave her some milk. She heard Eva walk into the child's bedroom.

"Morning, Zoe," Eva said.

Isabella smiled upon hearing her mother's familiar voice.

"Morning, madam," Zoe said.

"Hi, my darling," Eva took her child from her maid's arms.

An awkward silence ensued. Eva could tell Zoe didn't have the same brightness that morning. The usual light in her eyes had dimmed.

"I want you to know that I am not for the new laws," Eva said. "I respect you and appreciate you."

"Thank you, madam. The shackles of apartheid are upon us. In this black man's continent, we are chained to the lowest ranks of society. We are now divided, you and I, black and white. If we don't separate, we will be forced to...white power will be preserved by all means."

"The world can be a terrible place," Eva said. "I have been on the receiving end of hatred, and I know how you feel, Zoe, but I know I cannot relate. I do know how it feels to feel inferior, to be hated for who you are, and for what you believe in."

Zoe nodded. Tears welled in her black eyes.

"You will never know what it feels like to be black in this country, madam," Zoe said. "To live in squalor, to barely make ends meet, to not know when your next meal will be or where it will come from, to go to sleep at night and sometimes hear gun shots, to only have the opportunity

Monique Roy

to dream, knowing the chance of your dreams coming true are near to nothing."

Zoe paused. She walked to the window and set her eyes on the manicured garden.

"You can't believe the pain I felt…" Zoe began to cry.

"Imagine what it felt like to find my daughter curled up in a ball in the corner of our little tin shack because she had been raped. Bruised and bloody…her innocence taken from her."

Tears dripped down Eva's cheeks.

Behind the bedroom door, Inge stood, silently listening in on the conversation. She knew it would be wrong to intrude at that very moment. Instead, she stood listening in shock and disbelief.

"Imagine that, madam…finding your daughter like that and not being able to turn to anyone for help because there is no money for medical care and no one who can help you. Rape is an everyday occurrence in my world. It's like a disease, an epidemic."

"I couldn't imagine, Zoe. I am so sorry. I wish you had told me. When did this happen?"

"Remember when I did not show up to work and I had told you Zola was ill."

Eva nodded. "Yes, I remember."

"I felt so ashamed," Zoe said. "I was terrified and I felt as though I did not protect my daughter as well as I could have."

"That's a shame," Eva said, putting her arm around her maid's shoulder. "I am so sorry, Zoe. You are a wonderful mother. Please know you can come to me for anything."

"Thank you, madam," Zoe said. "No one has treated me this well. I am just the maid, that's it."

"Most whites don't care about how we feel," Zoe said. "They don't consider us human."

"I am not like most whites, Zoe," Eva said. "I know how it feels to be hated."

Inge quietly walked away from behind the bedroom door. She felt sadness for Zoe and her daughter, but she felt greater sadness for her family. Was South Africa the right place for them, she wondered? Her family had survived the war and now they faced a war of another kind.

# chapter

# EIGHTEEN

Max sat on the long flight of steps of the majestic Jameson Hall at the University of Cape Town, adoring the splendid view of the city. A soft cloud edged itself gently against the mountain. The white faces of students walked past him as he waited for his brother-in-law. Some sat near him on the steps, relaxing in the sunlight. He often met Isaac on the steps to discuss his courses, eat some lunch, and enjoy each other's company. Soon, he saw Isaac and waved.

"Hey, *laaitie*," Isaac sat down next to Max.

"Hello, Isaac!" Max shook Isaac's hand.

"How are you?"

"I'm well, Isaac. How's the professor?"

Isaac sighed.

"I am surrounded by a citadel of white privileged students who care nothing of the world, only of themselves, their wants and needs," Isaac said, crossing his arms. "Young men who have grown up without lifting a finger, with everything served on a silver platter. There is only one opinion they hold—that apartheid is right and is needed in this beautiful country.

They have grown up to believe that this rich land they live in is theirs and that the non-whites are needed to cultivate the land and enrich the nation."

Max nodded.

"I know them well," Max said. "They sit next to me in class. I am sometimes in disbelief that we breathe the same air."

"If you had grown up here, you would know no different," Isaac said. "You would be just like them. You would probably support apartheid."

"You're probably right," Max said. "Or, I would support it just to fit in, so I wouldn't stick out like a sore thumb in the crowd. Like the Germans had to do when the Nazis came to power…they conformed to Nazi rule."

"And if they didn't, they would have been severely punished," Isaac said.

A young student who was sitting near them overheard their conversation, glared at them from behind his glasses, and stormed off from the steps.

"I can't sit still, Isaac," Max said. "I need to support the black cause in some way."

"Your parents would not be happy with you getting involved," Isaac said. "It's ugly out there. It's dangerous. You must concentrate on your studies."

"You know, I cringe when I hear our maids say 'master' and 'madam'," Max said. "Everyone seems to accept this without a blink."

Isaac opened a bag with chicken sandwiches and handed one to Max.

"I love Zoe's sandwiches," Isaac said.

"They're delicious," Max said.

They sat quietly eating their sandwiches, while enjoying the peacefulness of their surroundings. When there was nothing left in the bag, Isaac dug deep in the bag and retrieved a milk chocolate bar.

"Want some chocolate?"

Max laughed. "Yes, thank you. I can't refuse chocolate."

"Your sister loves to hide little treats in my lunch bag," Isaac said.

Isaac gazed at his watch. "I have class to teach. I must run."

"See you soon, kid." He then disappeared beyond the steps that led into Jameson Hall.

Max didn't have class for another 45 minutes. He could work on his studies, but the day was far too pretty to be wasted. He had no desire to bury his face in a boring textbook. But he enjoyed reading books by a well-known Austrian author Stefan Zweig. He grabbed Zweig's book *Amok* from his bag and lay flat on one of the steps. He drew in a deep breath. As he closed his eyes, Max listened to the chirping birds in a nearby tree.

His mind wondered back to the girl he saw the day before last, the girl who interrupted his focus in class. It took just one look to get him hooked. She looked as if she had floated down from heaven. Her rolling, golden brown curls cascaded over her shoulders like waves. Her face was as clear as dawn with eyes that mesmerized him, a deep blue color that could only resemble the color of the sea. Her eyes laughed as she spoke. He remembered feeling envious of the young man who sat next to her, who could easily make her laugh.

His eyes shot open as a leaflet drifting in the wind landed on his face. When he sat up, he noticed several leaflets had blown across the Jameson steps.

"So sorry," he heard a voice from behind. "I didn't mean to wake you."

"No, it's quite okay," he said, turning toward the voice. "I need to get to class before I am late."

Her back was to him as she was gathering the leaflets she had dropped.

"Can I help you?" Max called out.

"No, thanks," she said, climbing some of the steps to grab the remaining leaflets. "I'm a bit of a klutz sometimes."

He laughed. She turned around. Max noticed it was the girl from class whom he thought about often and wanted to talk to, desperately. Their eyes met briefly. In shyness, they both looked away.

He approached her. "Here are some more leaflets."

"Thank you," she smiled. "These are pretty important. They can't just blow away in the wind."

"I understand," he said. "I think we got them all." He looked about him at the steps.

"You look familiar," she said. "Are we in the same class? Mr. Van Rensburg's class?"

"Yes," he said. "My name is Max."

"I'm Sara."

"Nice to meet you, Sara."

He shook her delicate hand.

"Here is a leaflet, only if you are interested though," she said. "I don't know what your thoughts are on...well, the politics of this country, but there will be a student demonstration tomorrow."

"A demonstration...I am interested," he said. "I sort of peeked at the leaflet that hit my face."

She smiled. "Wonderful."

"Might I ask, what is NUSAS?" He looked into her deep blue eyes anxiously awaiting the answer. "Sorry, I am new to town." He blushed.

"The National Union of South African Students," she said, noticing his unique hazel eyes. "We are an anti-apartheid resistance group. Where are you from? I sense an accent—German, perhaps?"

"Yes, I am from Berlin," Max said, quickly changing the subject. "I'd like to attend the demonstration. What's happening in this country is pathetic."

They both laughed, sensing they shared the same feelings about South African politics.

"May I get your phone number?" he asked.

"Sure," she said.

They exchanged phone numbers.

That night at dinner Max sat with his parents as they discussed matters at the diamond center. Oskar was having a problem with a member of his staff.

The phone rang and their maid, Rosie, interrupted the meal.

"Master Max, the phone call is for you," Rosie entered the dining room.

Max rose from the table and took the phone from Rosie's hand.

"Hello," he answered.

"Hello, Max," the voice answered. "It's Sara."

"Hey, Sara. How are you doing?"

"Well, thank you. Max, will you be joining us at the Sympathy Street March tomorrow at 11:00 o'clock?"

"Yes, maybe…" He cleared his throat. "I think so."

"What do you mean you think so?"

"Well, I have class at that time," he said.

"We all have class," she said. "That is the point."

"Yes, true," he answered. "I will see you tomorrow then."

"Great," she said. "Meet at the Jameson Steps."

"Alright, see you then," he said.

Max returned to the dinner table and began eating his pea soup.

"Who was on the phone?" Helene asked.

"Just a friend, Mother," he said.

"Ah," she said. "Making weekend plans?"

"Something like that," Max answered.

"Pardon me, I didn't hear you," Helene said, looking at her son.

"Nothing, Mother," he said.

Rosie, Oskar and Helene's third maid and the one Oskar finally trusted, walked into the dining room, carrying a serving dish filled with chicken and mushrooms, along with a large bowl of rice.

"Would you like a drink, Master Max?" she asked.

"Please don't call me 'Master', Rosie," he said. "Please just call me Max."

"Yes, Master Max," she said.

"Rosie!" he exclaimed, slightly agitated.

Oskar stared at his son with wide eyes.

"Aag, man," she said with a giggle. "Sorry, Max. It's a habit."

"Break your habit for me, Rosie," he said.

She nodded. Helene sipped her wine, sort of amused by it all.

"What was that about?" Oskar said, pointedly.

Max stared at the large gold loop sitting on the table that held keys to cabinets that limited the maid's access to necessities like cubes of sugar, salt, and even chocolate and wine.

"Nothing, Father," Max said. "It just doesn't feel right to be called 'Master'. That's all."

"It's just respectful that she does," Helene said.

"That's just it," Max said. "It's not respectful, not to her. She is not a slave. May I be excused, please?"

"Yes," Helene said, meeting Oskar's eyes.

Oskar sighed as he grew impatient with his son.

Oskar and Helene ate in silence.

≈∽

The next morning as Max approached the Jameson steps, his eyes widened at the swarms of people, students and teachers who had convened at the steps ready to protest. Most held striking posters denouncing apartheid support. His eyes set upon one with a black fist crushing a white stone that read "Apartheid Parliament" with the words "Don't Support Apartheid", printed at the bottom of the poster.

"Sara!" Max yelled out.

One girl with blonde hair turned around. "Sorry, I am looking for someone else," he said. He began to climb the steps to the top. He looked around and could not find Sara. Dismay set in. He wondered if he should leave now and not be a part of this. It was a sympathy march after all, what could really go wrong? He analysed the crowd. The majority of the people were students, a few he recognized from several of his classes and many he did not recognize.

"How's this for a poster?"

He turned around to find Sara's laughing eyes staring at him. He smiled back. Max held the poster in his hands and read the black, bold words:

*"South Africa, wake up! It's either democracy or tragedy!"*

"Perfect!" Max laughed.

As he held the poster in his hand, Sara grabbed his arm, winked at him, and led him into the thick crowd. He felt his pulse quicken. He hated crowds. They made him nervous. People were pushing and some were shoving, trying to get in the front of the demonstration. A few tripped on some of the steps. Sara kept pulling him through the jam of people down the steps, towards the front, or it could have been the back, he could not tell what direction was what. He closed his eyes as Sara continued to lead him and then he felt her force his arm upwards.

"Raise the poster, Max!"

He raised it as high as he could in the air and opened his eyes. He noticed the Jameson Steps to the right as they marched down a street past the library.

He smiled and began shouting what the others shouted, "End apartheid!"

He noticed Mr. Van Rensburg standing on the side of the road, yelling at the students. His index finger jabbed in the air. "Stop this now!" he shouted. His body jolted as he shrieked at the marching crowd. Three other teachers joined him. Their tyranny of screaming was lost against the loudness of the demonstration and shouts of students.

Max looked to his left and noticed Sara was no longer beside him. Somehow they weren't able to keep up with each other. Suddenly, his eyes fixed upon several police trying to break up the crowd. He could hear the sounds of barking dogs. He decided to slow down his pace to make sure he was not a target.

In seconds, he was on the ground on the side of the street. Someone had accidently tripped him and when he looked up, a policeman was inches from his face. A rubber baton struck his shoulder. He flinched, grabbing his shoulder as pain shot through his arm. He felt his fingers go numb. When he looked up again at the policeman, he saw the grim face of a Nazi officer. He stuck his hands in the air as the officer grabbed his shirt collar and raised the baton in the air as if he would strike Max again.

"Please don't hurt me," Max cried. "Please don't do it."

Max closed his eyes and awaited another blow to his body. A second or two passed and nothing happened. By the time he opened his eyes, the policeman had walked off towards the demonstration.

He rested for a moment. A pang of pain ripped through his shoulder.

Then, he felt someone from behind grab his arm and help him to his feet.

"Thank you," Max said, as he felt a gentle pat on his back.

"No, thank you," the voice said and laughed.

He turned his head and noticed the person who had helped him was a homeless "bergie". The poor black man smelled of whiskey. He gave a toothless grin before walking off, followed by a scrawny, dirty mutt.

"Hey, wait! You forgot your hat!" Max screamed after the man.

But by then, the man had disappeared into the shadows. Max dusted off the dirty patches from his pants. As he looked up, he saw Isaac approaching him, and he didn't look happy.

Isaac grabbed Max's arm and led him up the steps into Jameson Hall.

"I told you not to get involved," Isaac spoke softly, but pointedly. "I warned you."

As they neared the hallway that led to Isaac's office, Professor Henry Lutz turned the corner, almost colliding into them.

"Ah, Isaac, did you hear about the demonstration?" The professor eyed Max.

"Yes, word spreads like a wildfire," Isaac put his arm around Max's shoulder, trying to change the topic of conversation. "This is my brother-in-law, Max."

The professor held out his hand. Max shook it.

"Max is a humanities student," Isaac said.

"How do you like it, young man?"

"I'm enjoying it very much, thank you," Max said, still trying to catch his breath.

"Do you know any students involved in that march?" The professor asked Max.

"No," Max shook his head. "I don't know anything about it really."

"I heard it got brutal out there," the professor said, looking from Max to Isaac. "Apparently, they made a few arrests."

Max tried to not react. Concern overcame him. Was Sara in danger?

"As far as I am concerned, those kids can bark all they want and march the whole of South Africa, but no one is listening," the professor said. "What they don't understand is apartheid is as much for them as it is for us and for future generations, so that there is a future for them. Without it, their future is at stake."

Max forced an agreeable smile. The professor brushed back his silver hair.

"Black and white people are fundamentally different," he said. "They need to be kept separate."

"Don't you agree, Isaac?"

Isaac inhaled deeply.

"Yes," Isaac cleared his throat. "It's probably the right direction for this country."

The old professor laughed.

"Probably...yes...probably it is," he ridiculed Isaac.

Max and Isaac exchanged quick glances.

"Will you excuse us, professor?"

"Certainly," he said.

"I have to prepare for class," Isaac said.

As they sat in Isaac's office, there were no windows to see what was going on with the demonstration. Isaac handed him a silver flask.

"It will take some of the pain away, calm the nerves," he said.

Max grabbed the flask and took a gulp of the brandy.

"Thank you," Max said.

"You have come too far, Max," Isaac said. "*We* have come too far to jeopardize your future, our future. This interest you have in the black cause is refreshing, but dangerous. Sometimes I wonder if danger is in your bones...anything to fight for a hefty cause. I know you want to help. I do, too. But we are not nearly powerful enough. You must concentrate on your studies. And forget about the pretty girl. She is not for you. She will get you in trouble. Trouble you don't need."

For a moment, Max sat pensively. How could he forget her? From the moment, he met Sara, all he could think about was her.

"Do you know Sara?" he asked his brother-in-law.

"Who doesn't?" Isaac said, chuckling. "We all know Sara. Pretty, smart, and the list goes on. Do you understand? This is not her first parade, if you know what I mean. She is known to stir up trouble."

"Don't tell my parents," Max begged. "Please, Isaac. My father will be furious."

"Relax," Isaac said. "That is the last thing I'd do. Just promise me that you will focus on your studies from now on."

"Promise," Max said, with a boyish grin.

"Now, get out of here," Isaac said jokingly. "I have to prepare for class."

When he left Isaac's office, Sara was the only thing on Max's mind. He ran out of the building and noticed the demonstration had ended. The area was heavily patrolled by the police with dogs in tow. Sara was nowhere in sight. That evening, Max called her, but her father said she was unavailable. He wished there was a way to find out if she was okay, but today was Friday and he knew he was out of luck. He would have to wait until Monday when he would see Sara in class.

❧❦

As the sun set on Shabbat, they once again turned their attention to what opened their hearts. They lit the candles, said the Kiddush prayer, and came together around the table as a family.

Shabbat became their weekly family ritual, a reflective time, a time to catch up with each other's lives and enjoy a festive meal. It was a special time to bring the family together.

"Max, why are you moving your arm like that?" Helene asked. "Are you hurt, darling?"

"It's nothing, Mother," he said. "It's just a sports injury. I was playing rugby with some friends after school."

"Rugby?" Oskar questioned. "I have never known you to like sports much. Rugby, they say, is a thuggish game played by gentlemen."

Carmen and Isaac laughed.

"I would think tennis or maybe cricket would be more your style, Max," Carmen voiced.

"Same to you, Carmen!" Max joked with his brother-in-law. "You're no gentleman thug either."

"I am sorry to change the subject, but Isaac and I have been talking about our future," Inge said.

They all looked up from their plates and turned their eyes toward Inge.

"What of the future?" Oskar asked, putting down his fork.

Helene smiled, hoping the news had to do with a baby.

"We are thinking of moving," Inge said to her family.

Their faces froze. Oskar turned pale.

"Did I hear you correctly, Inge?" Oskar said.

"Yes, Father," she said. "We are thinking of moving to New York."

Inge looked at her sister. Eva looked heartbroken.

"No, Inge!" Eva cried out. "No!"

Oskar slammed his hand on the table. His face grew angry. "No!" he yelled. "No, you will not! You cannot leave your family. Not now, Inge. Not after all we have been through."

Tears streamed down Inge's face. Isaac grabbed her hand.

"I didn't expect this sort of reaction," Inge said. "I thought you would be happy for us."

Eva swallowed hard. She felt her throat constrict.

Oskar crossed his arms.

"Why would you want to leave your family," he said. "And live in a place thousands of miles away?"

"I don't understand," Helene said, searching for answers. "Please, Inge. Isaac?"

"We are not certain South Africa is for us," Isaac said. "We fled a regime where our lives were in great danger, only to land in another country with its own set of challenges."

"What place is immune to challenges?" Oskar said. "I don't know of any, do you?"

"America," Isaac said.

"America..." Oskar said. "There is nowhere on Earth that is free of challenges, wars, hatred, and the list goes on."

"It's your lives, of course," Helene said. "But please think about it carefully."

"We have come so far together," Oskar said. "I cannot have my family split apart, not now and not ever. Do you understand?"

Oskar rose from the table and grabbed his glass of whiskey.

"Is this not enough for you, life here?" Oskar asked. Before Inge or Isaac had time to respond, Oskar left the dining room. Helene followed him.

"Please, Inge," Eva said. "We vowed to never be apart. Please don't leave. I beg you."

"I know, Eva." Inge said. "I know. You know that no matter how far we are, we are always close, in each other's hearts."

Eva eyes welled with tears.

"If you went to America, I don't know how often I would see you," Eva said. "It's so far away. The distance is immense and I worry it would come between us...our closeness."

"I realize it's a great distance, but nothing could come between us, dear sister," Inge said. "I just don't know that we are happy in Cape Town."

By then, the rest of the family had left the table. Eva moved next to her sister and took her hand in hers.

"What is happiness, really?" Eva asked. "Isn't all of this happiness: our family, our lives together? I want you to really think about this. New York can be harsh for immigrants. Language barriers and cultural clashes. Do you really want to start over again?"

"Not really, but America might have better opportunities for Isaac," Inge said.

"I thought he was happy working at the University," Eva said.

"He is...well, he was," Inge said.

"What do you mean?" Eva asked.

"With the eruption of apartheid, there is a new, inherited culture that makes it difficult to teach human rights to a hostile environment, filled with privileged white faces," Inge explained. "It is a major challenge to teach in a neutral manner. Isaac has his own feelings towards apartheid."

"Yes, I understand," Eva said. "Isaac is a great teacher and I am sure he can overcome this challenge. It's not like America doesn't have its own similar challenges. Hatred is everywhere, Inge."

Eva stood up. "I know you have a lot to think about," she said. "Do what is right for you and Isaac. I will support whatever you decide."

As Eva was walking away, Inge grabbed her arm.

"Wait," she said. "I have something else to tell you."

Eva sat down again.

Inge smiled and looked down at her belly.

"I am having a baby," she said.

"Inge!" Eva said, excitedly. Eva grabbed her sister in a tight embrace.

"Inge, I am so happy," she said. "I know you have wanted this for a long time."

Eva held her sister's delicate face in her hands and said, "You will be a wonderful mother."

"I have had a great role model," Inge said to her sister.

Alone at the dining room table, Inge stared at the old grandfather clock as it chimed away. She couldn't let the night slip away without confronting her father.

Inge found her father in the study. She sat down next to him.

"*Vati*," she said. She had not called him that since she was a little girl. "I'm sorry to have upset you."

Oskar turned to his daughter. She could not help to notice how tired he looked. His fine lines formed a map of his life, some deeper than others, some just beginning to form.

"Inge," Oskar patted her arm. "It's okay, darling. I'm sorry I got so upset. It breaks my heart to hear that you are not happy here. Your mother and I only want you to be happy."

Inge laid her head upon her father's shoulder.

"We faced great challenges getting here, in addition to much danger," Oskar said. "It was the best place to come to at the time. It's not like we had a world of choices."

"I know, Papa," she said.

"South Africa is a beautiful place, Inge, but not a perfect place. So far it's been kind to us. It's brought us some peace of mind, a small sense of community, and more prosperity than I could have hoped for. Above and beyond that, I wanted us to find happiness and peace. Sometimes, Inge, we have to look at the larger picture, not just at what's before our eyes, not just at the challenges we face. If you look beyond what is in front of you, you can see a small piece of perfection, a glimmer of light, some happiness. The clouds are not always grey. The sun is shining just behind it."

Inge broke into a smile.

"If I know you, Inge, and I feel I do, I know that moving away may seem like the right thing to do, but in fact, I don't think it's the right decision at all. And your family needs you. Think about what I just told you and do what's in your heart."

"I need my family very much, *Vati*," she said. "Isaac and I are having a baby."

Tears welled in Oskar's eyes. He kissed his daughter on the cheek.

"That's happiness," he said. "Tell your mother. She will be thrilled."

As Oskar watched Inge walk away, he prayed that his daughter would not leave him.

৵৽৽৻

Isaac and Inge needed to make a decision. Should they stay or should they go? The question whirred around in their heads. Of course, their family wanted them to stay, but it wasn't their decision. They were looking for answers, but the answer was in their hearts.

Saturday was a picture-perfect day. The sun was bright and the day was breezy and warm. The ocean sparkled in the sunlight.

Heading away from Seapoint, Clifton beach and the city, the Volkswagen Beetle hugged the winding road ahead. Inge looked out at the sun-kissed buttresses of a series of peaks known as the Twelve Apostles, an extension of the Table Mountain range. They drove up Cape Town's Kloof Nek Road to the 'Nek', which led them to Tafelberg Road on which the lower cable station of Table Mountain was situated. They were quiet in the car, consumed in their own thoughts. Inge was enamored by Table Mountain's ruggedness and grayish, purple shades. The huge slab of sandstone, granite and shale rose from the sea more than 250 million years ago. It was mystical and beautiful.

With a short wait, the cable car came down. Isaac grabbed Inge's hand and held it tight as they entered the cable car. It was empty except for a couple touring the area and two men. As the cable car traveled upward, Inge looked down watching everything in the city get smaller and smaller. With that, the "Mountain of the Sea" became more real and touchable. Almost six minutes later, they arrived at the top. The blue sky stretched high above them. They walked from corner to corner on the flat top of Table Mountain, taking in the views over the city and the beaches. The panorama stretched from Cape Point in the south to the peaks of the Hottentot Hollands in the east.

"I will definitely miss the beauty," Inge said.

"Me, too," Isaac said.

They continued to tour the mountaintop, from its back table forests to its shrub-like vegetation and hundreds of rare plants. Isaac pointed out the best known specimen, the king protea, South Africa's national flower. Isaac snapped his camera so that he could at least keep the beauty in a picture.

Unexpectedly, some weather closed in on the top of the mountain. This was not an unusual occurrence, but risky to walkers or sightseers who might become lost in the network of paths. The wind on Table Mountain was very dangerous and could turn the top of the mountain into a deadly maze. As they headed down the mountain, Inge looked up at the top of the mountain one more time, thinking it was her last.

They continued on Kloof Nek Road, which is linked to Lion's Head Mountain, connected by a lion's body to a rump known as Signal Hill. From the road, they could see views of the Atlantic Seaboard. The pathway up Lion's Head passes through rare silver trees and flowers. Isaac slowed the car, so they could get a better look. They parked at Signal Hill. It reminded

Inge of a lion's sphinx. They stood on the hill amid tourists and fellow South Africans. Little children ran around.

On their way home they drove Chapman's Peak, the twists and turns of the route that clung to the cliffside along the Cape Peninsula's western edge. It was glorious, the vertical and rugged sweep of the mountains on one side and the deep, blue ocean on the other. As Inge looked down along the sweep of the beach, a fisherman waded into the cold waters. The scene was a feast for the eyes.

"Do you want to leave?" Inge looked out at the ocean that stretched beyond the horizon. It was endless and magnificent.

"What does your heart tell you?" she asked, looking into Isaac's eyes.

"The thought of moving was an exciting one, but suddenly, leaving seems daunting and challenging," Isaac said. "Starting over is never easy. I am not certain the time is right. We are having a baby. And it feels like yesterday that we stepped off that ship as immigrants."

He stroked Inge's cheek.

"I think peace means a lot of things to a lot of people," Inge said. "Maybe this is peace."

Inge turned her head, looked out the window, and absorbed the ocean's sparkle and the ridged mountain passes as they sifted downward around the bends and curves toward home.

"Before we return home, Isaac, let's stop by my parents and tell them we are staying," Inge said. "My father still seemed upset when we left last night."

When they turned into the street, they were surprised to see a police car parked in front of the house.

Inge grabbed Isaac's hand. "Oh no, Isaac! I hope everything is okay."

"Oh, shit!" Isaac exclaimed. "I know what this is about...that damn professor!"

"What are you talking about?" Inge asked.

"You will soon find out," he said as he parked the car.

Inge ran to the front door and furiously knocked, not even bothering with her key. Helene answered.

"Mother, is everything alright?"

"Not really," she said, lowering her voice. "It seems your brother is in some sort of trouble."

"What!" Inge gasped.

"Come in, but stay in the kitchen," Helene pulled her daughter and son-in-law inside the house.

Officer Pieter Granger sat in their living room, Max directly opposite him. Oskar sat next to his son. Pearls of sweat developed on his forehead.

"The march was an illegal gathering," the middle-aged officer said, as he crossed his legs. "It's prohibited by law."

"I understand, sir," Max said. "I apologize for any wrongdoing on my behalf."

"Were you a planner or participant?" the officer asked as he opened his notebook.

"I was a participant only," Max said. "I never meant any harm."

"Did someone inform you of the event? How did you become involved?"

Max hesitated. He did not want to tell on Sara. He froze.

"Speak up!" Oskar yelled at his son.

Tears welled in Max's eyes.

"Might I remind you that South Africa has strict internal security laws," the officer said. "The laws authorize people to be detained for questioning indefinitely without charge and to be held in solitary confinement. I recommend you tell me everything."

"I joined into the march out of sheer curiosity," Max said. "It's the truth."

The officer laughed. "Don't fool me," he said. "I know that a leaflet was distributed to students. I also know many students knew about the march, days before it even occurred."

Max broke out in a cold sweat. Oskar began to pace the room. Helene sat grief-stricken on a side chair.

"Does the name Sara Marcus ring a bell?"

Max nodded. "I had just met her when she told me about the march. To be honest, I didn't even know her last name."

"Well, your friend, Sara, was held in solitary confinement and questioned as she is a strong activist against apartheid," the officer said. "Did you know?"

"No," Max said. "I had no knowledge of that. Like I said, I barely knew her."

"Are you sure?" Helene asked.

"Yes, Mother," he said.

"Let me be clear: do not oppose the government," the officer stated, rising from the chair.

"You will be arrested and even charged. Don't let us catch you again or you will be locked up for a long time. I will make certain of that."

"Yes, sir," Max said.

Max looked over at his mother apologetically.

Oskar led the officer to the front door. Max and Helene sat in silence until the car pulled away.

"My son is a fool!" Oskar yelled, returning to the living room. "I have sacrificed so much to give you everything and now you are willing to put yourself and all of us in danger. Are you mad? Don't ever see that girl again and you will never participate in such foolish things. You don't need to support this government, Max, but you need to obey it. Do you understand?"

Max nodded and stared at the floor. What had he done, he thought?

"Understand that if you are imprisoned for going against the government, I have no way of getting you out," Oskar said. "It would be almost impossible."

"I am sorry, Father," Max said. "It won't happen again."

"Make damn sure of it," Oskar said. "Realize that you are not off that easy. They will be watching you."

Max sighed. "Yes, Father."

# chapter

# NINETEEN

Nestled deep in the bush, a rural Zulu village dotted the majestic hills of eMakhosini, the "Valley of the Kings." Trudy watched as the morning sun illuminated the magical landscape beyond the unspoilt Zulu kingdom. The land was silent for a brief moment as the sun warmed the sloping terrain and jagged hills. Thatch-roofed *rondavels* cluttered together beneath beautiful shady *dawa-dawa* trees. Thickets of spiny shrubs and acacia trees surrounded the *kraal* or village, built on a gently declining slope.

The Zulus knew their land. One main entrance was situated at the lowest point of the kraal. Heavy rainfalls, dung and other dirt washed through the entrance onto the large vegetable plot below. Due to the slope, no rain water was retained, allowing the bare ground of the kraal to dry quickly.

The Zulus knew no fear. The weakest point of their village was the entrance. While enemies had to fight uphill, the Zulu tribe was at a strategic advantage. If they had to, they would shed rivers of blood to remain free on the land of their forefathers. They held the spirit of sacrifice and discipline that guided their nation and their people.

As the traditional, primitive community came to life, eventually silence was replaced by squawking chickens, mooing cows and bleating goats. In the distance, the roar of lions could be heard. Trudy smiled at the loud coo-cooing of the turtledoves. A man shouted in Zulu. Herdsmen struggled to control a group of grazing cows, and then disappeared over the brow of a hill. Children emerged from rondavels, ready to embrace their day, a day consumed with helping their parents and elders with chores. From a young age, children learned to show respect towards their parents and elders in the village. Everything surrounded the promise of education, for education was a privilege. The men and women, boys and girls of the kraal had well-defined duties and chores, and for the young, these chores and responsibilities were an important part of growing up and becoming responsible adults in the society.

Trudy took in the surroundings. It was another world compared to what she had always known. She embraced the change, but it challenged her in more ways than one. She was amazed at how happy everyone in the community seemed, yet they lacked the simple things in life, like electricity, running water and telephones. The comforts of home, of Germany, were unreachable, but for the first time, Trudy did not mind the inconvenience or the lack of things she had grown most accustomed to. Like the people in this community, she too would rise above the lack of limited resources. She looked forward to getting back to the simple things in life. When the world was at war, life became complicated and terrifying. Somewhere in the midst of it all, she had lost her sense of self, and the things that were most important to her.

Trudy stood just beyond the low doorway of her rondavel. She sipped a cup of honeybush tea, taking in the life around her. She heard distant drums. A bowl of *samp*, dried maize kernels, sat uneaten on a small table in the darkness of the rondavel. Her eyes caught the sight of a trail of ants traveling through a vein of the mud and dung ground of her dwelling. A large cobweb dangled from the steeple that supported the dwelling. This life was primitive and simple, yet uncomplicated.

She watched as the children gathered under the large, leafless African Baobab tree. Its thick roots stuck out in the air and provided much-needed shade. Trudy joined them, like she did each morning. She stood amid the large trunk of the tree as the children smiled back in anticipation. She had to be creative to teach in this environment as they were challenged with nothing—nothing to write with, no chalkboard, and only a few books.

"What is your dream?" Trudy asked the children.

She waited patiently for someone to answer. The little faces looked at each other, hesitant to speak.

"Don't be afraid," she said. "Everyone dreams. Don't be scared to dream. Don't be afraid to chase after your dreams."

"Would you like to be a scientist?" she asked. "A doctor, perhaps? Or maybe an athlete or a teacher, like me?"

Excitement came over the children's faces. Trudy smiled back at them. She focused her attention on Thulile, the shy, quiet girl who lived with her older sister. What opportunities would she have in life, here in this place? Thulile's mother died during childbirth and her father, a herdsman, vanished for days on end. Trudy wondered what the sweet, thin six-year-old girl dreamed of each day when she awoke and when sleep took over at night.

"Thulile, what do you want to be one day?" Trudy asked the girl. Thulile's big black eyes stared back at Trudy. Too shy to answer, she hid her head in her hands.

"It's okay, Thulile," she said. "You can tell us. We all want to know." Some of the children giggled.

"I know you love to gaze at the stars, Thulile," Trudy said. A smile came over the little girl's face.

"Maybe you want to be an astronomer?" Trudy asked. "An astronomer is a scientist who studies the stars and planets in the sky."

Thulile nodded with excitement.

"Now we are dreaming big," Trudy said. "Doesn't it feel great?"

Trudy pulled out her compass and a map from a bag. The children only knew of this place and nothing more. Did they know just how big and diverse the world really was?

"Gather around, children," Trudy said, motioning the children to come towards her. She spread out the map on the ground.

"Does anyone know what this is?" She held up the compass in the air. The children stared blankly at the instrument.

She explained what the instrument was and then pointed on the map where South Africa was located.

"Where are you from?" a boy asked.

Trudy pointed to Berlin, Germany. Suddenly, a strange feeling came upon her. Berlin felt like worlds away, a place that had lost its meaning as her home. A place she felt ashamed of, and penitent to be German. In the midst of this primitive place, she realized that people are more alike than not, that there should be no hate, only love.

Her mind drifted to the pendant necklace that was hidden away in a pair of socks in her bag. She thought of her mother, alone in Berlin. She felt a sharp pang of guilt for leaving her. She would write her a letter that day to tell her about her adventure in Africa. Trudy hoped her mother would join her at the village.

Trudy's mother had hoped to pick up the threads of her old life, but Berlin was a sea of devastation. The café she once frequented weekly with old friends was no longer and even her friends seemed worn. The city lay under a permanent gray cloud—a city so far from the brightness and sereneness of Africa.

Trudy thought of Eva. She wasn't certain if Eva was dead or alive.

Trudy knew in her heart that she wanted to disappear from Germany for good, from the harsh effects of the war, from the familiar places that brought back horrifying memories.

"Trudy," a booming voice startled her back to reality. "How are the children today?"

"They are doing well," she replied, smoothing her hair.

"*Unjani?*" he asked. (How are you?)

"*Ngikhona, ngiyabonga!*" she said. (I'm fine, thanks!)

As she taught them English, they in turn taught her Zulu.

"*Ngiyabonga,*" she said. (Thank you.)

The head teacher of the village glanced at the children.

"They seem happy," he said, as Trudy stared at his *inJobo*, long animal skin worn around his waist. She was fascinated by his decorated headband worn only by married men. The men of the Zulu tribe were very noble and traditional.

After reading to the children, the boys joined the men who busied their days raising cattle. It was their duty to look after their fathers' herd. After sunrise, they left the kraal with the cattle and returned sometime in the morning. Then, they would take a break and sit with Trudy and the other teachers to learn how to speak English and learn the ways of the Western world before returning to their duties. They milked the cows, and then the boys would go back to the pastures until sunset. Most had survival instincts of grown men.

The girls joined the women and were gradually introduced to household chores. Initially, each girl was given a small gourd and accompanied her mother, her teacher, to the water source. There, the mother first filled her much larger container while the daughter watched and filled hers under the patient eye of her mother. Next, the mother braided two head supports (*inkatha*), made of grass, to enable them to carry the load comfortably on their head. The child, not having yet attained a great sense of balance, usually arrived back at the kraal wet, slightly agitated, and with little water left in her gourd. After a few lessons, she quickly learned the trick and carried varying loads, eventually becoming a healthy, determined woman with a strong back. More lessons took place in the field. The child carried a small gourd filled with seeds, which her mother hoed into the soil. In time, the daughter mastered the correct technique of sowing and hoeing, and on her eleventh birthday is given her own light hoe. At this age, she knew what firewood to collect on the slopes of the hills that would make a good fire for cooking. She could prepare some dishes and look after her younger brothers and sisters.

The girls also learned the time-honored skill of basket-weaving. They absorbed knowledge from the skillful master Zulu basket weaver, a title given to one of the elder women in the village. This title often took decades to accomplish as weavers perfected their skills over many years.

Trudy was fascinated by this age-old craft that spanned generations. She assisted the women in preparing and dying the palm fibers. Then, she sat back and watched as the women pulled and weaved the threads of Llala Palm. Eventually, the women created beautiful baskets with unique patterns, each with their own meaning. Some of them were so amazing, especially the ones created by the "masters". These baskets could be exhibited in a museum.

❧

The day started with just a hint of cold in the air. Once Trudy left her rondavel, she could tell it was no ordinary day. The men of the village had congregated in the kraal and sat around large three-legged pots, bubbling away with steam that escaped from their broken lids. Trudy was offered a seat facing the men. She looked around nervously.

The ceremony began with a low hum from the men, and soon as others joined in, the hum turned into shrill chanting. Villagers stomped their bare feet. Trudy could hear the rhythmic thundering of cowhide drums behind her. She had no idea what was happening. One of the village elders smiled reassuringly at her. Trudy forced a smile back. She was then served some pap by one of the younger women who carried an infant on her back. Trudy almost choked on her meal when a goat was slaughtered before her eyes.

The village's traditional healer, *sangoma*, appeared before them. She wore a goat's gallbladder tied into her hair at the back of her head. The gallbladder came from the goat slaughtered at the time of the sangoma's graduation and is said to "call the ancestors." A cluster of goat horns and beaded containers filled with an assortment of herbs and medicines hung around her neck, shoulders, and body. The village elders were shrouded in animal skins and swayed and danced, singing in guttural voices. Unsure what to do, Trudy clapped her hands with the others.

The ceremony became louder when the initiate arrived. She was a special person chosen by her ancestors through a dream. She became the link to the physical world and the afterworld of the ancestors. Sangomas were called to heal, and through them, ancestors from the spirit world gave instruction and advice to heal illness, social disharmony and spiritual difficulties.

The initiate was wrapped in white cloth with a crown of willow branches wrapped around her head. Her face was painted white. She wore strips of goatskin taken from the initiation goat that crisscrossed her bare chest. Trudy felt even more uneasy when a group of bare-chested unmarried girls chanted and danced beside her. Unmarried girls (*intombi*) wore only a short skirt made of grass or beaded cotton strings, and went bare-chested, regardless of her size, weight, or small or large bosom. Zulus did not contribute any sexual meaning to the naked breast, but rather to back of the upper thigh. The young girls made up for their nakedness by sprucing themselves up with beadwork. Beads conveyed messages in the Zulu land, such as grief, death and love. Young women who have been chosen or engaged, let their hair grow and covered her breasts with a decorative cloth as a sign of respect to her future family. Married women covered their bodies completely, signaling that she was off limits.

Sangomas were steeped in ritual. They worked in a sacred healing hut or *Ndumba*, where their ancestors reside. The initiate underwent *Thwasa*, a period of training including learning humility to the ancestors, purification through steaming, washing in the blood of sacrificed animals, and the use of *Muti*, medicines with spiritual significance. At the end of *Thwasa*, a goat is sacrificed to call to the ancestors and appease them.

When Trudy could not stand it anymore, she disappeared into the dancing and chanting crowd and went beyond into the dark, open foothill of the kraal. As she approached her rondavel, she noticed a presence by her doorstep. A line of cigarette smoke sifted into the air.

"Hello!" Trudy yelled out as she got closer. She noticed the figure stand and dust off her pants.

"Hi there," the young woman said, extending her arm to Trudy. "I'm Sara."

"Hi," Trudy said, shaking the woman's hand. She noticed her golden brown curls that hung over her shoulders and the deep blueness of her eyes.

"I'm the new volunteer," Sara said. "Looks like we're going to be roommates, I hope that's okay."

"Roommates?" Trudy peered at the small space in which she slept.

"Yes..."

"Ah, sure," Trudy said. What option did she really have?

"Sorry to intrude on your space," Sara said. "Unfortunately, there does not seem to be much alternative. It's either here or maybe in the field with the cows."

"I'm sure one of the villagers would take you in, but you will be more comfortable here," Trudy smiled.

"Thanks," Sara said, as they entered the rondavel. Sara looked around the dwelling. "Wow, it's roomier than I imagined and very cozy, indeed."

"It's not so bad," Trudy said. "Please, make yourself at home. Would you like a cup of tea? Are you hungry? I'm sure you're tired from your long journey."

"Not a bad journey from Cape Town," the girl said. "I am not so hungry, but would love a cup of tea. Thank you."

"Cape Town?" Trudy said. "I hear it's very beautiful there."

"It's extraordinary," Sara said. "What was happening in the village?"

"A sangoma initiation," Trudy said. "A ceremony for the traditional healer. It's been quite a day actually...The ceremony has been going on for hours. Amazing and terrifying at the same time. It's interesting to learn about the culture here."

They sat down on some reed mats and drank their tea.

"What brings you here, Sara?"

"I got into some trouble at school," she said. "This was cheaper than boarding school."

Trudy laughed. "What happened?"

"It's a long story," Sara said. "I'd hate to bore you."

"How long are you here for?" Trudy asked.

"My father told me I would stay as long as it took to reform me," Sara said. "A few weeks, I suppose."

"And it will," Trudy said. "It's changed me. It's opened my eyes to many things and has shown me what is important in life."

The girl nodded. She finished her tea and grabbed a sweater from her bag. Trudy handed her a blanket.

"Thank you," Sara said. "It sounds like you have enjoyed your experience so far."

"I have," Trudy answered.

A knock sounded on the door of their rondavel. A Zulu woman stood before them. She came bearing gifts. She held a large wooden bowl filled with fruit. By the door stood a traditional Zulu beer basket crafted out of Ilala Palm and woven with colorful patterns. The gesture was to welcome Sara and to thank Trudy for her work in the village. They could tell by her dress and beautiful red, beaded headband that she was married. She was a large woman and the fifth wife of the Zulu chief. She said, "I am wife, wife, wife, wife, wife," ticking off with her fingers five times. Sara laughed in response.

"*Ngiyabonga kakhulu!*" (Thank you very much.) Trudy smiled at the Zulu woman.

Sara stared wide-eyed at the generous portion of fruit in the wooden bowl. "The village has several fruit orchards," Trudy said to Sara. Not knowing what to say, Sara grinned at the Zulu woman and waved.

"*Kulungile!*" (You're welcome) the Zulu woman said. "*Sanibona!*" (Good evening)

"*Sawubona!*" Trudy responded.

The woman walked away into the night.

"That was amazing and so nice," Sara said.

"The Zulus are friendly people when you are on their side," Trudy said.

They each grabbed a piece of fruit and settled in for the night. Sara laid down on her *icansi*, the Zulu sleeping mat made of reeds, and fell asleep. Trudy sat at a small, wooden table and worked on her lesson plan for the children before turning in for the night.

The next day, after they had finished teaching the children, they sat alongside a group of Zulu women as they created spectacular beadwork. One of the younger women was hard at work creating a love letter (*incwadi*) made of beads to be given to the man in which she felt passion. Zulu beadwork formed an intricate system of communication where colors and designs, a blazon of beads, told a story. The woman assorted the beads in such a way that they geometrically symbolized, through triangular and other shapes, that she was unfulfilled, unmarried. She included red beads to represent her passion and love, as well as white beads for purity and spiritual love.

"Trudy?"

"Yes?"

"Have you ever been in love?" Sara asked.

Trudy took a deep breath.

"Once," Trudy said, staring into the distance. "It was great until it... well...ended. Then, it was just horrible. Love can make you feel so vulnerable, so out of control."

"It can also be very exciting," Sara added.

"Absolutely!" Trudy eyed Sara. "What's his name?"

"Max," Sara said. "The minute I saw him, I was intrigued."

"I knew someone named Max once," Trudy said. "He was my best friend's younger brother. I was very fond of him. He was sweet, good-natured and innocent."

"What happened to them?" Sara asked.

"I don't know," Trudy said. "I wish I did. The war tore us apart." Trudy's eyes welled with tears.

Sara nodded. "Are you okay?" she asked.

"Yes," Trudy said. "I'm fine. When you mentioned the name Max, some distant memories came to life again—bittersweet memories of my past."

"Where are you from, Trudy, if you don't mind me asking?"

"No, not at all," Trudy said. "I am from Germany." She cleared her throat. "Berlin."

Silence ensued. Trudy hoped that Sara would not ask any more questions about her life.

As if a light bulb had turned on in her head, Sara eyes grew wide. "You know, thinking back to when I met Max, he may have said he was from Berlin."

"Are you certain, Sara?" Trudy asked, suddenly brimming with excitement.

"I think so," Sara said. "He spoke with an accent, a definite German accent."

Trudy wondered if they were talking about the same person.

"Did he have twin sisters?" Trudy asked.

"I'm not certain," Sara said. "I didn't really know him well or anything about his family, but he left a strong impression on me."

"Where did you meet?" Trudy asked.

"At the University of Cape Town," Sara said. "We were in the same class."

"I see," Trudy said, shocked by this newfound knowledge.

"Is the Max you know Jewish?" Trudy asked.

"Jewish?" Sara pondered, looking at Trudy.

"That's a tough one," she said, closing her eyes in thought. "I don't know what religion he was, but I know he read a lot and whenever I saw him, he was reading a book by Stefan Zweig, a prominent Jewish writer in the 1920s and 1930s."

"Yes, that sounds a little more like the Max I once knew," Trudy said.

"What about his hair? What color was it?" she asked, eagerly.

"Dark and wavy," Sara said. "He's a handsome young man."

That night, she could not sleep a wink. She felt a mix of emotions and she had to know if the person Sara knew was truly Max. She heard barking dogs coming from inside the kraal, probably the lions mocking them again. What are the chances, *she thought*? She was half-way across the world in a Zulu village and her connection to her past slept a few feet away on a reed mat.

As Sara stretched sleep away, she noticed Trudy drinking tea in the doorway of their rondavel.

"Good morning," Sara said.

"Good morning," Trudy turned to Sara.

"Have you been up for long?" Sara asked.

"A little while," Trudy said, as she watched the village stir back to life. "I couldn't stop thinking about our conversation."

"Still thinking about Max?" Sara asked.

"Yes," Trudy said.

"Is it that important to find them again?" Sara asked.

"Yes, very important," she said, thinking of the hidden diamond and emerald necklace in her bag. Trudy's thoughts drifted back to the night of the book burning, seeing Eva there, and the disappointment written all over her face.

"Tell me one more thing, Sara," Trudy turned to face her new friend. "What color were Max's eyes? Do you remember?"

"Yes, that I do remember," she said with a grin. "A dreamy hazel..."

Before she could rethink her decision, overanalyze it, or think it silly, Trudy was whisked away in a rusty jeep from the Zulu village in which she had grown fond. The driver, John, was a British volunteer who often went to Cape Town to visit his girlfriend and pick up supplies for the village.

As John adjusted his seat, a Zulu man with a spear got into the back seat.

"Our body guard," John laughed.

Trudy giggled, looking back at the Zulu.

"Good, I feel safe now," Trudy said.

The Zulu man not understanding their humor just stared back at them with a blank look.

"*Umlondolozi*," (Protector) John said to the man.

"*Yebo*," (Yes) the Zulu said.

As the jeep sped off, Trudy looked in the rear-view mirror at Sara who stood in the middle of the dirt road and waved. As dust from the unpaved road kicked up in the air and fogged her view of the village and of Sara, excitement and nerves infiltrated every inch of her.

Trudy feared not finding Eva. She wasn't even sure if Eva was in Cape Town. It's possible that Max was alive, but did Eva survive the war? She feared rejection. She feared seeing her for the first time. She hoped for forgiveness. Most importantly, how could Eva explain the things she did, the life she led, the horrible things she saw?

"So, why Cape Town?" John asked. "I know it's beautiful and all, but..."

"I am visiting some old friends who I haven't seen in a while," Trudy said.

"Nice," he said. "You will enjoy Cape Town. It's quite a change from the Zulu village in which you have grown accustomed."

"So I hear," she said.

"How often do you go to Cape Town?" she asked.

"I try to go once a month," he said. "My girlfriend lives there and I load up on supplies at the same time. As the old saying goes, 'kill two birds with one stone.'"

"What?" Trudy said. "What does that mean?"

John laughed.

"It basically means performing two tasks at the same time," he said.

"I like it," she said.

Trudy pulled her hair back from her face and stared at the unfamiliar landscape. She was amazed by the allure and mysticism of Africa as the land stretched beyond the horizon, from the rugged landscape of the imposing Drakensberg Mountains to the endless bushlands.

After a 2,000-kilometer drive from KwaZulu Natal via the Wild Coast, and the scenic Eastern and Southern Cape, Trudy arrived in Cape Town.

"This is one of the most beautiful places I've ever seen," she said. "Instantly, I'm reminded of something the explorer Sir Francis Drake said about his first impressions of this part of the world in 1580."

John cut her off, "This cape is the most stately thing and the fairest cape we saw in the whole circumference of the earth."

"You stole my line," she said.

"I did," he said, proud of himself.

The weather forecast printed in a small, but readable box in the Cape Town newspaper was clear and mild. That meant that the view of Table Mountain would be glorious. As the mountain came into sight, it was undoubtedly majestic. Table Mountain was the epitome of Cape Town.

Upon arrival, John dropped Trudy off at a small, cozy hotel by the sea.

"Here's the number of where I am staying," he said. "I'll be heading back to the Zulu village in a couple of days."

"You're coming back, right?" he asked.

Trudy cleared her throat.

"Uhm...I think so," she said with a reluctant smile.

"You don't sound so sure," he said. "Should I be concerned?"

"I will call you," she said, evading his questions. "Thank you for the ride."

She waved to the Zulu warrior. He waved back, awkwardly.

She laughed. They drove away.

*Now what*, she thought. She was in Cape Town and had no plan. She suddenly felt infinitely small and unimportant as she stared at the modern city before her.

Soon, Trudy found herself sitting on a bed in a musty hotel room. She was exhausted from the journey and sat motionless. The late afternoon sun had disappeared behind Table Mountain. She ordered room service two hours prior and hungrily ate *boerewors* (farm sausages) and potatoes, and washed it all down with a local red wine. Lost in thought, she nibbled on small pieces of *biltong* (dried, salted meat).

Trudy grabbed the black sock from her bag and pulled from it the treasured emerald and diamond pendant necklace. She enclosed it tightly in her hands. As her hands trembled, she held the necklace round her neck and was lost in the beautiful reflection in the mirror.

"So this is what it feels like," she said, admiring the gem. "It's magnificent."

After a few minutes, she hid the necklace in the black sock and placed it back in her bag. She returned to bed and heard rain drops falling, as the clouds roared out loud.

When Trudy's eyelids grew heavy and she fell asleep, everything tormented her dreams. Sangomas. The concentration camp commandant. Ravensbruck's head training overseer and her whip. Even Eva.

∂∞∫

In the morning, a soaking rain fell from the grey sky. Trudy waited, but it did not let up, and she desperately needed fresh air. The rain didn't stop her. She got dressed and left her hotel room. The hotel concierge ordered her a taxi. When it arrived, she asked the taxi driver to take her to a tea house. She craved a strong cup of tea, scones and tea sandwiches. The taxi driver dropped Trudy off at a popular English tea room, near the Cecil Rhodes Memorial.

By the time she was seated by a window in the tea room, the clouds had lifted and the storm had passed. Trudy watched as a group of amateur artists set up their easels, capturing the backdrop before them, the grandiose shrine of Cecil John Rhodes and the forest surrounding the Northern slope of Table Mountain.

As she quietly sipped her tea, a little girl and her mother caught her eye. The girl clad in a red rain coat and brown boots, pointed to a fallow deer as it ran into the grove of oaks and stone pines. Trudy set her tea cup down as she focused on the pretty little girl, and noticed the woman grab her daughter's hand and ascend the line of steps flanked by bronze lions. The girl turned away stubbornly, unwilling to climb the steps. Trudy laughed to herself. Then, she noticed something unbelievable as she leaned closer to the window. Were her eyes playing tricks? While the woman's back faced Trudy, she was sure of one thing.

The little girl reminded Trudy of Eva. It was easy to see the resemblance. Her delicate little face told it, her blonde hair tumbling half out of a blue ribbon that tied her hair back. Her blue eyes were striking from every blink. Blue eyes true like her mother's.

Quickly, Trudy pulled out some money, dropped it on the table and she jumped from her chair. She ran out of the tea house toward the woman and her child. In her rush, she sprinted into an older lady, knocking her to the ground.

"I am so sorry!" Trudy exclaimed, helping the woman to her feet. "Please forgive me. I was not looking where I was going."

The lady dusted off her skirt.

"Are you hurt?" Trudy asked.

"No," the woman said. "Thank you. I am alright, dear."

Trudy hung onto the woman's arm, ensuring she had her footing.

"Sorry, again," she said. "I am in somewhat of a rush."

"It's okay, dear," the woman reiterated.

Before she could finish, Trudy dashed off towards the memorial. As she approached the very spot where she saw the little girl and her mother, they were nowhere to be found. Her eyes darted in all directions. Trudy rubbed her temples and sighed as she felt a headache emerge.

"*Scheiss!*" Trudy said, throwing her hands in the air. She sat upon the steps feeling discouraged. Was her plan just a hard-to-reach dream? Maybe she should return to the hotel, pack her bag, and return to the Zulu village, she thought. Finding Eva seemed impossible, like trying to find a needle in a haystack. She glanced up at the bronze statue of Energy at the base of the memorial, commissioned as a tribute to Cecil Rhode's determination and drive. She too must stay determined. Trudy gazed out at the magnificent view facing northeast, which can be imagined as the Cape to Cairo road, Rhodes's imperial dream of a British colonial Africa.

Trudy walked from the memorial to the University of Cape Town, nestled just below at the foot of Table Mountain. For now, she would let fate lead the way as she took in the sights of this magnificent city.

# chapter

# TWENTY

Zoe placed the crystal-clear glass pitcher filled with freshly-squeezed orange juice on the table in the garden. She poured a glass for Eva as she proudly watched Isabella play with Inge and Zola. The little girl chased after a red ball Inge threw to her. Her little hands were still too small, but she was quick to scoop it up from the ground and throw it back. Her joy came from running barefoot in the green grass, while the others cheered her on.

"I can't believe how quickly she has grown," Eva said. "I remember bringing her home so vividly as if it was only yesterday."

The little girl giggled as she threw the ball back to the others.

"They grow up so fast," Zoe said. "You have to make the most of these precious years."

The spirited girl's face lit up as she said, "Mommy," and ran into her mother's welcoming arms. Both mother and daughter could not stop smiling. "May I have some water, please?"

"Yes, my love," Eva said.

As Zoe poured the little girl a glass of water, she said, "Thank you."

"For what," Eva asked, looking up at her maid.

"If you had never found me that day when I was sitting on the steps, I don't know where we would be," Zoe said. "You have given us a home, a place to be, for outside these walls, the world is filled with hate. I am forever grateful. Zola and I are finally at peace."

Eva placed her hand upon Zoe's hand. "Thank you," Eva said. "I feel as though we have inspired one another, challenged one another, and been there for each other through thick and thin."

Eva held her daughter tight upon her lap.

"The world has been harsh to both of us," Eva said. "We've both been discriminated against. Out there, you are ruled by the color of your skin, identified by a passbook that denotes if you are white, black, or coloured. Here, surrounded by these walls, you are a beautiful woman with a huge heart. Never forget that and stay true to who you are, Zoe."

"Thank you, madam," Zoe said.

"And Zoe," Eva said. "Please call me Eva. I can't bear to be called 'madam.' What right have I earned?"

"*Ag man*!" Zoe laughed. "I could never call you by your first name, madam."

"Oh, Zoe, you must!"

❧

Before his last class of the day, Max sat alone and ate a quick lunch on the steps in front of Jameson Hall. He could only think of one thing—Sara. There were still days he'd catch himself hoping that he would find her running after demonstration pamphlets as they floated in the wind. Then he would have to force her out of his mind again. He took one last bite of his Marmite sandwich and placed it down before picking up his textbook. A shiny African bird swooped in and snatched a piece of his sandwich.

"Oh no!" he shouted, half-laughing.

The bird then had the audacity to land a yard from his feet and eat what it had captured in its little mouth. He laughed as the bird nibbled on the bread. Max threw tiny bits of his sandwich at the bird, its black beak shining in the sun. Eventually, it flew away.

He picked up his textbook and laid it on his lap. For a few minutes, he read about Greek mythology. Then, his concentration was broken.

"Remember me?"

Max turned around and looked up at the man. His stomach twisted in a knot.

"Officer Granger," Max said, closing his book. "What a surprise."

"Hello, Max. Beautiful day, isn't it?"

Max rose from the steps.

"May I help you with something?" Max asked, unsure how to proceed.

The officer shook his head. "Not at all," he said. "I was just finishing up some investigative work on the march."

"Oh," Max responded, tucking his hands in the pockets of his pants.

"By the way, were you one of the lucky ones who carried a poster during the march?" the officer asked.

Max swallowed hard. Shit, he thought. He stared for a moment at the step below.

"Well...yes, I did," he said. His heart began to beat faster and his face turned pale.

"What did it say?" the officer asked, crossing his arms.

Max cleared his throat.

"Something like 'wake up, South Africa,'" Max said.

"Wow," the officer said. "Wake up, South Africa? Was anything else written on that poster?"

Max looked down at the steps again. "No, sir," he said.

"What do you really think?" the officer responded. "Should we wake up? Are we asleep? From what I have heard around campus, you are a smart student, Max?"

"Asleep or awake...well, I stand with the government, sir," Max said, eyeing the officer. "And for whatever is best for this city and country."

"Did you feel that way on that day?" the officer asked.

"Yes," Max said.

"Then, why did you carry the poster?"

"You win, officer," Max said, as irritation and fear grew within him.

"I win," the officer said. "Don't know about that. I won't win if we don't control the problem in this country. Nor, will you. If we don't take control of this problem, we will be a small minority. We will suffer greatly. Understand?"

"Yes," Max said.

"And I know you know of these things...a certain kind of people being a problem," the officer said.

"What do you mean?" Max asked.

"A German Jew, right?" the officer asked, pointedly.

"Yes," Max said, staring at the officer. Anger began to seethe from within.

"My point exactly...good day, Max," the officer said, tipping his hat.

Monique Roy

As the officer walked away, Max yelled, "Why don't you arrest me already? Why delay it any longer?"

The officer continued to walk as Max watched his every step. Then, he stopped and turned toward the young man.

"Isn't this more fun?" the officer grinned.

Max stared at him, pitied him.

"Don't you have more important things to attend to, Officer Granger?" Max asked.

"Such as what?" the officer smiled slyly.

"Perhaps, making sure there are no blacks wandering the streets without passes, stirring up mass chaos," Max said. "Whatever it is you do with your day."

The officer laughed.

"You are a funny one," the officer said. "They're better off under the chains of apartheid, you know? We must cement control over this chaotic social system. Whites must have complete supremacy over all other racial groups, and if not, chaos will prevail. Maybe one day you will realize that, and hopefully not the hard way, like discovering your neighbour or even your loved one slaughtered to death in the driveway of their home. Or, someone you know raped and murdered."

"I don't think they are better off," Max said. "And what a gruesome way to explain yourself."

"Well, I would rather lay it out on the line for you," the officer said. "The truth is, blacks, when integrated into white societies, drastically lower the general standard. They just can't make it in a white man's world. Apartheid ensures that like lives with like. We shouldn't feel guilty, Max. We are all better off in the end."

"You're a bastard!" Max yelled. "You think that segregating natives and coloureds, and depriving them of their citizenship will bring peace and harmony. I think it will create more chaos, backlash and uprisings. Giving these people no rights will be costly down the road."

"The whites of this country have a privileged position and we must run South Africa," the officer said. "I refuse to feel guilty. Now, I have important work to do. In the meantime, you be a good boy or else...I will make sure there is a little jail cell for you, perhaps next to a nice black man."

"Just warnings, Officer Granger?" Max asked.

"For now," the officer said. "You know, I see potential in you and jail is not the place for you. Plus, you remind me of me when I was younger. Take it easy."

Just like that the officer walked away and Max never saw him again.

Max sat back down on the steps and held his head in his hands. His head began to ache.

Trudy watched Max from behind a tree, unsure of her next move. How would he react, she thought, if she approached him this very minute? A part of her wanted to and the other part of her wanted to watch him and plan her next move. She instantly noticed how he'd grown into a mature and handsome young man.

Out of nowhere, a couple, in love, ran towards Trudy and disappeared behind a nearby tree. They began to kiss. Embarrassed, Trudy froze and bit her lip so she would not laugh. A car drove by and honked at the couple. They laughed and then noticed Trudy.

"Hey, what are you doing over there?" the young man questioned.

"Nothing," Trudy answered. "Just enjoying the pleasant day."

"Behind a tree...," he remarked.

She shrugged her shoulders.

Max watched it all unravel. He ran down the Jameson steps as he noticed his friends.

"Hey, Brian!" Max called out.

"Hey, Max!"

"Howzit!" Max said. The young woman appeared from behind the tree, buttoning her shirt.

"Howzit, Shelley!" Max said to the girl, grinning at her.

She smiled back. "Hi, Max. Wipe that smile off your face."

Trudy held her breath. This was not the way she had planned it. Suddenly, she sneezed, twice.

"Who is that?" Max asked. "Is someone there?" He focused on the tree.

Her heart raced, her feet froze to the ground. Her hands began to tremble.

"Who's there?" Max asked. He walked over to the tree.

Seconds later, they stood face-to-face.

Trudy stared into his sparkling hazel eyes. He stared back in astonishment.

"Max..." she said his name. His face became flushed upon hearing her voice.

"Do you two know each other?" the young man asked.

He continued to stare at her, studying every inch of her face. She was still beautiful.

By then the couple had walked off. Trudy walked up to Max and hugged him.

He pulled away from her.

"I don't know what to say," he said. "This is so sudden, so unexpected. My God, Trudy...I never expected to see you here. What on earth are you doing here?"

She nodded. "I apologize for startling you."

"My heart is racing," he said. "Why are you here?"

"Mine, too," she forced a smile. "I can explain, if you will let me."

"Were you spying on me?" he asked her with concern.

"No," she said. "I was walking around the campus when I saw you on the steps. Seeing you again took my breath away. I couldn't face you, so I hid behind this silly tree."

He let out a nervous laugh.

"This is crazy!" he said, placing his hands in his pockets.

"What are you doing in Cape Town, Trudy?"

"I've been teaching English in a Zulu village..."

He cut her off.

"Oh, I see," he said. "I suppose Nazi life didn't turn out as you had expected. How are all your Nazi friends these days?"

She looked down at the grass, feeling ashamed.

"It turns out that Nazi life was not for me," she said, as tears formed in her eyes.

"Really?" he said. "You were born to be a Nazi, like the rest of them."

"No," she said. "I was born to Nazis. I am *not* a Nazi."

"I wish I could believe you, Trudy."

"I am glad to see you, Max. Is everyone well?" She swallowed hard, trying to change the subject and fearing what he would say next.

He looked straight at her. "Yes," he said softly.

"I must see Eva," she said.

He shook his head.

"I don't know, Trudy," he said. "I'd hate for her to feel the pain of old wounds."

"I'm not here to hurt her or anyone for that matter," she said. "I am here to make amends."

"Does it matter now?" he asked, looking into her eyes. "The war is over. We are trying to move on with life. Berlin is in our past. We faced horrible struggles and terrible times."

"I must see, Eva," she said again. "Please let me see her. I have something that your family treasures."

"What is it, Trudy?" he asked, slightly irritated.

She opened her bag and pulled out a black sock. Max watched carefully as she pulled from it the glistening emerald and diamond necklace. Max's hand flew up to cover his mouth as his eyes widened with shock.

Tears flowed down his cheeks. She gave the necklace to him, his hands trembling as he held it.

"Is this a dream?" he asked.

"No," she said.

"Where did you find it?" he asked.

"It's a long story," she said. "I will tell you, but please take me to Eva."

He could not refuse.

A car passed by.

"Let's put it away," Max said. "I'd hate for it to go missing again."

Trudy placed the pendant necklace back in her bag.

"Let's hurry or we'll be late for Shabbat dinner," he said, grabbing her hand.

She looked at him steadily, and said, "Wait, maybe I shouldn't go. I don't want to upset anyone, especially on Shabbat."

"You wanted to see my sister, right?" He dropped her hand. She nodded.

"You've come too far to turn around now," he said. "You've brought back something we cherish, greatly. For this, my family will be truly grateful."

She followed Max to the bus stop that was marked "Whites Only." They sat on a bench for a few minutes in silence. He smiled at her now. As a bus came into sight, Max stood from the bench.

"This is our bus," he said, extending his hand to help her to her feet.

They sat together in the middle section. Almost every seat was taken. They weaved in and out of traffic. The street lamps were lit already; it was getting dark.

Every inch of Trudy trembled inside. A cold shiver ran up and down her body.

She looked at Max.

"I can't get over how handsome you are," she smiled. "You look so much like your father."

"Thanks," he said with a shy grin.

"What do you think of Cape Town?" he asked. His eyes fixed on Table Mountain.

"It's glorious," she said. "It's picturesque in every way. I didn't realize that it was so modern."

"Yes, it is a nice city to live in," he said. "We've enjoyed it so far."

"When did you leave Berlin?" she asked.

"We left shortly after Kristallnacht in 1938," he said. "It was a frightening time. We went first to Antwerp, then to Rio, until Cape Town finally became our home. We always thought how far we would have to go in the pursuit of peace."

"I understand," she said.

He looked at her with bewilderment.

"How could you possibly understand or even relate to that?" he asked.

She looked at him then and saw his frustration.

"No, I will never know what it was like to be a Jew, living in Hitler's Germany, but I do know what it was like to be a German who hated her country for what it became," she said. "I am ashamed, Max."

When she said that, he saw sadness in her eyes. He looked away.

They meandered through the Rondebosch center, around the cast iron fountain, and into the lush neighboring suburbs at the foot of Table Mountain. Trudy felt a warm breeze upon her cheeks as she stepped off the bus.

They strolled through curvy, narrow roads of an exclusive suburb in Rondebosch. Soon, they stood in front of the home. It was quaint and situated in a quiet cul-de-sac. She breathed deeply, her mouth closed. When she entered the home, she could smell the warm, inviting aroma of chicken soup.

"Wait here," Max said.

Trudy stood in the entry hall and gazed around with fascination. She stared at an old grandfather clock and a feeling of nostalgia came over her. The old house in Berlin where Eva, Inge and Max grew up had a similar clock.

She heard familiar voices in the next room. Eva and Inge chatted with their mother.

"What should we do tomorrow morning?" she heard Helene ask. "Your father has to work."

"Carmen does, too," Trudy heard Eva say.

"We have a visitor," Trudy heard Max tell his family.

"Who is it?" Oskar asked.

Trudy's heart began to race. She glanced over at the door, planning her escape.

"An old friend," Max said.

"But it's Shabbat," Inge said. "Why are they here?"

"Well, don't just stand there," Carmen said. "Invite them in."

Without any more hesitation, Trudy invited herself in. Suddenly, she found herself standing in front of everyone as they looked at her in complete shock.

"Trudy!" Eva said as the color drained from her face. Inge stared at Trudy with wide eyes. Helene looked like she had seen a ghost. Isaac and Carmen looked at each other in utter confusion.

"Hello," Trudy said.

"What are you doing here, Trudy?" Eva asked. "I mean, what a surprise!"

Instead of answering, Trudy walked over to Eva and embraced her. She whispered in Eva's ear, "I am sorry."

Eva pulled away. Trudy went to greet Inge, Helene and Oskar.

"What do you want, Trudy?" Oskar asked, holding a glass of whiskey.

"Give her a chance," Max said. "She is here for an important reason."

"Would you like a drink?" Carmen offered, trying to be nice.

"Yes, please," she nodded. "Something strong, perhaps." They smiled at each other.

"Please, sit down," Helene said. "Zoe!"

The maid entered the room. "Yes, madam."

"Mom, I told you not to yell at her," Eva corrected her mother. "Zoe, we have a visitor who will be joining us for dinner."

Zoe smiled at Trudy.

"No problem, madam," Zoe responded.

"No," Trudy said. "That's okay. I hate to intrude."

"Don't be silly," Carmen said.

"It's good to see all of you," Trudy said. "It's been a very long time."

"Likewise, dear," Helene cleared her throat and sipped her wine.

After an awkward silence, Trudy reached for her bag.

"I have something very precious," she grabbed the black sock.

Everyone looked on with curiosity. She pulled from it the emerald and diamond necklace. Oskar stared in disbelief as she walked towards him with the gem.

Oskar took it from her. He held it tightly, analyzing every inch, every detail.

"This can't be true," he said.

Trudy watched him, tears welling in her eyes. She heard sniffles coming from Inge and Eva.

"I can't believe it," Oskar said, eyeing the jewelry. "I never thought I would ever see it again."

He looked up at Trudy, half smiling, half crying tears of joy.

"I am so thankful," he said, as their eyes met. "The gem was my father's, you know? This means the world to me."

Trudy nodded.

Helene joined Oskar to admire the piece.

"Thank you, Trudy," Helene said, hugging Trudy. "This is a wonderful surprise."

"Thank you," Eva said, realizing her old friend had done something amazing. "It's a miracle that you found it."

Their eyes met briefly, and for a mere second the pain of the past diminished.

"Why don't you tell us where you found the pendant over dinner?" Oskar said. "I am very curious, as we all are, and hungry." He looked at his family.

Trudy nodded as Oskar led her to the dining room as the rest of the family followed. When they took their places, Eva realized she had not introduced Carmen and Isaac to Trudy.

"Forgive my rudeness," Eva said. "This is my husband Carmen and Inge's husband Isaac."

"It's a pleasure to meet the gentlemen who has captured the hearts of my dear old friends," she said.

Trudy watched as Helene, Eva, and Inge lit the Shabbat candles, covered their eyes, and recited the blessing, to reflect the beginning of the Sabbath. She felt sentimental about the moment. She missed those special times when she joined the family for Shabbats when they were in Berlin. Now that they had survived the war, Shabbat had a deeper meaning, of togetherness, and of true survival and tradition.

Trudy thought it was beautiful how they kept their traditions alive after all they had been through and how they came together as a family, in good times and in bad. They were quintessential survivors. Even after the ravages of war and the evils of the Nazi regime, some things remained.

Oskar recited the Kiddush as he held the rich wine, a magical bridge from the week to the day of rest. Then, he lifted two challah loaves in the air and recited the *Ha-Motzi*.

Once they began to eat the delicious meal laid out before them, their attention shifted to Trudy.

"Where shall I begin," she asked, staring at her soup bowl.

"From the beginning," voiced Isaac. "Tell us everything."

"Let the girl eat," Oskar said.

"No, it's alright," she said, laying down her spoon.

"I want to start by saying that I am *beschämt*," she said. "I am so ashamed of my country and of what I became."

She looked at Eva.

"Now, I am not able to apologize for the failures of a whole nation of people, but I would like to apologize for hurting you all, especially you, Eva."

She cleared her throat. For a moment, it seemed like she was going to cry.

"I made the choice to become who I was when I had the power to choose," she said.

"Did you though?" Max asked. "Did you really have the power to choose to be anyone, but a Nazi?"

She paused. Everyone had stopped eating.

"I think so," she said. "But my father was a Nazi and the choice was made for me at a young age. I knew the road I would travel."

"What about your mother?" Inge asked. "What happened to her?"

"My mother went along with it, but then it began to upset her and weigh her down. My father left us to be an SS officer at a camp. I haven't seen my father in a long time."

"Tell us about the pendant necklace," Oskar said. "I can't wait any longer."

They laughed.

"I first became an *Aufseherin* at Ravensbruck. I couldn't handle the role. I was forced to whip prisoners and I just couldn't do it. I was dismissed from my duties and sent to be a maid at a sub-camp in Buchenwald. I worked for the camp commandant. It was there in the commandant's home that I stumbled upon the jewel. When I saw the pendant, I knew I could not leave that home without it. It was a gift to his wife. When he gave it to her, the clasp was broken. The commandant told me that a jeweler would come by to pick it up for repair. Luckily, the jeweler never came. I devised a plan to steal it and escape. And that's what I did."

Oskar began to laugh, a deep laugh from the pit of his belly.

"That is amazing!" he said. "I am so thankful...I feel so blessed! You risked a lot to do that."

"You are very brave," Helene said, as she laid down her knife and fork and pushed her plate away.

"I knew I had to bring the necklace back to you," she said. "You were like family to me."

"How did you get to South Africa?" Eva asked.

"The evening I escaped from the commandant's house, my mother picked me up from a deserted road, just outside the camp. When we arrived at our apartment, I found a leaflet on the floor about teaching English in an African village. Germany was losing the war and there was nothing left for me in Berlin. So, a few weeks later, I packed my bags and landed in an amazing place, a Zulu village in the Valley of the Kings."

"That sounds incredible," Isaac said.

"Isaac is a humanities professor at the University," Inge added.

Trudy smiled at him. "Do you enjoy your work?"

"I do enjoy it most days...when the students listen to me," he said.

"There is still a gap in your story," Max said. "How did you know we were in Cape Town?"

"Well, that's the most interesting part," she said, raising an eyebrow at Max.

"I had no idea where you were or even if you were alive, and became discouraged many times. I kept the hope alive and let fate take its course, hopefully leading me to you," Trudy said.

"I don't understand," Oskar said.

"I needed to find myself again and believe in myself. I knew that one day we would cross paths again. But then something lucky happened. One night, when I was returning to my *rondavel* in the village, a pretty, young woman was waiting for me. She had come to the village to teach English as well. Her parents had sent her to be reformed since she had been expelled from school, that school being the University of Cape Town."

Trudy turned her eyes to Max who was suddenly too busy eating.

"Her name is Sara," Trudy said.

Max looked up, still chewing on his food.

"Sara?" he asked.

"Yes, Max...Sara," she said.

"Who is Sara, dear?" Helene asked her son.

"My God," Max said, dropping his fork.

"Your Sara," Trudy said.

"Your Sara?" Eva looked at her brother.

"The girl who Max has fallen for," Isaac said. "She is a student at UCT. A bright girl...she organized the recent anti-apartheid rally and was expelled from school."

"Is she well?" Max said. His eyes glued to Trudy.

"Yes, she is very well," Trudy said sincerely. "She will probably be home soon. And I am quite certain that she would like to see you again."

He smiled back at Trudy.

Oskar raised his glass of red wine. "Trudy, tonight I raise my glass to you," and the rest of the family followed. "Thank you for bringing home one of my most prized possessions, other than my family, of course."

Laughter spread around the room.

"When the Nazis took the necklace from me, it felt like they had taken an important part of me," he said. "It symbolized so much, everything I had worked towards. Those diamonds symbolized love and hope. Those emeralds symbolized stability, balance, and creativity."

"That's beautiful," Helene said, touching his hand.

Oskar looked at Trudy.

"I want to ask you something and get your thoughts," he said. "When I was forced to close down my diamond center, I hid some valuable jewelry in pastries. As I was locking up for the last time, the Nazi guard asked me what was in the bag. I answered pastries for my family. Then, I offered him one. He slipped his hand into the bag and grabbed a warm pastry. I walked away, unsure if he had taken an empty pastry or one that hid diamonds. I fretted and panicked, and when I arrived home, we tore through those pastries looking for the diamonds. We found all, but one, a glittering pendant. I thought the Gestapo would come for us that night. But they never came. If the guard had taken the jewelry, why did he not report me immediately to the Gestapo?"

"Many would have reported you," Trudy said. "You were lucky. He saw it as a prize. We were in a war and most likely he would have bartered it for food for his family. A diamond like that could have fed his family for a long time. Food was for survival, a diamond was just a means."

☙◈

The next morning, it seemed like the world was perfect, even if it was just for a moment. The sun shone brightly. Birds chirped from atop trees.

Eva smiled as she watched Inge plant flowers in the garden with Isabella, planting the seeds of the future. Her little girl mimicked Inge's movements as she dug into the soil. Soon, Inge would have a child of her own, creating a new generation of hope.

Eva was instantly reminded of the 'Dreidorn' badge when she heard the sound of the rake, scraping up fallen leaves from the lawn. She had forgotten all about the silly metal badge that had forced many memories to resurface. She retrieved it from its hiding place in the back of a drawer and asked Charlie to dig a hole for it under a tree. It didn't matter anymore where the 'Dreidorn' badge was buried.

When Trudy arrived for tea, Eva felt it was the perfect time for them to bury the symbol of the past. And as they turned the soil over the 'Dreidorn' badge, Trudy gently took her friend's hand.

"You know that I had no choice," Trudy said to Eva. "I had to obey my parent's wishes to not see you. My father threatened to send me away if I did not obey him."

"Yes," Eva replied, looking into her friend's eyes that now beamed with warmth and kindness.

"I tried to disobey…to see you," Trudy said.

Eva patted the soil.

"Remember the day you came to my home after you had not heard from me?" Trudy asked.

"I will never forget," Eva said.

"I had fought with my mother to see you," Trudy said. "I tried to reason with her, but she forbade me to ever see you or be associated with you."

Eva swallowed her tears. Trudy looked into Eva's beautiful eyes.

"I am sorry, Eva," she said. "I know your family dealt with much strife."

"I forgive you," Eva said. "Let's put the past behind us, so that we can all live in peace."

Just then, from a neighbor's open window, Eva was taken by the sound of Beethoven's Ninth.

Eva smiled at the joyful sound, and for a few seconds, her mind drifted back to that evening she spent at the symphony in Berlin many years ago. A bittersweet evening of firsts—the first time she saw Hitler and her first glimpse of the emerald and diamond necklace that became an invaluable family treasure.

Now the future awaits and everything is possible.

With a piece of the past buried, and as if she was saying a prayer, Eva said: "One day when the badge resurfaces again, it will hopefully bring an understanding of the past, compassion for all humanity, and provide hope and courage to move forward *across great divides*."

# About the Author

Monique loves writing that twitches her smiling muscles or transports her to another time or place. Her passion for writing began as a young girl while penning stories in a journal. Now she looks forward to deepening her passion by creating many unique stories that do nothing less than intrigue her readers.

Monique holds a degree in journalism from Southern Methodist University in Dallas and is also the author of a children's book *Once Upon a Time in Venice*. In 2008, she was chosen by the American Jewish Committee's ACCESS program to travel to Berlin, Germany, on the 70th anniversary of Kristallnacht, to explore German and Israeli relations along with 20 other Jewish professionals from across the U.S.

Monique was born in Cape Town, South Africa, and her grandparents were European Jews who fled their home as Hitler rose to power. It's their story that inspired her to write *Across Great Divides*.

Discover more at http://www.Monique-Roy.com